Common Sense

& Other Tales of Disillusionment

Aj Saxsma

Copyright © 2024 by Aj Saxsma

All rights reserved.

No part of this publication may be reproduced, distributed, or transmitted in any form or by any means, including photocopying, recording, or other electronic or mechanical methods, without the prior written permission of the publisher, except as permitted by U.S. copyright law.

The story, all names, characters, and incidents portrayed in this production are fictitious. No identification with actual persons (living or deceased), places, buildings, and products is intended or should be inferred.

For Mom & Dad

TABLE OF CONTENTS

Drive You to Violence 1

Curse the Writer 59

He Had a Receipt 115

Common Sense 157

What's in Your Head, Chris Cooper? 207

Drive You to Violence

Linda arrived home from the office five past the six o'clock hour. Dusk burned near, and it burned far, and it had begun arriving earlier and earlier and colder and colder. The small, boxy home with dirty windows and slanted shutters and dead bushes, to which she arrived, had all the outward signs that this particular home, where inside her family waited, was in a growing state of lapse.

When she came in, Ed was across the couch in sweats and a baggy sweatshirt, watching television in the dark with the kids, seven-year-old Kevin and nine-year-old Donna, who were lying on the floor under blankets on big pillows, the good decor pillows, which were no longer good decor pillows but regular, misshapen, fraying pillows.

From being lain on too much.

'Mom's home,' Ed said.

He didn't lift his eyes from the TV. Nor did the kids.

'Guys, Mom's home,' he said.

The kids said hi, Mom.

Their greeting was lazy and without investment.

Linda pecked the kids on the cheek. From Ed she chased a kiss, competing with the TV for attention.

'Kiss me,' she said.

He finally did.

'Hamburger is thawing in the sink,' he said.

'Oh. Okay.'

'Box with the noodles and spice packet I set out too.'

'I'll get dinner going then,' Linda said.

'Can you follow the directions on the box?'

'Hm?'

'The box tells you how to make it on the side,' Ed said.

'Well, it's easy. I just make it.'

'No, I know.'

'The instructions anyone can do, they're easy,' Linda said.

'Sometimes you add a step, sometimes you take one out.'

The kids said yeah, sometimes it's good, sometimes it's not good.

'Guys,' Ed said, 'be nice to Mom.'

From the TV, an audience laughed graciously.

'I like when you make the box dinner helper, but can you follow the box instructions? Each step? Don't add steps or take steps out. Just follow the box.'

Linda smiled, but Ed wasn't watching.

She changed out of work clothes into comfy clothes and shuffled through the boxy home, picking up messes the kids and Ed had made, and she shuffled around and flipped on lights in the living room and hall and, when the home had been somewhat reset, she shuffled into the kitchen and started dinner.

Night filled windows and the slide door to outside. It shone Linda cooking back at her, she watched herself off and on against the black glass.

When dinner was ready, she called out it was ready.

Ed corralled, with very little energy available to him, the kids to the island between living room and kitchen and up on stools.

Plastic plates and plastic cups and silverware waited.

'Hey, hon, the hand towels are for drying hands,' Ed said.

He pointed at two hand towels bunched by the stove.

Cooking juices and spills had soaked in each from Linda's cleaning.

'Mm-hmm,' Linda said.

'Prolly should toss those in the hamper, hon.'

'Mm-hmm.'

'Prolly shouldn't let those sit too long.'

'Mm-hmm.'

'They're for hands, not spills, hon,' Ed said.

'Mm-hmm.'

Ed rolled his sleeves and looked dinner over.

In the kitchen, in the light, the rashes across his arms were clear, as well as the areas where he'd done excessive scratching and left dark-red peeling trails. Also clear were the patches in his dark hair, which had thinned worse than others and shone glimpses of scalp.

Linda worked at not looking. Mostly she was successful.

'Food looks good, right, guys?' Ed said to the kids.

Kevin sipped milk, and Donna sipped soda, and both sat atop their island stools and made no comments.

'Shannon, come eat,' Linda said out into the hall.

Ed served himself.

Linda served the kids first, then herself.

Ed and the kids began chewing and clinking and chewing and laughing and chewing and smiling and chewing and burping and chewing and sipping and chewing and chewing.

Linda picked at her food and watched everyone else eat.

Several moments into dinner, Linda's younger sister, Shannon, emerged.

She'd moved in several months before, having run into hard times living on her own.

Sunset hair hung down her back. A large, wrinkled men's T-shirt and large, wrinkled men's boxer shorts covered her thin, candle-white frame.

Sleep hung in Shannon's eyes, as if she'd just woken.

She sat left of Ed, at the end of the island. She did not speak. She was four years Linda's junior.

Linda prepared her a plate.
The family consumed at uneven paces.
'Hon, you follow the steps?' Ed said.
'Mm-hmm.'
'This tastes different.'
'I followed them,' Linda said.
The kids said it tastes like she added a step.
'Tastes different,' Ed said.
He worked food in his mouth and made faces that were neither pleasant nor unpleasant.
'Tastes like you added a step,' he said.
The kids said they bet she added a step.
They said it wasn't good.
'Guys. Be nice to Mom,' Ed said.
Shannon, who had been eating quietly, said, 'It's good.'
Sometime into the meal, Ed made a face at Linda. He gestured about Shannon at Linda, without Shannon seeing. He gestured several times in a row until Linda understood.
Linda ate a moment longer, then said, 'How'd interviews go this week?'
Shannon moved food around her plate. Small bites she took, big bites she left. 'No interviews,' she said.
Ed made a new gesture at Linda without Shannon seeing.
'You put in job applications?' Linda said.
'Just ones week before last.'
Ed rolled his eyes at Linda; he rolled his head too, sitting right next to Shannon, who this time saw.
Dinner concluded in silence not long after.
Before sleep, she and Ed lay in bed in the dark. Moon and starlight could not find a path inside.
Ed was fresh from a shower.
Linda snuggled against him and smelled soap on his skin and in his hair, and she held him tight, and when she found her grip loosening and slipping away, she tightened her grip and snuggled him again.
Everything inside Linda was quiet, everything inside at peace.

Here lay a man who belonged to her and belonged only to her and belonged to no one else, and her arms were around him.
Claiming him, in sleep.
Ed let her hold him.
Then, some minutes later, he rolled from her and drifted to sleep.

Over the kitchen island, the family consumed breakfast in similar habits and paces as they had dinner.
But for Shannon.
She ate cereal in the living room.
The family was each dressed to enter their respective days, the kids for school, Linda for the office, Ed for the clinic, not as staff but as patient.
But not Shannon.
Shannon sat cross-legged on the couch in the same men's shirt and men's boxer shorts she'd worn the night before, and the day before too, and the day before that, and the day before that, and the day before that too. Sleep lingered on Shannon's face and in her long hair, and it was wrinkled into her clothes.
Ed gestured at Linda about Shannon with looks of his eyes, widening and squinting them, with little finger movements pointed at the living room.
Linda pretended not to see and busied herself through the kitchen, keeping herself pretending not to see, and Ed followed her, trying to get her to see the widening and squinting of his eyes and his little finger movements pointed at the living room. During this, Linda's father, Ray, unlocked the front door and came inside.
Using his own key.
To Linda and Ed's home.
Ray came right in and said mornings around the kitchen and helped himself to a plate of breakfast and brought it to the

living room, where he said to Shannon, hey sweetie, sitting on the couch beside her while she ate cereal, him with his plate, his demeanor bright as morning. 'Linda feeding you?' he asked.
'I'm feeding her,' Linda said. 'She's eating now.'
'Cereal, Linda. She's eating cereal.'
Ray traded Shannon the plate he'd made for the cereal without her consent.
'There's a decent breakfast,' he said.
Ed was tucked behind the fridge, from Ray's view, hovering over Linda but spying out into the living room.
'Is he staying then?' Ed said in a low and irritated tone.
Linda called over the island and into the living room. 'Dad, are you staying then?'
'Yes, I'm staying then.'
'He's staying,' Linda said.
'For how long?' Ed said.
'For how long, Dad?'
'I don't know, I got a key, so.'
'He's got a key,' Linda said.
'I know he's got a key, hon,' Ed said. 'I know that. He didn't knock.'
'Well.'
Linda moved left-over breakfast to the fridge.
'Ask if he knocked,' Ed said.
'Dad, did you knock?'
'No, didn't knock, I got a key.'
Ed made another face. 'Ask about applications,' Ed said.
'Dad, ask Shannon how her job interviews are going.'
Ray did and Shannon answered him low; Linda could not hear.
'She says good,' Ray said.
Ed made a face.
'She said good?' Linda asked her father.
'She said interviews are good,' Ray said.
He draped his arm over Shannon and gave her a squeeze. He said, 'That's great, sweetie.'
'Ask how many she's putting in today,' Ed said.

Linda pretended not to hear Ed.

'Who's back there talking?' Ray said. He twisted around, looking back over the couch. 'Ed back there?'

'Yeah, Ed's back here.'

'Hey, Ed.'

'Hey, Ray.'

Ed drifted out, waved, then drifted back.

He said, 'Hon, ask how many she's putting in today.'

'Dad, ask Shannon how many job apps she's putting in today.'

Ray did. Shannon answered softer than Linda could hear.

'She said none today.'

'None today?' Ed said.

'None today, she says,' Ray said. 'She's got a headache, she says.'

Ed made a face and rolled his eyes at Linda.

Ray gave Shannon another squeeze. He said, 'Take today and relax, sweetie, okay? Take today.' Ray stood and wandered toward the kitchen.

'It takes time, you're making discouragements out loud, Linda, you know that?' Ray said. 'Getting going again takes time.'

'I'm not making discouragements.'

'I think you know you're making discouragements of your sister out loud.'

Shannon was looking at Linda.

Then she went back to the TV.

In the car to the clinic, when normally Ed was loud and talking over the radio stations or singing along to music Linda neither sought nor cared for, he was, instead, violently quiet.

He was quiet when they walked into the small, uninteresting medical building, which sat on dying grass, and he was quiet when they exchanged information that was needed to check in, and he was quiet when he and Linda were walked through sad, silent halls to the sterile room with all the chairs, and he was quiet when he sat in the bigger chair with the cushions and blankets and reclining mechanism that did not quite recline fully, and the tubes, the tubes that ran here and there, and he was quiet when Linda sat in the smaller, less comfy chair beside him.

Then Ed was still quiet.

Violently.

He was quiet when they hooked him in and fed his veins cancer-killing chemicals.

Two hours the pair sat at length, in gross and unsettling quiet.

Then Ed was no longer quiet.

He was losing breakfast into a pail provided by the clinic, long and wet heaves of it. Gagging took tightly his body.

Linda sat by and watched the episode, passing a paper towel and then taking the dirty-vomit-chunky paper towel back, and doing no more, no patting on his back, no caressing of his back, no comments to ease his vomit, none of these but for passing fresh paper towel and taking the dirty-vomit-chunky paper towel back, passing one for the other only as needed.

Ed had, the last session, asked that she stop the caressing and comments.

None of it helps, he had complained.

None of it.

Gagging and heaving released him.

Linda passed fresh paper towel.

Ed collected his breathing and sat quietly for a time longer, connected via tube to diluted poison.

'I thought you told your dad about knocking.' He all but blurted it out.

'I told him,' she said.

'He talked like you didn't tell him.'

'Well.'

'I thought you told him,' Ed said. 'You said.'

A nurse came with a new bag of chemicals. Ed settled.

'Don't you think Shannon needs to move out?' he said.

He again all but blurted it out. 'You've been thinking it, hon?' Ed said.

'No.'

'You haven't been thinking that? Hon?'

'No. I haven't been thinking that,' Linda said.

'She hit a snag with a boyfriend, a dirtbag boyfriend, you helped with a roof, hon. Our roof. For some time. You done your share if you're asking me, hon.'

'Oh.'

'Your share and then some.'

'You want her out?'

'You haven't been thinking that it's been long enough?' Ed said.

Linda said nothing.

'You should tell her it's been long enough; you done your share.'

In her hand, she forgot she was holding soiled paper towel.

'It's hard doing this and having stress at home,' Ed said. 'All that chaos in the house.'

'The house feels chaotic?'

'It's my space, my recharge and quiet space.'

'Well. Yeah.'

'It's hard doing both, hon, both treatment and the stress at home.'

Linda rose from her chair to comfort Ed, but he said no, it doesn't help.

So, she sat.

'I think you set a deadline with her. Start with that,' he said.

He returned to quiet.

Before the session ended, he said the following with a cracked voice and at a slow, pained pace.

'I need to be at one hundred percent for treatment. Remember when doctors said that? Ed, they said, you need to be at one hundred percent if we're going to beat this? If we're going to beat this, hon. They put *if* right at the start. I'm starting with an unfair advantage here. I'm starting with an *if*.

And when I'm doing both this and stress at home, your dad and sister, I mean, I'm not at one hundred percent, hon. I want to live, hon. I want to live.'

There was such a begging in his tone, *I want to live.*

Linda stopped herself from rising and comforting him and instead sat holding soiled paper towel and said nothing.

'You haven't been thinking she should go?' Ed said.

A daydream filled Linda's head with warmth and distraction. She had dropped Ed home to rest then driven the half hour into town, where the unimpressive office building in which she worked stood some three unimpressive stories tall alongside other unimpressive office buildings that also stood three unimpressive stories tall.

Linda was at her desk, on the third story, filing and typing on her workstation but not seeing the files she filed or the computer screen.

She saw daydream, warm and distracting.

One desk over, Janine filed and typed on her workstation. Both desks faced the door to Carol and Dave's shared office, which was shut.

Somewhere, somewhere else in the office, always somewhere else in the office, a phone was ringing.

Gary from accounting was squatting and fingering through the bottom drawer of a four-drawer filing cabinet.

He was not finding the file of his search and made disappointed comments, mostly to himself, the longer his search ran on.

Each morning began in this fashion, Gary searching and making disappointed comments, mostly to himself, and Janine and Linda working at their workstations while Linda daydreamed.

If Janine daydreamed was unknown.

But likely.

The office was thin and narrow and was a dull beige. Doorframes were painted a lighter beige than the beige carpet but a darker beige than the walls, and placed about the office at varying intervals were fake plants, short and tall and bushy. They were the sort of fake plants that made no attempt at looking real or smelling real and looked, to anyone who took a moment, fake and smelled fake. Someone, no one seemed to quite know who, someone from a time before each individual's employment, had placed the fake plants in positions from which they had not moved, not once.

Like ancient natural formations, they had simply always been.

Time and again they were dusted but no one seemed to know who dusted them. All that was known was the plants had been placed long ago and had not moved, not once, and, with no one actually seeing, were dusted regularly.

Gary made huff and puff noises, fingering through files. 'Such a mess,' he said, mostly to himself.

He made louder huff and puff noises.

'I can't work with you making those noises,' Janine said.

'Nothing's where it should be,' he said.

'You're the only one in that drawer ever.'

Gary said no more. He moved up a drawer.

'Ed hanging in there?' Gary said to Linda.

'Sorry?'

'I always thought highly of Ed.'

'Yes, Ed is fine.'

'That's got to be something awful,' Gary said.

'We make due,' Linda said. 'Like anyone.'

'Yeah, because I always thought highly of Ed, something awful like that, that's just got to be ...'

He said no more.

'I can't work with you making huff and puff noises,' Janine said.

'I wasn't making huff and puff noises.'

Gary found the file of his search, then followed the thin hall out.

Sometime later, Janine spoke. 'I got a letter from my brother.' She dug in her purse for a lozenge.
'I didn't know you had a brother,' Linda said.
'He's visiting from Maryland week after next.'
'How lovely.'
'That's not a cheap plane ticket either,' Janine said.
'I didn't know you had a brother, how lovely.'
'Last we spoke was seven years ago, April.'
Janine fed a lozenge to her mouth and made sucking noises.
'And now he's visiting?'
'Week after next,' Janine said.
'Well. That must have been just lovely, a letter after seven years.'
Janine made sucking noises and typed on her workstation.
'Never fit in the family, my brother,' Janine said. 'He stuck out, like he made a point to stick himself out, like he thought he was better. I thought that, that he thought he was better. I mean. You got to take my brother at his actions. Never joining get-togethers. Never participating when he did join get-togethers. Always sticking out, my brother, that's how you got to take him, at his actions, and he put my family through it, like, really put us all through it. And then I get this letter. After seven years, come April.'
'What did it say?'
'That he's visiting, week after next,' Janine said.
'Was there a falling out?'
Janine held the question, making sucking sounds and typing, then dug back in her purse for a pack of cigarettes and a lighter.
'You could say. You could say there was a falling out.'
She slid out a cigarette.
'I didn't know you smoke,' Linda said.
'I don't,' Janine said.
'When did you start?'
'When I got the letter,' Janine said.
Janine exited the building and smoked in the parking lot.
Linda looked at the cigarette pack poking out of Janine's purse, then returned to daydreaming, warm and distracting.

Mrs. Hornsby was outside tending flower beds next door when Linda pulled in from work. It'd been a warm day; the flowers were sun beaten, and Mrs. Hornsby let them drink heavily of the hose.

The day had been long on Linda. Carol and Dave had come out the office saying there was an emergency meeting, and it had worn Linda right out.

Mrs. Hornsby came swiftly from the hose to the border between her and Linda's homes, calling out she needed a moment. Her white hair was thin as spun sugar. Her makeup was overproduced.

Linda hadn't the energy to offer a greeting and so shone a smile in its place, a tired smile that reached into tired eyes.

Mrs. Hornsby pulled cash from her pocket for Linda. Forty-five dollars.

'She is so sweet, that sister,' Mrs. Hornsby said.

'Sorry?'

'Your sister wouldn't take it.'

Linda looked at the money given her.

'I says I insist, I says you're so sweet, take it sweet girl, but—' Mrs. Hornsby gave a shrug.

'I'm saying I held right to her the forty-five dollars for all the help she'd been this afternoon, over my place, you know. She was out in your backyard, and I made chat with her, small chat, you know, and then I was saying about how I need help inside, and that sweet sister a yours said she'd help and then she got dressed and then she was helping this afternoon, over my place, and, oh, and so I held right to her the forty-five dollars, and that sweet sister a yours turned my offer right down.'

'Got dressed?'

'What?'

'My sister got dressed?'

'Yeah, she got dressed, and then she was helping, over my place.'
'Why did she need to get dressed?'
Mrs. Hornsby began to go. 'She wouldn't take that money. If she still won't, just use it to buy something real nice for that sweet sister a yours.'
And then she waddled inside.
Linda was left with the money.
And questions.

Linda ran the shower and brushed her hair and looked at herself in the mirror, the tired reflection of herself. She slid back the shower curtain and stepped in when water was warm, and still warming further, and steam was rising over her. She closed her eyes and let warm water, and still warming further, wash troubles and thoughts and tension from her body down the drain.
Into warm and distracted daydreaming Linda returned.
Until she heard the door open and someone enter.
'I'm in here,' she said, wiping water from her eyes, listening through water's white noise.
The person in the bathroom did not respond.
Linda heard them lift the toilet lid and their weight sit and she heard and smelled them use the toilet.
'I'm in here!'
She poked her head out of the shower.
Kevin was on his Game Boy on the toilet, kicking his legs and moving his bowels and ignoring Linda.
'I'm in here!' Linda lost a bit of temper.
'I'm almost done,' Kevin said.
He continued sitting and kicking his legs and moving his bowels and playing on his Game Boy, continued ignoring Linda, whose head was still stuck out of the shower. Steam climbed and rolled above her head.

She knew warm water was limited; soon water from the shower would be cold, and her daydream, warm and distracting, could not continue, not in the shower.

She snapped again, saying she was in here, goodness Jesus.

'Okay!' Kevin said.

He wiped and did not flush and exited, leaving the door half open.

'Kevin!' Linda shouted, her head still stuck out. 'Kevin!'

He did not respond or return.

'Goodness Jesus,' Linda said out into the bathroom half open to the hall. She sealed herself back behind the shower curtain and ran water over her head, moving on, moving back into daydreaming.

Warm and distracting.

Then someone was urinating in the toilet. The flow started in spurts into the toilet, to Linda they sounded strained, maybe painful.

'I'm in here,' she said up and out the shower.

She heard tiny sprinkles in the toilet water.

Then the flow deepened and ran heavy and long, and it was louder than the shower water.

'Goodness Jesus!'

Linda poked her head out of the shower again.

Ed was over the toilet, his pants half down his ass. He was looking at his dick and urinating.

'Someone went in here and didn't flush,' Ed said.

'I'm in here!'

'Almost done, hon,' he said.

Warmth was leaving the shower water.

'Goodness Jesus,' she said.

She looked where Ed's pants were half down his ass. Deep bruises beneath the skin, some purple as eggplant and some yellow, reached and mingled up and down his backside. She knew more were hidden lower and higher than his ass; she knew they led up his back and down his legs.

She'd caught him one morning, looking nude in the mirror. Taking inventory of both his illness's and treatment's reach. Turning and twisting to see all of himself.

She refrained from snapping at Ed; for him her patience was wide and forgiving of most things.

All things, really.

There was, in fact, nothing he'd done that she'd not forgiven, or at least said she'd forgiven, for there are things one might forgive that remain recorded in oneself as unforgiven. So, that is to say, nothing Ed had done, mistakes and the like, and there had been mistakes and the like he'd done that required forgiving, mistakes and the like both small and large, both by accident and on purpose, both painless and painful, none of which had, for the duration of their courtship and marriage, gone unacknowledged as forgiven, out loud, by Linda.

And so.

Ed operated as though the slate were clean.

Linda did not.

Though quite often she said she did and, quite often, made a point of saying she did.

But internally, she did not. Internally, the slate was unclean.

Her head was still stuck out of the shower, and the water was still losing warmth, and Ed's urinating, deep and heavy, went on.

And on.

Ed made wincing noises.

'Are you all right?'

He made more. Linda could see hints of blood in the toilet bowl, in the urine.

'Hon?'

'I'm fine,' Ed said.

He cut his urination short and exited.

That night, before sleep, Linda was lying against Ed in the dark.

He was quiet, his eyes shut.

The window was open to the night. The street slept, stirred by cars passing now and again and also, now and again, by the Johnsons' dog barking several blocks away.

Linda reached below the sheets, in Ed's sleep shorts, and took him in her hand and gently worked him, tugged him. It was meat in her hand and, after a moment of working and tugging, was still meat in her hand. She slid her head below the sheets, to take him in her mouth, to help him, but Ed put a stop then and there.

'Not tonight,' he said.

'Are you all right?'

'I'm fine, just not tonight.'

Linda slid back out of the sheets and removed her hand out of his sleep shorts and lay there while Ed turned away without another word and found sleep rather easily.

Linda found sleep much later and with great difficulty.

The following morning, Linda fed the kids breakfast and got them on the school bus while Ed slept in. He had woken briefly with Linda, the two greeting the new day with fuzzy thinking and bargains, and he had tried to rise from bed but had finally said he was having a "tired day" and made no further attempts at getting up.

Shannon was eating cereal in the living room. A new men's shirt and new men's boxers drowned out her bone-thin figure.

'You probably don't like staying here, huh?' Linda said.

Linda was finishing the remainder of her morning coffee, which was no longer warm but not quite cold. It was between. It wasn't enjoyable, but neither was it unenjoyable.

'I kinda like staying,' Shannon said. She was eating and not looking from the TV. 'I kinda really like it,' she added.

'I mean, you probably don't like sharing a living situation with so many. Two adults and two kids. And then there's you. You probably don't like coming into a space and having to share it with noise and kids' toys and me and Ed. I mean, especially since Ed is–' Linda spoke softly, so as not to carry her voice down the hall to the bedroom where he was still in bed, '–sick and all.'

'I don't mind,' Shannon said.

Her cereal chewing was loud.

'I don't mind at all.'

'Oh.'

Linda sipped lukewarm coffee, which edged on cold.

Like the shower.

Warmth had left.

'Ed was thinking maybe we put a deadline on paper,' Linda said.

'A deadline?'

Shannon stopped chewing; she was looking at Linda.

'Well. Yeah.'

'You want me to leave?'

'Well. No. We just thought you probably don't like staying here.'

'But I do.'

'Well. Sure. But Ed was thinking maybe we put a deadline on paper.'

'Ed said that?'

'Well, you know–' she spoke softly again, '–he's sick, so.'

Shannon said nothing. She looked at Linda.

'So,' Linda said. She sipped cold coffee. 'Should we say, like, three weeks to find a place?'

'Ed said that?'

'Well.'

'I like it here, kinda really.'

'So, should we say three weeks then? Is that time enough, Shan?'

'You want me to just leave then?'

'Well. No. But. Ed just. Ed was saying, and he's sick. So.'

Shannon put the cereal bowl in the sink and retired down the hall, into the guest room, and quietly shut herself in with no production or drama, just in, quiet as a mouse, and the door shut, soft and silent.

Linda stood where she was a moment, processing and analyzing, then walked up and said into the guest room door, 'So we'll say three weeks then. Shan?'

There was nothing on the other side.

'Shan?'

Dead silence.

'I'm going. So. If I don't hear otherwise. We'll say three weeks then.'

No response followed.

Linda poured out her cold coffee and began her day.

Somewhere in the office, the phone was ringing, from everywhere and nowhere. It rang on and on.

Somewhere it was answered.

Not long after, another phone was ringing.

Somewhere.

Linda and Janine were typing on their workstations and clicking with their mice, not more than a few words crossing between Linda's or Janine's desks and back again.

Carol and Dave's office was shut. A sign hung on the doorknob. It said *Open Door Policy, 24/7.*

Shortly after noon, the women took lunch outside in the sun and rolling, comforting breeze that was neither rough nor gentle but was both, in spurts from around the building. They chatted and ate and finished their food, and Linda joined Janine around the building while she smoked out of breeze and out of sun.

'I'm not seeing my brother when he visits,' Janine told Linda. She blew smoke.

'Oh.'

'He's here next week, remember? I'm not seeing him.'

'Won't he be disappointed?' Linda said.

'Quite frankly, I don't much care. Quite frankly, I don't much care one bit.' She blew more smoke.
'Oh.'
'But I may see him,' Janine said.
'You may?'
'I may, I don't know. But if I don't, and he's disappointed, quite frankly, I won't much care. But I may see him.'
'Well,' Linda said.
'He sued me, you know,' Janine said.
Linda said nothing.
Janine pulled on her cigarette. 'He did.' Smoke fell from Janine's mouth while she spoke. 'He sued me.'
'Who's heard of family suing family?'
'Served me right at the house, his lawyer, some fella from town, real shady fella. Rang the doorbell and served me then and there.'
'Right at the front door?'
'You never seen a thing so cold-hearted.'
'Goodness,' Linda said.
'Yeah, goodness! Sent us right to bankruptcy, me and Lester! Right to it. Me and Lester were scraping the barrel already. A lawsuit on top put us right in bankruptcy. Seven years digging ourselves out, buried in bankruptcy and we're finally all dug out, and now the son of a bitch wants to visit. I'm not seeing him. Well. I may. I don't know.'
'What made him do a thing like suing his own sister?'
'Don't know I can say,' Janine said. 'That's part of it, I think. Don't know I, or Lester, bless his little old heart, my Lester, don't know we can say the particulars. Part of the suit, I think, forbidding us talking about it. So. And I ain't giving that son of a bitch brother a mine any ammo, so.'
'Goodness,' Linda said.
'So. I may see him. I may not.'
The women were quiet while Janine smoked.
'Ed asked that Shannon go,' Linda said.
'Oh boy,' Janine said. She blew smoke and said again, 'Oh boy.'

Sometime later, the women came back in stinking like smoke. Janine popped a lozenge, and the two worked quietly, clicking on their keyboards and clicking on their mice.

The door to Carol and Dave's office opened, and first Carol then Dave came in hard, as if they'd been catapulted out their office.

They were similar in appearance, in eyes and ears and nose and hair, and to conclude they were brother and sister was not difficult, even to perfect strangers. Of their age, one might guess they were closer than they were apart. They did not speak over one another but were perfectly in sync. When one's sentence ended, the other's began without delay.

'We were in the office talking, and some concerning items were brought up,' Carol said.

Dave said, 'Very concerning items, and we were talking them over, and we thought it might be great to have another emergency meeting for the remainder of the afternoon.'

'We thought that would be great, hunkering down for the remainder of the afternoon and hashing out all the concerning items,' Carol said.

Dave said, 'Going to be working hard through the afternoon. The concerns we were talking over are many, and we have to go through each one.'

'Was someone smoking in here?' Carol said.

Dave said, 'I was smelling that too.'

The following Sunday, the family rose and enjoyed breakfast together, then, with Linda's parents, made nine a.m. service at the Our Lord & Savior's Lutheran Church, down Larton way.

But not Shannon.

She had not come out of the guest room.

Ray had told them, no, let her alone, let her sleep, but Linda had asked through the door anyhow, was she wanting to come to church with the family, as a family, and had received no response from inside. During service, while the preacher read verses aloud, Ray, who was seated on Linda's right, said in something louder than a whisper, 'What's this about asking Shannon to move out?'

Linda's attention remained raised and focused on the preacher atop his pulpit and his words spreading over the congregation, and she did not engage with her father.

'Shannon calls day before and says you want her to leave.'

'Well. I only just mentioned, maybe, getting a move date on paper.'

'She calls me in tears, Linda. In tears.'

Ed, who was seated on Linda's left, said in something louder than a whisper, 'What's he saying now?'

'He's saying nothing,' Linda said.

'She's in tears on the phone day before, Linda,' Ray said.

'We said three weeks.'

'No. She says *you* said three weeks. She says she said nothing at all. She didn't say three weeks.'

'Well. Ed was saying we done our share,' Linda said.

Ray listened to the service and did not respond.

'Is he saying about Shannon?' Ed said.

Linda pretended not to hear Ed.

'You want her out?' Ray said.

'Well. Ed and I been thinking it's been long enough.'

Ray said nothing to this, and Linda felt compelled to say more. 'It's hard with Ed doing treatments and having stress at home,' Linda said. 'All that chaos in the house.'

'Ed say that?'

'Well.'

'What chaos in the house? There's no chaos in the house,' Ray said.

'There's chaos,' Linda said.

'What's he saying over there?' Ed said.

'You should let her stay,' Ray said.

'Dad,' Linda said.

'You should really let her stay, that's your sister, Linda.'

'Well, I need to think of Ed, so.'
'That's a raw deal, Linda. It really is raw. That's your sister, Linda.'
'Ed needs to be at one hundred percent. Remember when doctors said that?'
Ray said no more.
Linda's mother, Deena, who was seated on the right of Ray, said, 'Is she saying about Shannon?'
'Yeah, saying about she wants Shannon to leave,' Ray said.
'Is he saying about Shannon?' Ed said.
Linda pretended again not to hear Ed.
Sometime into service, Ed was mentioned in prayer, folks asking the Lord to take from Ed his illness and to replace it with light, good and holy.
The kids and Ed and Linda and Deena bowed their heads.
Ray did not.
After service, Ed and the kids piled around the kitchen island at home, still wearing church clothes, while Linda started lunch.
Linda knocked on the guest room and called Shannon out to eat.
Inside was silent.
'Shan? Lunch.'
Linda tried the knob. It was locked.
This puzzled Linda, as the door was not equipped with a lock. She tried the knob a second time. It turned not at all.
'Shan?'
She tried the knob a third time.
'Hon?'
Her voice traveled up the hall.
'The door is locked,' Linda said out loud.
Ed came down the hall and tried the knob.
'I don't think she's home, hon,' Linda said.
'Shannon?' he said.
Inside the guest room was still silent.
Ed tried the knob a second time.

Then Ray unlocked the front door and barged in, calling out hello.

'Good Christ! Your father didn't knock,' Ed said to Linda.

'Dad, you didn't knock just then,' Linda called out.

'Well, no, I got a key.'

Ray came down the hall. A moment later, Deena came in the front.

'Shannon put a lock on my guest room door,' Ed said to no one in particular, but he said it at Ray.

Ray tried the knob. 'Sweetheart?' he said.

'She's not home, Ray,' Ed said.

Ray tried the knob a second time. 'Well, Linda, I don't know what to tell ya,' Ray said. 'It's a raw deal. The whole of it.'

Ed tried the knob a third time then moved back up the hall, cursing under his breath, saying good Christ, good God damn.

'She's safe here, Linda, that's the big thing of it; she's safe here. She loves it here.'

'She does not,' Linda said.

'She does, she told me so.'

Ed interjected, he said she's thirty, Ray, almost thirty-one.

Ray did not acknowledge Ed in the slightest.

'You want your sister out, you need to help, Linda,' Ray said. 'She calls me crying, just out her mind, Linda, crying right out her mind over how raw a deal this is and, I'm just, you need to help, Linda.'

Deena took Linda aside and said she'd talk to Dad, she'd talk to him about the Shannon stuff and about the knocking stuff, okay, honey, don't with that long and lost face, honey; she said she'd talk to Dad.

Linda made lunch so the family might quiet and pause discussions that might progress matters further, and she felt a sort of doom.

Linda stepped around. And avoided it. The doom.

One of the kids said Mom looks tired today and the other said she looked so so so so so so tired, haha, her eyes and hair, and the other said Mom's eyes look so tired, haha.

'Be nice to Mom,' Ed said.

But the kids weren't; they continued.

Ed repeated a number of times to be nice.

Ray and Deena ate then said goodbyes, and Ray left a message for Shannon to call him when she's home. The kids finished and ran out to play in the street with the neighbor kids.

It was Ed and Linda left in the kitchen.

'Hand towels are not for spills, hon,' Ed said.

Linda said, 'What?'

'You just used a hand towel for that lunch spill. Now it's got to be washed, hon.'

'It's fine,' Linda said.

'Don't forget Doug's coming this afternoon.'

'Oh yeah?'

'I told you yesterday.'

'You weren't home yesterday,' Linda said.

'He's taking me down to Mackie's. Thought we'd shoot some pool.'

'You did not tell me yesterday,' Linda said.

'Well, I did,' Ed said. 'He's coming this afternoon.'

'Doug's taking you to Mackie's?' Linda said.

'Don't, Linda,' Ed said.

'I didn't.'

'You're doing it.'

'All I asked was Doug's taking you to Mackie's.'

'I can hear you thinking it even when you're not saying it, I swear.'

Linda was quiet.

'It's just me and Doug, no one else,' Ed said.

Linda cleaned up lunch and put leftovers in the fridge and said no more on the matter.

'No one else but Doug,' Ed said at Linda's back.

'No drinking,' Linda said.

'I'm not drinking.'

'You can't be drinking with your treatments.'

Ed left the kitchen.

His brother Doug came to the house late afternoon. He pulled up in a tired little car and came in the house like a hurricane, dragging in all manner of chaos and volume, and he riled the kids and got them full of energy and bounce, then took Ed up the road to Mackie's, which sat on the corner and advertised various brands of beer on tap. The short building flashed neon colors over the road running alongside every day as soon as the sun died.

A little after dark, Shannon came in the front door.

Linda was reading while the kids watched TV.

She did not bring up the lock.

She offered small talk to Linda, it was taken, answers were parsed and few.

The kids begged Aunt Shannon to watch TV with them, and she agreed and joined them on pillows on the floor. Seeing her sister with the kids on the floor, Linda said, 'Remember when we watched TV like that? On the floor on pillows like that?'

Shannon said she barely remembers.

'We would watch TV like that. Me and you on pillows.'

Shannon engaged with the kids about the show on TV.

'Can I help you find a new apartment?' Linda said sometime later. 'I would like to.'

Shannon said sure.

'Good,' Linda said.

She sat back and got comfy and continued reading.

Later, much later, when the kids were in bed and Linda was in bed and Shannon was in bed and the home was in differing stages of sleep, Ed stumbled in.

Linda heard him come through the front door.

She heard him laughing.

She heard him in the kitchen, then up the stairs, then in the room.

The light came on, she heard him stumble in, then he said sorry and shut the room light off.

She heard him strip.

She heard him climb in bed.

She smelled him, the alky stink of him, the hops and liquor wafting off him.

The feeling of doom returned.

After an hour sitting with it, it departed, and she soon fell asleep.

Out of exhaustion.

The following morning, the kids were sent to school, and Shannon was still in bed, and Ed was coming out the hall, dressed for the clinic, and Linda was waiting to take him, and he came out of the hall with his car keys.

She looked at them in his hand, dangling from his fingers. Linda had always driven, since the first appointment.

She was waiting with her keys.

He came out of the hall with *his*.

'Oh, I can drive, hon,' Linda said.

'I was thinking it would be just me today.'

'Oh.'

Ed put on one shoe then the other, slow and steady and with effort.

'Today's a long one. So. Be home late.'

'You never do long ones.'

'Well, today's a long one. So.'

His face was pale; he wore a long sleeve. Bruising poked from under his collar. His eyes were bold and sad.

'I'll drive, and I got a book.'

He showed her his book, *Defeating Cancer in Your Head*.

'Was it just you and Doug last night?'

Linda said it straight as a dagger. It'd just come out, really.

'I knew it,' Ed said. 'Good Christ, I knew it. I knew you were thinking it right when I said.'

'Well. You come in last night and, I thought, you know–'

'It was just me and Doug, no one else. But you don't believe me.'

'Well. No. I just. When you come in–'

Then Ed said it, straight as a dagger back at Linda. 'There were no women last night, Linda. I swear it. Just Doug.'

Linda said nothing.

'It'll be after dinner before I'm home,' Ed said.

'I don't mind driving you and sitting with you.'

Ed stood in the doorway open to the morning. It was plain he meant to leave on his own but lingered impatiently, not even looking at Linda.

'I like sitting with you and being with you, next to you when you need me.'

'I would prefer it just me today, hon.'

He kissed her cheek then left her at the front door.

Linda stood and felt like a tool that had lost one of its uses, few of which remained. She did not leave for work straight away; she watched Ed leave from the kitchen window then sat for a time.

Midday at the office, Linda and Janine had just returned from lunch to work routines and moving through their own individual workloads, which at the moment were not light, when Dave and Carol emerged from the office and announced to both Linda and Janine's desks they were doing a brother-sister trip and would be out for one week.

They said they discussed who would be in charge in their absence, as this would greatly impact future promotions, and had decided Linda would manage business matters until their return, and they offered a little applause.

Janine seemed thrilled and said it's just as well; she didn't want the weight of the office, what with all the stress she's already under anyhow, what with her brother and all, she said, then she went outside to smoke.

Dave and Carol took Linda in their office a moment to review tasks required of her while they were out.

The tasks were many.

When the workday was ending, Janine was first to depart. She said, before she went, that Lester, her husband, was looking for some help in his mechanic shop, up in Clinton City. The gal who'd been doing his office work, she said, was let go for stealing out of the cash drawer. With all the business with her sister, if Linda thought Shannon was interested in some work like that, office work, Janine said, she would put the word in.

Linda liked the idea and said she'd talk to Shannon. In fact, she said why don't you go ahead and mention it to Lester, and we'll get Shannon on board, either way.

'Have her stop at the shop in the morning.'

Linda said thank you and she would have her stop at the shop.

Linda picked up groceries and then stopped for sandwiches for dinner on the way home and found Shannon watching scary movies with the kids when she came in the house.

'Maybe we turn that off,' Linda said.

Both Donna and Kevin said, very loudly, Mom, no!

Linda listened to their complaints and plated sandwiches at the island, then called the kids up to eat. Shannon came uncalled.

Linda mentioned, while Shannon ate, about Janine's husband's shop, how he needed help and how she thought that would be good, to get working, earning money, and the work would be easy enough, and she said how she was going to take her apartment looking day after next.

Linda wrote the shop's address.

'You stop by in the morning, okay. It's a free job,' Linda said.

'Clinton City?'

'What's it, like, twenty minutes?'

'Yeah, but it's Clinton City.'

'Janine's putting in the word for you; that's a nice thing she did. You could at least stop by.'

'Let me talk to Dad first,' Shannon said.

'It's a free job. You just stop by in the morning. Nothing else.'

'Yeah, I heard you.'

Shannon put the address in her pocket and continued eating. She said no more of it.

Sometime later, Linda said, 'So, are you thinking you'll stop by in the morning?'

Shannon said could she eat please?

'Well, it was just a nice thing Janine offered, putting in the word for you.'

Shannon ate.

Some more time later, Linda said, 'Did you say Ed was home?'

Shannon said Ed hadn't been home once all day then finished her sandwich and closed herself in the guest room.

Linda heard the knob lock.

While the kids did homework and watched TV in the living room, Linda phoned the clinic.

A woman answered the other end. Her voice was young. Pleasant.

Linda straight out lied; she said she was so sorry to phone, she had forgotten to confirm her husband's appointment for today. It was for today, right? She said she'd had such a busy week, it had simply slipped her mind, just slipped right out, haha, his appointment was today, wasn't it? She said that would be under Ed.

'Yes, we received Ed this morning just fine,' she said.

'Wonderful, oh, and that was a long dose today, right? I know he's only been doing short ones, but today wasn't a short one?'

'Ma'am?'

'Oh, I was just meaning about how long he was supposed to be there today, if it was a short treatment today or a long one, that was all. I don't usually forget but, you know, haha.'

'You'd like to know if your husband was here for a short period or a long period?'

'Well ... yeah.'

'One moment please.'

The other end was quiet. It sounded as if Linda had been placed on hold, but there was no music, only quiet, a quiet that was quieter than quiet. But it seemed there was something on the other end, was it muffled? Was it talking?

Or was it nothing?

The other end returned. This voice was less pleasant, less young.

It apologized but the information requested was considered private and medically protected and was not able to be shared.

'Oh. Yeah. Okay. I was just—I had just forgotten to confirm was all, and everything sounds okay then.'

The voice said no worries, thank you for calling, then hung up.

About forty minutes later, Ed came in, appearing quite lively. There was a smile on his face, and it seemed there was some color too, a little bit of warmth and life in his cheeks. He said hi hon and moved about the house with little announcement. He ate the sandwich Linda put in the fridge for him, standing in the dark kitchen and eating it bite after bite in the open fridge, Linda watched him do it from the living room, she had stopped reading her book to watch.

Later, Linda lay in bed with the TV on. It was set atop the tall dresser next to a wooden jewelry box and a few of Ed's watches, which he rotated wearing.

The TV was on mute.

Ed came in fresh from a shower, his hair and body still wet. The bruises were many, but they were faint tonight. There was some color there too, through his body and in his skin that stood apart and over the bruises in a manner.

He dropped the towel he'd walked in wearing and slid on underwear and then flowy sleep shorts and then slid in bed, next to Linda, apart from Linda.

He made noises until he stirred no further.

'I like this episode, turn it up,' Ed said of the TV.

Linda turned the volume up.

She slid close. He was still warm from the shower. Together they lay in TV light, not talking, watching for some time, not long. She started kissing his neck, with purpose, traveling up to his ear, then down, and down, and down, and he stopped her.

'Not tonight,' he said.

She read disinterest all over him. Linda pulled away.

'I just have a headache, hon,' he said, 'and it was a long day.'
'Maybe we could tomorrow?'
'Maybe tomorrow.'

❖

At the office, Linda made herself more available to Dave and Carol. When she'd gotten in, she'd poked her head into their office and asked if they needed anything from her, and when they had said they did not, she had said how she looked forward to tending the office in their absence and had said how pleased she was to have inherited the responsibility, and she had lingered until they asked she please go and shut the door behind her.

In the afternoon, Linda and Janine made coffees in the break room and took them outside to sit on the concrete benches along the side of the building, under two tall trees that gifted lovely shade.

Janine smoked. She offered one to Linda.

Linda declined.

'Nothing melts stress like a smoke,' Janine said. 'I'm saying I tried it all. Stress balls, yoga, meditation. With a smoke, stress just melts.'

'I'm not stressed,' Linda said.

'I'm looking at you. I'm seeing stress.'

'Oh, no, no. No.'

Janine slid a smoke out for Linda.

'Not for now, unless you want it now, but for when you need it.'

'I don't need it,' Linda said.

'I'm seeing stress, all over you.' Janine passed the cigarette anyhow. 'Just keep it. For when you need.'

Linda said thanks.

'You can try this one?' Janine said. She offered her lit cigarette.

'No, thank you.'

'My brother is here in a few days,' Janine said. She put out her cigarette and lit another.

'You decided to see him then?'

'Just for breakfast, just to talk. Lester won't see him, after he sued us into a hole, he won't, says he'll kill the son of a bitch.'

'Oh my.'

'Yeah, so. We'll do breakfast and, if it goes well, we'll see.'

Linda nodded and smiled and studied the beautiful day.

'Dad tried to kill him. My brother sued him and Mom too. After he sued me. I can't talk details; that was part of when he sued me too, I can't talk about my suit and I can't talk about Mom and Dad's suit. So. But, golly. He sued them into a hole too. Just. Golly. Dragged them through it all, the whole thing of it. I'm. Yeah. So. Dad took him out in the middle of nowhere, where the roads are gravel and everything is just trees, just trees every which way, and Dad tried to kill him. Dad's been in jail since.'

'Oh my God.'

'Nothing drives a person to violence quicker than family, all a family's mess stewing and heating up in a person, the years of buildup and disappointment and lying and favoritism and neglect and anger and sadness wearing a person down, so, we'll see how breakfast goes.'

Linda returned to studying the beautiful day but found the day was beautiful no longer.

The workday busied and continued past Linda's quitting time, on Dave and Carol's request, but she made no complaints and stayed until the work was done.

Ed was at her when she came in the house from work, saying she needed to tell her dad *again* he can't just come in whenever he likes, letting himself in, unannounced he was saying, not knocking, just coming in with no heads-up and no notice whatsoever and just planting himself like he lives here, saying her dad don't live here and saying she needs to say something! Ray was sitting in the living room in Ed's chair watching TV. Ed's complaints became whispers in the kitchen, lower than

Ray could hear, and he nagged Linda from the kitchen to the bedroom to the bathroom then back to the kitchen.

Linda said fine!

She marched over to Ray and plucked the TV remote out of his hand and shut the TV off and told him to get up, and when he did not, and when he looked at her confused, she said again to get up, and he did, and she told him to go out on the front porch. Ray and Ed stood still and quiet. Linda stood still and quiet, too, and quite serious.

After a moment, Ray followed her direction, Linda followed and shut the door behind him, closing him outside.

'Knock!' Linda shouted through the door.

Ray didn't.

'Knock!'

A small, quiet knock came against the door.

Linda opened the door to Ray.

'Hi, Dad, would you like to come in?'

Ray didn't answer straight away, but he said, 'I would.'

Linda stepped aside so he could enter and asked for his key.

Ray handed it with no friction and returned to the chair and TV.

Linda passed Ed the key and said there, happy?

Ed said, 'Well. Geez.'

Linda started dinner.

Shannon came in the house after they'd eaten and after Linda had cleared leftovers. She plopped on the sofa. She said she was exhausted and received comfort from Ray for her exhaustion, and she said she'd stopped by the shop that morning and had gotten the job and ended up working the whole day.

She offered a smile to Linda, but it was frail and forced.

'That's wonderful, sweetheart. I'm so proud,' Ray said. He made no effort to hide or whisper what he said next. 'Probably it's best to be getting out of this chaotic house anyway, I think.'

In the middle of the night, while Ed slept, Linda lay wide awake. She had not even so much as approached sleep. She rose from bed and took from her purse the cigarette Janine had given her and lit it behind the garage with her candle lighter.

She coughed at first, she coughed horribly, and she coughed at second and third, horribly, but halfway through smoking, the heat in her throat was smooth, and her body was calm, and the dark world was quiet and, as promised, stress melted from her bones.

Just melted away.

❖

Linda crawled through her morning routine. She had not slept well, and was late to the office, and it was immediately noticed by Dave and Carol, who were at Janine's desk.

'Sorry, sorry!' Linda said, getting settled at her desk.

Both Dave and Carol watched her with concerned looks.

Dave said, 'You won't be late next week, correct?'

'We're out beginning Monday,' Carol said, 'We don't need you coming in to the office late while we're out.'

'No, no, it's, no, I won't be, sorry!'

Both Dave and Carol said it's fine, this time, but next week, she's in charge and the person in charge, while they're gone, cannot be late, okay?

That evening, Linda stopped for cigarettes.

She smoked one before going in the house and another after dinner. Both Shannon and Ed were out, and she got the kids in front of the TV and smoked behind the garage after the sun had set, and she peeked out now and again to see if the kids were fine or if they were coming or if Ed or Shannon had come home.

She showered and, from the bathroom, heard Shannon come home and rummage in the fridge then lock herself in the guest room.

Ed came in later, when the house was quiet and Linda was on the couch reading with the TV on and the kids had gone to bed.

'You're home late,' she said.

'Yeah, I know.'

'You and Doug go to Mackie's again?'

Ed kissed the top of her freshly showered head. Then sniffed. 'Are you smoking?'

'Janine at work started smoking,' Linda said.

Ed rummaged the fridge and nibbled leftovers. He said, 'Smells like you were smoking, hon.'

'I'll pick up stronger shampoo.'

'Yeah, because with me on treatments, that would be really bad, if you started smoking.'

'No, no, no, I know. It's Janine. She started.'

Linda adjusted how she was sitting to better see Ed in the kitchen. 'You guys go to Mackie's again?'

'Sorry, hon, I'm so tired. I still need to shower.'

Ed moved to kiss her head, sniffed, then did not kiss her.

He went in the bathroom and showered.

❖

Early afternoon several days later, Linda was driving Shannon through town for apartment showings. Ray had insisted he come along and, since her husband had insisted, so had Deena. The four of them were in Linda's car, Shannon in the front and their parents in back.

Before lunch they had seen three units in middle-income areas, where the streets were wide and where there were parks with children at play and parents laughing and talking from afar, and where everyone was smiling and waving.

The units they had seen were in newer buildings, one as young as five years old, and were private and gated, and the units themselves were spacious and had updated finishes and new appliances and long countertops and light hardwood floors of real walnut that filled the space with a clean scent, and along the walls were tall, big windows allowing in generous and wandering natural light.

Linda had been quite keen on these newer units in newer buildings, and as they walked through each, she pointed out positive qualities in rooms and kitchens to Shannon, things she thought Shannon would love and things she could do or things she could bring in and things she wished she had in her own house and how great would this place be, Shannon, she had said in each unit.

And in each unit they had seen, whenever Linda had highlighted a positive quality, Ray had followed with a highlight of his own in rooms and kitchens, pointing out to Shannon it would cost a fortune to warm such large spaces in winter and expressing concern over waterproofing and pointing out gutter faults on building exteriors and expressing concern over plumbing, saying these newer buildings always skimp on the plumbing.

Upon exiting each newer unit, Ray had also said it wasn't in budget.

Deena kept quiet in each unit. She nodded her head but said not a word.

Shannon had said, in each unit, couldn't she just stay in Linda's house. She liked the noise and the movement inside its walls; she liked the feeling of people around.

After lunch, Linda drove them where neighborhood incomes were lower, and where much of town had been neglected for one reason or another, where sidewalks were cracked and split, like broken teeth, and where parks were enclosed in chain-link fences and locked when not in use and where the people kept to themselves and sat outside because inside was too warm and the means to cool inside was too expensive or not available, and where homes and businesses barred their windows at ground level. The apartment buildings here were dirty faced and old and not private. Each apartment building was easily accessible and open to the community, and each building's landscaping was ignored and wild with growth and weeds in places and dead and barren in others.

The units were cramped and with unkempt finishes and the appliances were outdated and the carpet was dark and frayed and coiled and the walls were scuffed and marked and chipped and, for some, yellowed by cigarette smoke. The windows were dusty and collected cobwebs in corners. Dead bugs piled in the sills. And each room also smelled stale, like the common halls, like air didn't move in there. One unit in particular contained the previous tenant's furniture, which building staff offered to any tenant moving in, but it was terribly outdated and in poor condition. In these lower-income units, Linda's highlights were few and quiet, and Ray's were many and loud and relentless.

Shannon had stared out of the windows of each unit and had said, of each unit's neighborhood, she did not feel safe, could she please just stay with Linda and Ed and the kids?

And Ray had said what a raw deal, Linda.

Linda collected applications from each unit they toured and brought them home and left them in the guest room for Shannon to fill and submit, seeing as how, she reminded Shannon, the deadline was coming due, remember they had said three weeks?

'You said three weeks,' Ray said.

That night, while Ed slept, it seemed just out of reach for Linda, and for hours, she lay in bed and reached for it and failed until she was frustrated and then was out behind the garage.

Smoking.

Melting the stress away.

Like flame to candle wax.

❖

The following morning, after a third night of awful sleep, Linda slept through her alarm, right through it.

It woke Ed, and he woke Linda.

'You stink like smoke,' he said.

Linda's morning routine was disjointed and out of order, and steps were forgotten, and she was late again to work, though Dave and Carol had left on their trip, and the office was hers to manage.

Janine was deep in work when Linda finally arrived. Throughout the day, Linda struggled to get ahead, and never did, not before the workday ended, and so she stayed late to catch up and went home tired and made dinner tired and showered tired and lay down tired and woke tired and went to work, again, tired.

'I'm seeing stress all over you,' Janine said from her desk.

'I'm not stressed.'

'I'm seeing it in your forehead and your fingers and just all over.'

Linda turned from Janine's view.

'Did you smoke the one I gave you?' Janine said. Linda did not answer, and Janine said, 'Would you like another?'

Linda said after a moment she had her own, and the two took a smoke break, and for the two, stress dissolved.

For a bit.

Janine lit a second and said she was seeing her brother tomorrow, and how, within the last day or two, she had come to look forward to it, that whatever had happened in the past, she said, it was no longer important, and how she was open to bonding with her brother, starting something new, maybe.

After all these years.

After all the bad memories.

❖

Ed and Linda were in bed together that night. Linda kissed him good night on the lips, and he kissed back, and then she gave another kiss and he kissed back, and then she gave another, fuller kiss and he kissed back and he said what, hon, and she gave another kiss with her open mouth and tongue and his

mouth did not open to hers and she gave more kisses to his closed mouth until he said hon, hon, hon!
'Linda paused.
'I can't, okay.'
'We haven't made love in a while.'
'I'm tired.'
'Kiss me,' Linda said.
Ed was quiet in the dark.
'You taste like cigarettes,' he said.
'Always an excuse. I'm sorry, but. You've always got an excuse.'
'You smell like smoke, hon. It's all I smell, it's in my nostrils, I'm smelling smoke on me. You're one big cigarette to me right now.'
'It's been months, Ed.'
'You stink.'
Linda rose from bed with no care for how she left her side of the bedsheets and said well, you know what she started smoking, okay, and she liked it and she wasn't quitting, so, and then she went out and smoked behind the garage, free from stress in a pocket moment.

Sometime into smoking, a breeze came through, and she was reminded how much she loved this house once, and she thought how easy it is to hate something you thought you'd love forever.

She brushed her teeth in the bathroom to get cigarette taste from her tongue. Before returning to bed, she found Shannon's apartment applications wadded up in the trash can under the sink.

Linda looked at them for a time, then unwadded and smoothed them and kept them herself.

❖

Heading to work the next morning, Linda was stopped by the neighbor, Mrs. Hornsby. She was drinking coffee on her front porch when she flagged Linda.

'That sweet sister a yours,' she said.

'What's that?'

'I said that sweet sister a yours.'

'Yeah?' Linda said.

She waited a moment for Mrs. Hornsby to continue.

'I'm just here with my coffee and I seen her coming out to go to work, and she calls up to me here saying good morning,' Mrs. Hornsby said. 'Saying how she hopes my day is wonderful.'

Linda was smiling and nodding and waiting for a point.

'You never do that,' she said to Linda.

'I have.'

'You haven't.'

'We've said good morning,' Linda said.

'No. We haven't.'

The conversation paused.

Then Mrs. Hornsby said, 'You really shouldn't kick her out. She's so sweet, that sister a yours.'

'We said good morning the other day.'

'No. I seen you come home from work, and we exchanged words there in your driveway, but no good mornings. Ten years, not one *good morning, have a wonderful day* from you.'

Linda was unsure what to do with the criticism, so she got in her car and started it and, after a moment of thought sitting behind the wheel, rolled down the window and said, 'Good morning, Mrs. Hornsby, have a wonderful day!'

Then she rolled the window up and said, in a conversational tone, to fuck off.

Janine did not show to work that morning, and she did not answer Linda's calls.

Work piled on Linda from the moment she entered the office until after the office had closed, and it continued to pile while she sat at her desk after hours and worked on Janine's tasks and the tasks Dave and Carol had left, her areas of responsibility, and the tasks tested Linda and tried Linda and hassled Linda and caused Linda to sigh and say come on, over and again until she left.

Late.

Again.

Once home, Linda found Shannon had gone out and Ed took the kids for pizza.

She brewed tea and made dinner for herself and sat at the kitchen island in the quiet.

And then Shannon was back from going out with friends.

She sprawled on the couch for a moment and then collected herself and came in the kitchen and said, 'Are you going to tell Ed if I drink his wine?'

'Ed doesn't have wine,' Linda said.

Shannon used a chair to get at the cabinet over the fridge. In the back was a bottle of red and a bottle of white and a bottle of bourbon. Linda watched her bring down the bourbon, not the wine.

'Would you like some?'

She didn't wait for Linda's answer; she grabbed two glasses and poured.

Linda said no thanks, then said okay, maybe a little, but just a little.

It went down smooth for Shannon, but Linda made a gag noise and shook her head and said oh dear. Shannon poured again and Linda said no, she was good, no thank you, I'm really fine with—okay, all right, well, maybe one more is fine, and it went down smoother and without gag noises and, in fact, the next three went down quite easy for Linda. Conversation progressed and sank below surface-level chatter, and the sisters talked as they had not talked in years, openly and honestly, and they admitted wrongdoings to one another and they apologized for grudges that had gone decades without reconciliation, and with more pouring and smooth drinking and with the kitchen falling quiet, Linda said, 'I don't think Ed thinks about me.'

'I'm sure he thinks about you.'

'No. I don't think he does.'

Linda put her glass before Shannon for another pour.

'I think when he thinks and needs to make a decision in his day, he doesn't think about me, I mean. I think he doesn't consider me when he makes a decision.'

'He thinks about you.'

'He messed up years ago. He didn't think about me then, when he messed up, when he decided to mess up. And if he did think about me, he didn't think enough about me to *not* mess up. Like, if only he'd thought about me more, he wouldn't have messed up. He admitted he messed up, and he wanted to tell me about the woman, and I said I don't want to know anything about her, don't you tell me one thing; that's what I said then. I didn't want to know a thing about her, but then for a long time, it was all I thought about. What does she look like, what does she do for work, what's her name, where does she live, when is she home? But I stopped all that. Because I think about him in everything, when I'm grocery shopping, when I'm working, whenever *I* make a decision, I consider him always, automatically. He doesn't need to tell me to consider him, and I don't think he does the same for me because I'm always learning about his decisions where I'm left out.'

'Let's get the wine down,' Shannon said.

'I'm always left out.'

Shannon used a chair to get down one of Ed's wine bottles. She poured more for Linda. And listened while Linda opened private scars and grievances. Shannon listened to *all of it*. And encouraged Linda to share more.

❖

Linda slept through her alarm again, and when Ed finally woke her, there was a throbbing in her head and in her limbs and in her bones, and any movement caused it to worsen. Her mouth was arid, and there was a taste stuck on her tongue; it was bourbon and wine and cigarettes.

Ed didn't allow her time to sit up or process the morning. He said, 'It's past the deadline.'

'What?'

'You said you talked to her, and you said three weeks, and it's been three weeks.'

'Did my alarm go off?'

'You weren't waking.'

Linda saw the clock; she was already late to work.

'We gave her time, Linda.'

Linda said she wasn't feeling well, and she needed a minute.

'Well, for God's sake, Linda, quit your smoking,' Ed said.

He left the room. He poked back in the room. 'And say something to Shannon. She needs to go.'

Linda slowly pulled herself from bed and slowly pulled herself in the bathroom and slowly pulled herself through makeup and dressing for work and slowly pulled herself down the hall to the kitchen and slowly pulled herself to say good morning to Shannon and slowly pulled herself to say, exactly as Ed had said to her, 'It's been three weeks.'

Shannon was eating breakfast and ignored the remark.

'Remember we said?'

'Well. You said,' Shannon said. 'I didn't say three weeks. You did.'

'Well. It's been three weeks.'

'Well. I haven't heard from the apartments, so.'

'Well. You didn't submit the applications.'

'Well. Yes, I did.'

'Shannon.'

'What?'

'You didn't. They were in the bathroom trash.'

Shannon said nothing.

'Shannon.'

'What?'

'It's been three weeks,' Linda said.

'We had such a good night last night, and then you want to bring this stuff up? I thought last night was really good for us, between us, and you want to ruin all that by telling me I missed the deadline?'

'Well,' Linda said, but she had no more to add.

Ed came out of the hall. He was not wearing his usual comfy clothes but nice clothes.

'Linda thinks you don't think about her,' Shannon told Ed.

'What?'

'She thinks when you make decisions, you don't think about her at all, that you only think about yourself,' Shannon said.

Ed looked at Linda.

'She told me last night, and we got into your liquor, but she drank more than me, and she told me so much about you.'

'I'm going for treatment,' Ed said.

'Ed,' Linda said.

'Don't Ed me.'

'Ed,' Linda said.

'How dare you say I don't think about you.'

'Ed!'

'Don't Ed me! I'm going for treatment.'

Ed stormed out of the house in his nice clothes.

Shannon said she was fired yesterday, that's why she went out and why she got into Ed's liquor and what is she supposed to do? Hm? How is she supposed to afford a place? Where is she supposed to go and, goddamn, she couldn't talk about this now.

Linda, after a moment, slowly pulled herself to the office and found Janine *again* did not show and did not call and did not answer any of Linda's calls.

Sometime after lunch, her phone rang.

A machine voice said to hold for a call from Larton County Jail.

Linda held.

Unpleasant music played for five minutes then stopped for a voice.

'Linda?'

It was Janine.

'I only have a few minutes, so. Making my way down my call list.'

'Sorry. I'm just ...'

'Yeah. So, I'm probably not going to be in office for a while.'

'Jesus, Janine.'

'Well, I told you I was going to breakfast with my brother. And. I went. And. We was talking. And. Remember I said I was open to bonding with him, starting something new, you know, building something, maybe. After all these years. After all the bad memories. And. Right at the start, before we ordered food even, he's right into saying stuff he always says and doing things he always does, chipping at me, I'm saying, like he always does. And–'

A machine voice interrupted Janine's audio and said there are three minutes remaining.

Janine was still talking, as if the warning was only given to Linda.

'–going on about the lawsuit and my bankruptcy and Mom and Dad's lawsuit and bankruptcy, just going and going and going and going and going about it. It's all he was saying; he wasn't saying anything about bonding and building together, no, he was just saying what he always says, and I guess I took a knife from the table and tried, they're saying, to kill him. I don't know. I don't much remember.'

Linda was quiet.

'Linda?'

Linda was still quiet.

The machine voice interrupted to say one minute remaining.

'Linda?'

'Sorry. I'm just ...'

'Yeah. So. I won't be in for a while. I just got so mad, and I couldn't see anything, couldn't see what I was doing.'

Linda wasn't sure what to say, so she said the first thing she thought. 'How's your husband taking it?'

'Gosh. I just want a cigarette.'

'Is he handling it well?'

'Lester is, you know, I mean, with the shop short-staffed, he's about had it, I think. Gosh, I wish I had my smokes.'

'I'm so sorry it didn't work out with Shannon. Maybe he'll have an easier time.'

'What do you mean?'

'Shannon was fired.'

'No. No. I told you to have her come and meet Lester, but she never came, so, and he hasn't hired anyone for the office so, he's drowning.'
'She never came?'
'Can you let Dave and Carol know I won't be in for a while, maybe a long while? Also, do you think you could drop some smokes by the county jail?'
'But Shannon said she was going?'
'No. Lester's been managing the whole thing his own self.' Janine paused, then said, 'You know the brand I like, do you think you could drop some cigarettes here?'
'Shannon's been going to work, though?'
'I like the menthol ones, you know that, right?'
'But Shannon's been—'
The voice interrupted to say the call was ending, goodbye.
The line ended.

❖

After work, Linda stopped at one of the apartments they'd toured in the low-income area with bars on ground-floor windows and with old furniture in poor condition in the unit, and dropped an application she'd filled using Shannon's information, along with a deposit and first month's rent. She said she'd also prefer the furniture stay; she didn't mind the state of it, not one bit.

She was given the keys to the unit, and she drove home and walked straight in the house, straight to Shannon sitting in sweats on the couch watching TV and eating a bowl of cereal, and placed the apartment keys on the coffee table at her feet.

Shannon looked at them, then at Linda, then at the keys again.

'Your apartment keys. I'm keeping a key, by the way, because I know you.'

Shannon stopped chewing cereal. 'I don't have apartment keys.'

'Or a job,' Linda said.
'Yeah. I was fired.'
'Shannon.'
'What?'
'Shannon!'
'What!'
'I want you packing and calling up Dad to help you start moving, and I'm giving you one week. We said three weeks, and we gave you three weeks, and you get one more and no more. So. And I'm keeping an extra apartment key, because I just know you. You'll lose it or lock yourself out. So. Better start getting stuff out of storage.'
'Please,' Shannon said.
'Just where the hell have you been going during the day?'
Shannon said nothing; she just looked at Linda.
'Shannon?'
'What?'
'Just where the goddam hell have you been going during the day? You tell me you're going to work and leave out the door, but that's not where you've been going!'
Shannon said nothing. Just looking.
'Shannon?'
'What?'
A knock came at the front door, and the house fell to stillness.
A gentleman whom Linda did not know was standing on the porch when she opened the door. His hair was buzzed and thin, and he wore vivid wrap sunglasses and an athletic polo and baggy cargo pants and had an envelope, which he held with both hands.
'Are you Linda?' he said.
'I am.'
'Linda Lonsky?'
'Yes. That's me.'
'Served,' he said.
He handed her the envelope.

Linda accepted the envelope with no idea what she was accepting.

'Sorry?' She almost laughed, as if there was humor to be found here.

'Served,' he said. 'Witnessed.' He pointed to Shannon on the couch. Then he said good day and departed.

In the envelope were legal papers, which Linda skimmed there at the front door, opened to the neighborhood and sun.

Shannon was suing her.

'You're *suing* me?'

'Well.'

'You're goddamn suing me!'

'Technically I'm a legal tenant, the lawyer says I've been here longer than thirty days, so you can't just force me out.'

'You have a lawyer?'

'Well. You wanted to know where I was going. So.'

'Shannon!'

'What?'

'Shannon!'

Shannon said nothing.

'You got a lawyer, and you're goddamn suing me!'

Linda took the cereal bowl from Shannon and dumped it in the sink. 'Out!'

'What?'

'Get out!'

'You said I get one more week!'

'You're goddam suing me, Shannon!'

'The lawyer said you can't throw me out until the lawsuit is settled in or out of court!'

But Linda didn't listen. She took Shannon by the arm and dragged her out and shut the front door behind her, then locked it. Then she took armfuls of Shannon's clothes out of the dryer and unlocked the front door and threw them on the porch, and Shannon said what the fuck, but she took Linda's fury and made no effort to resist.

Then Linda locked the door again.

Then she wrote down the low-income apartment's address and unlocked the door and threw the paper out, then locked the door again.

Through the door she said there's the address to the apartment.

'I don't feel safe there!' Shannon said back through the door. She knocked and said it many times, *I don't feel safe there.*

But Linda was already down the hall in the bathroom, smoking out of the window, and so she did not hear Shannon shouting through the front door that she was absolutely terrified to be alone, please, please, Linda, shouting how is anyone ever supposed to be okay doing all this on their own? Shouting, Linda!

Later, when the shouting stopped, Linda came out of the bathroom and sat at the kitchen island, thinking and looking at nothing at all, just looking in space, feeling like she might just float away, and it seemed to her that not a person on this planet can abstain from a lie, not your mother or your father or your sister or your husband or your kids or your job, not one of them can stop themselves from telling lies, that the whole world was perfectly comfortable lying, absolutely keen on it, in fact, and it seemed to her so pointless, the whole of it, the whole of everything, it seemed so pointless.

Linda checked the front. Shannon was not there, and her belongings were no longer strewn across the porch, and all traces of her were gone.

Mrs. Hornsby came over from her house. 'Goodness, Linda,' she said. 'What did you do?'

Linda wasn't sure how to answer.

'We heard her shouting, you didn't hear?'

'No.'

'Goodness, Linda. That sister a yours was 'bout in tears!'

'Well. It was time she go, so.'

'Oh, I heard, she was screaming all about it. About in tears. You shouldn't have done that. You shouldn't have kicked her out. I'm telling you. We heard it from in the house and we just, you shouldn't have done that.'

'Well. Ed said we done enough, so. And Ed's, you know, he just needs all the support we can give, and it was time. So.'

But Mrs. Hornsby was shaking her head, not listening, saying you shouldn't have done that and not like that, and how she just couldn't believe that, that was just ... and then she went back up to the house and shut her door to the cold dusk.

Linda started dinner, and Ed came in with the kids from his mother's.

'You didn't say you were going to your mom's.'

Ed seemed to ignore this.

He got the kids settled in their rooms and came back into the kitchen.

'Are you smoking in the house? I smell it everywhere.'

Linda made a dinner spill.

Ed said, 'Did you kick Shannon out?'

'She left.'

Ed was quiet.

Then he said, 'You kicked her out?'

Linda did not answer.

'I got Ray calling my mom up and down. Shannon told him I was at Mom's, and he called and he called and he called.'

'You told Shannon you were going to your mom's?'

'Linda?'

'You didn't tell me.'

'Did you grab her by the arm and drag her out?' Ed said.

Linda, again, did not answer.

She was using a hand towel to clean the dinner spill.

'Hand towels are for hands, not spills, hon.'

She kept wiping.

'I got an apartment for her.'

'What apartment? Which apartment?'

'One in her budget,' Linda said.

'Christ, Linda,' he said.

'You said you needed this,' Linda said. 'You said you need to focus and fight this and get better, you said. *You!*'

'Yeah, but now I got Ray calling Mom and calling me, and he's going to show up at the clinic tomorrow, you know he will, and he's going to come at me because you dragged her out. When we talked, I said I needed peace, I needed out of this chaos, Linda. All you've done is make more, Linda!'

Linda wiped harder and wiped over more of the spill, making it worse and not better.

'How do I win with you?' she said.

'You need to wash that; you can't leave it out. Someone will use it, and they'll have dirty hands.'

'I really want to know. How do I win with you?'

'Geez,' he said.

'What?'

'I mean it, Linda, geez.'

She was digging the hand towel into the counter.

'I always lose with you, and it's not now and then or infrequent. You can expect a loss now and then with someone you love. I would accept that, that's healthy; some you win and some you lose, but with you it's every time I lose. I know because I keep track, and I'm confidently saying, with you, I have not won a single time,' Linda said.

'It's not a competition, Linda!'

'It is! It is because you make it one!' she screamed at him.

'The kids can hear you.'

'I didn't expect to lose every time when I married you.'

Ed was quiet for a long time.

Linda said, 'Well, aren't you going to say something?' She wanted to hear what he had to say about it. Could he say anything about her, she asked, could he? Could he think about her a moment, could he for one fucking moment?

And then Ed said it. Very simply. 'I slept with Shannon.'

'When?'

'Linda.'

Linda screamed, and her scream rammed into the windows and rammed through the house, she screamed *when!?*

'Linda.'

'How many times? Was it during the day? When she's at "work"?'

'Don't.'

'Goddamn you, Ed. Just. Goddamn you!'
'I swear it, Linda. Don't.'
'How many times, Ed!'
Ed kept from looking at her, looking anywhere else. She slapped him and earned his attention.
'When? What day? What night? Or is it days, Ed? Ed? Which days or which nights was it? Was it every day she was at "work," is that it? Every day?'
'Please don't.'
Ed tried to hold her, and she slapped his face. Then she slapped again. And a fourth time. 'Goddamn you, Ed!'
She wept openly, and the noise of it drew the kids from their rooms. She snapped at them to get back in, and Ed said nothing of her anger or her weeping; he allowed her the space.
He said he'd sleep on the couch tonight.

❖

Linda was late to the office the next morning, an hour late, and she had just sat at her desk when she noticed Dave and Carol were back and working in their office and there was a temp working at Janine's desk, a plain woman of young or old age, Linda wasn't sure which. Her face was old, but her hair was young. She wasn't working. She offered a half smile to Linda but no greeting. Dave and Carol popped open their office door.

The temp started working.

Linda said good morning to Dave and Carol and apologized for being late. Her eyes were red and swollen. Her makeup had run and smeared from crying in the parking lot, and she had cleaned and repaired much of it but not all, which had caused her to be late.

Dave and Carol called Linda into their office and said things look like they've slipped a little while they were out. Actually, they said, things look like they've slipped a lot. Timesheets, they said, showed that Linda had been late several days in a row and that this was not good, Linda, this was not good at all.

And then there was all the work that was behind.

Linda said she had stayed late many nights catching up, but there had been so much going on at home. She said, 'Look at the timesheets, they'll tell you how late I stayed to work, weekends, too," she said. 'That's all on there.'

'But the work's all backed up,' they said.

Linda apologized many times.

'This isn't good, Linda; things have really slipped.'

Before they spoke next, Linda heard her father out in the hall.

'Linda?'

He got louder.

'Linda in there?'

He came into Dave and Carol's office, Deena right after him, following him, asking him nicely but pointedly to come back to the car, please, hon, asking not to do this, and she had a polite hold on his arm, which he shrugged off over and over each time it returned.

'Jesus, Linda,' he said, getting eyes on her then Dave and Carol, looking them both over, then on Linda again. 'Tossing her out like a stranger, like a-a-a–'

'Come on, hon,' Deena said. She gently pulled him.

He pulled back.

'–like a-a goddamn stranger, Linda.'

'Mom, get him out,' Linda said.

Deena gently pulled again and said, let's go, dear, not here, but he pulled free again.

'That's your sister, Linda,' he said. 'Your goddamn sister. You don't do that.'

'Mom,' Linda warned.

'Yeah, hon, I know, I know. Come on, dear,' Deena said.

'Don't *come on dear* me,' Ray said, pulling himself free. 'She threw Shannon out like a goddamn stranger!'

'I'd do it again,' Linda said.

'Jesus, Linda,' Ray said.

'I'd throw her out harder if I could do it again,' Linda said.

'You hear that?' Ray asked Dave and Carol.

'Come back to the car, dear,' Deena said.

'And you know we got no room for her at the house, Linda, so now she's at that awful apartment because where else is she going and just in tears about it, you know, you've put her in tears about the whole thing, and that's all you're doing to her, always putting her in tears, and I'm just—and she's terrified in that place, you know that?'

Linda broke into weeping there, in front of her parents and Dave and Carol and the temp, who was leaning from the desk to see in the office.

'Jesus, Linda,' Ray said.

Linda's makeup ran from weeping.

'Mom! Get him out!'

'I'm trying, hon,' Deena said.

'We're just—your mother and I—you know—and then Ed was just, he didn't know what to say about the whole thing when we stopped at the clinic earlier. He just—I said you know Linda threw her sister out and that's what he said, he said he didn't know what to say about it.'

'You stopped at the clinic!' Linda asked Deena, not Ray.

'I'm not putting myself in the middle,' Deena said.

'And Ed said he's thinking some things,' Ray said. 'When we talked.'

'What things?' Linda said.

'Said he'd been thinking things for a while now. Thinking serious things, Linda. And that you've been smoking?'

'Come on, dear,' Deena said.

Linda wept once more.

'Jesus, Linda,' Ray said.

He let Deena pull him this time.

But he said, 'Like a goddamn stranger, Linda, that's your sister.'

'What serious things did Ed say?'

Deena escorted Ray out of the office and into the hall.

'What did Ed say?'

It was the only question she had.

Linda followed for answers but was suddenly aware of Dave and Carol and that she had cursed and cried in front of them, and so she did not follow her father.

She stayed in Dave and Carol's office, quiet as stone.

Dave and Carol said the trip they took showed the need for peace and for calm and, unfortunately, they said Linda brought too much chaos to the office.

Chaos at home finds its way to the office, they said.

They asked that she please collect her things and leave the building.

❖

Linda stood outside the house without going in for some time. Some of it she spent weeping, some she stood still; twice she put the key in and almost entered but stopped herself from going in.

Linda finally went in.

There were no TV noises; it was off, and the living room was dark. There were no children noises, no Ed noises.

The home was a tomb.

She searched for Ed and found some of his belongings gone. She looked where his shoes usually were, and they were gone. All of his shoes. She searched more and found more of his belongings gone. His dresser drawers were empty of socks and underwear, his clothes were absent from hangers, his medicine, his bathroom stuff, gone, and then she found the kids' belongings were gone too, their toys and clothes and their bathroom stuff.

Her heart ripped out.

On the kitchen island was a Post-it with Ed's writing.

I can't. Taking the kids to Mom's. Don't call - Ed

Linda read it a few times, then grabbed the ashtray and openly smoked in the house at the kitchen island, right where the kids usually ate. She was on the stool with the ashtray next to her, and she was smoking with the note before her.

She finished her cigarette and went into the garage and sorted through Ed's tools for a hammer. The head was rusted, and the wood of the handle was old and dried out.

Nothing drives a person to violence quicker than family, all a family's mess stewing and heating up in a person, the years of buildup and disappointment and lying and favoritism and neglect and anger and sadness wearing a person down.

Linda got in the car and drove to Clinton City, to the lower-income areas, with no music and no radio playing, driving directly to the apartment building where Shannon now resided, with the hammer resting on the front seat.

She parked and waited until dark, until late, until the world slept.

Nothing drives a person to violence quicker ...

Then into the building she went, with the hammer, up to Shannon's apartment, where she knocked and politely asked to come in, and when there was no response, she let herself in with the extra key, into black, into foreign smells, into a space that required slow, careful navigation in the dark. She bumped into this and bumped into that, whispering into the dark, half-whispering for Shannon, bumping into belongings and furniture that were not Shannon's, and then Linda was standing with the hammer in the dark, terribly confused, half-seeing in the dark a room full of things that were not Shannon's.

The years of buildup and disappointment and lying and favoritism and neglect and anger and sadness wearing a person down ...

Then lights went on.

A man in sleep pants and sleep shirt and with a gun was standing at the light switch.

Linda screamed out.

And the man in sleep pants and sleep shirt and with a gun startled and shot through Linda's nose.

Her body crumpled on the carpet.

At once, at an instant, the man shrieked.

He ran for the phone and, with it, ran out screaming into the phone, into nine-one-one, screaming she was wielding a hammer, a fucking hammer, and he shot her!

Screaming he just sublet the goddamn apartment that morning.

He just goddamn moved in, he shrieked, and my God, he screamed into the phone, my God the young lady who sublet the apartment said she didn't feel safe here, my God!

I shot her!

The man's screaming disappeared out of the hall, out of the building.

The apartment then fell to a harsh quiet filled with finality.

Curse the Writer

Up in the hills, behind single-lane roads that were winding and steep and quiet, the film director inhabited a home that was narrow and old and was, for the large sum it was worth, relatively tiny. On clear days, it took in full the sweeping valley below and city beyond. Most days, though, the sun could not reach in, and a broken dark lingered in the cramped rooms, the thin halls, and it crowded especially in the director's office.

The office above all else.

In the kitchen, the director paced restlessly one evening with a tightly rolled film script clutched in his hand. Colored Post-it notes protruded from its curled and dog-eared pages. The script's title, partially concealed by his hand, read *The King in Yellow*.

Over the phone, the director confirmed he'd gotten the script sent last week and confessed he'd read it in one sitting and then revisited it three more times over the weekend.

He said it's dark, it's brooding, it's a slow burn, that's for goddamn sure, but the dark and the brooding, he'd seen dark and brooding done before but not like this–and it was so devoid of cliches, he said. 'The themes really, truly, honestly resonate with me, way deep in my bones. I'm not kidding. They speak to me in ways nothing else ever has.'

A script like this, he said, not everyone gets a chance script like this.

'Studio wants to meet Friday,' his agent said from the other end. 'I heard from one of the assistants there's a real chance they're seriously considering you for this, really giving you a hard look.'

'Who else are they looking at?'

'I only heard a few names.'

'Like who?'

'Don't make me say.'

'Are they looking at Joe for it?' the director said.

'You always bring up Joe. Then you regret bringing up Joe.'

'They're looking at Joe?'

'They're always looking at Joe; everyone looks at Joe first.'

'Joe would mangle a script like this.'

'Go in Friday, chat with the studio folks. Bring your usual stuff, the tropes and well-worn plots, this script doesn't have any of those, so it needs some. Those studio folks adore predictable plot lines; they love knowing what's coming in the story. You're good at that in your directing, predictability, and if there's a way to weave in flashbacks, you should do that; you're really good at that, too, and I noticed there weren't any montages. Did you notice that? In the script? There's no montages.'

'I'd do this one different,' the director said.

'Different?'

'There's so much to work with in here, so much art and character work, good character work, so much to explore.'

'No one is asking you to do it different.'

'Did they bring in Joe yet?'

'Yesterday,' his agent said.

'Christ.'

'No one is saying for you to do it different,' his agent said.

The director wasn't listening.

'When you go in Friday, keep to stuff like you've done, okay? That's why they're bringing you in, they love what you've done, okay?'

The director began work in his office that evening, well into dusk.

After the sun had fallen below the rugged valley, he heard Dennis pull up.

He heard him come in the front.

The director waited, but Dennis did not come say hello and did not come give him a kiss or come discuss his day.

Discussion, lately, of any sort, led to arguments, bad ones, ones that went for hours, and so conversation had dwindled into stony, stained exchanges that were infrequent, until it was clear the relationship had ended, but neither could admit it.

The director heard him in the kitchen.

Moving around.

A house between them.

The director returned to the script, seated at his desk, and read of *The King in Yellow*, immersing himself once more in the unfolding scenes and characters and the sweeping, nightmarish landscapes described in the pages, the pivotal, artistic choices that needed to be made, reading and deciding what he wanted to inject from himself into the material, what ugly and terrifying reflection.

Near midnight, Dennis looked in and said he was sleeping on the couch tonight.

The director said no, take the bed.

'That's where you're sleeping.'

'Fine. Then don't,' the director said.

'Stop putting my balcony furniture in the garage.'

'I never liked it.'

Dennis said nothing to this, just looked at the director.

'I like to walk out there, and think out there,' the director said. 'It takes up all the space out there.'

Dennis was quiet in the office doorway. 'Are you working?'

'Yes.'

More quiet.

'Would you like to see?' the director said.

'No,' Dennis said.

After a moment. 'Are you sleeping in the bed?' Dennis said.

The director continued work but did not answer.

'I'm sleeping on the couch,' Dennis said.

Dennis left the doorway.

From the hallway, the director heard, 'And stop putting the balcony furniture in the garage!'

❖

Friday morning the director drove out of the hills, chasing cold and rising sun down into the city that lay like a waking beast and found his way into a waiting room with his storyboards and his ideas. He declined bottled water from the young woman at reception, who sat surrounded by logos and branding, then he changed his mind and asked for bottled water, please.

He was soon brought down long halls filled with office noise and taken into a conference room with a long, dark table and uniform chairs. One wall was glass and looked into the office, the other held successful film posters, the rest was window to blue sky and warmth that would not enter. It was cold, very cold in this room.

The director waited alone.

Muffled office noises filled the quiet.

Then a procession of men in suits filed along the glass wall and, one by one, entered and seated themselves, small-talking among each other and giving the director none of their attention until the man seated at the table's head formally began the meeting.

Then there was quiet.

The man at the head of the conference table thanked the director, so much, for coming, as did his entourage, and then asked what's he got, inviting the director to share his take on the script right at the start.

The director said, all right then, and led the room clumsily through his storyboard images, weaving the material's surrealism and horror and absurdity, and the madness of it all, behind it all, the absolute sheer madness of a cosmic horror script like this, and he wanted to put it through a lens of visionary imagination, subverting, he said, usual cinematic narrative for dreamlike visuals that were anything but quiet and mundane. And the ending, he gave precisely how he saw it all concluding, and it was here his passion was shown to the suits watching him, and he delivered to them every detail, every story thread brought to a chilling and upsetting close, and it was here he said that it would be up to the audience to interpret, that they weren't going to tell them the ending, you know, shove the ending in their face and digest it for them. He said he would let the audience do some of the work and interpret the ending how they did with the evidence he'd leave for them in the film, in the narrative.

When he finished, the room was silent.

The man at the head of the table was nodding, perhaps processing. The man, a very important man, adjusted how he was sitting and said you know what movie he loved of the director's, he said he absolutely loved *Safe and Sound*. 'Talk about eerie events and chilling discoveries, right? You had teens forming unlikely alliances but keeping those meet-cute moments, and the hero's journey, mentors and plucky sidekicks, and a-and a-and, what's it, a crisis, midpoint, heroes and allies at their lowest, and you still kept the humor and the villain, I don't remember his name, um, the guy with the mind control, and who would have seen when you brought him back for *Safe and Sound 4, Beyond the Ordinary*, I mean, what a treat. What. A. Treat. I really loved those films.'

The director smiled but did not offer thanks.

'Those films were so comfortable, weren't they?' the man said to the suits on either side of him. 'Weren't they light, undemanding? Didn't they get us out of our heads for some camp, some scares, some fun?'

The suits on either side of him agreed, yes, those films did those things.

The man said, 'And they each have a hidden gem, something for fans to cling to, something to brand, and it's kind of a charm, isn't it? It's a charm. Really.'

He asked the suits on either side, it's a charm isn't it?

They said yes.

'Yes, yes exactly,' he said.

Then he thanked the director for coming and said they'll be in touch.

He and the suits waited patiently and silently while the director collected his storyboards and items and waddled from the room, and they watched him through the glass wall, he tried not to look back, while he exited the office and had his parking validated.

❖

Weeks later, the director's agent phoned and said they wanted him, they sent an offer, he was sending it over now. He told the director it wasn't bad; he'd seen better, but lately, he'd seen worse too.

A lot worse, he said.

'I hadn't heard anything. I've been waiting.'

'Yeah, the offer just came through.'

'I didn't think they'd want me. I've been thinking that for weeks. This whole time.'

'Well, I guess there was a scheduling thing, they were waiting. I don't know, but the offer came and it's on the way. I think it's real good.'

'Christ. I mean it, Christ. This is, I mean, I was heartbroken about it the other day, I swear it. This whole time I'm thinking, Christ. What were they waiting on?'

'Ah, come on,' his agent said from the other end.

'What?'

'Don't make me say.'

'What were they waiting on?'
'Come on, we got an offer,' his agent said.
'Christ!' the director said.
'You always regret asking.'
'They were waiting on Joe?'
'Everyone's always waiting on Joe.'
'Well. Do they want me or they want Joe?'
'Everyone wants Joe. Okay? Everyone. They waited to see if he's available, but he's not. I wish you would stop asking about Joe and putting yourself down.'

'I mean I was heartbroken the other day, thinking I didn't get this,' the director said.

'We got an offer,' his agent said.
'So. I'm their second choice?'
'You don't want it?'
'No, of course I want it! But Christ, they were waiting on Joe?'
'Okay, I'm telling them you want it.'
'Of course, I do.'
'Okay, because them waiting on Joe has put production behind a bit, you'll see in the offer, but I still think it's good. I think it's real good.'

The director said nothing.
Then he said, 'Joe would have mangled this script.'

❖

The following week, the director was down at the studio, in a small building on the lot with offices and beat-up furniture and more framed film posters.

He was meeting the film's executive producer.

A gentleman only just entering his winter years was waiting for the director before he went in. He wore a faded, beat-up ball cap with the movie title *Safe and Sound* written in bold. It identified him as crew, specifically the director of photography. It noted the date of shooting, some eleven years before.

The man's movements and eyes yet had youth in them. They shook hands like teammates.

'What did you think of the script?' the director asked.

The gentleman, whose name was Lenny, said he read it, loved it, and said he was thinking, and he asked the director to hear him out, they should do this one completely different.

'That's what I said! That's *exactly* what I said.'

'This feels like one you don't ever get again.'

'I said that too, I said this one's, like, it's like a *Shining*.'

'It's like a *Shining*, yeah,' Lenny said. 'It's like a Kubrick, exactly!'

'Yeah.'

'I'm already thinking camera angles, framing, I got my camera guys already learning some really interesting techniques for act three.'

'Were you thinking cranes and wide angles?'

'I was. I was thinking sweeping, you know, but vast, wide angles.'

'Lots of them, right?' the director said.

'I was thinking lots, make the audience feel lost.'

'Yeah.'

'Remember what we did after *Safe and Sound*, with, what was it?'

'*The Visitor*?'

'No,' Lenny said, 'It was–?'

'You're thinking when we did *Possessed Toaster*?'

'No,' Lenny said. He plucked the cap off his head to think better.

'*Eerie Echoes*?' the director suggested.

'*Eerie Echoes*, the jump scares characters laugh off and the foggy cemetery, characters splitting from groups to search, I was thinking we don't do anything like that here.'

'No, no, nothing like *Eerie Echoes*.'

'There's something real in this one,' Lenny said.

'That's–that's where I'm going with this, you know, this one is, it's all in the craft of it; it's Cosmic Horror but it's, it's an artist's craft.'

'Whatever you're seeing in your head and planning, I'll make it happen for the camera.'

'You always do,' the director said.

The director shook Lenny's hand again, and the men went in with grins and waited in the EP's waiting room. The secretary apologized, but the EP was running a bit behind, and he would be on site any minute. She offered free water. Both men accepted. The director asked, more than once, logistical questions for images he saw and would like to see, and Lenny answered each with flexibility and positive tone.

The EP entered thirty minutes late and went right into his office.

A few minutes later, Lenny and the director were allowed back.

The EP was on the phone at his desk when they entered; he raised a finger and silenced greetings and welcomed them to sit.

Lenny and the director waited. The other end of the EP's phone call did all the talking and him all the listening, and he nodded and, now and again, said yep, yes, uh-huh, yep, yes, okay, yep, yes, yep, okay.

Then he hung up.

He stood and came around his desk and the men stood and he shook the men's hands and said it was marvelous to meet the director and his director of photography.

They sat once more and let greetings settle.

'Can I just say how personally thrilled I am we got you on board?'

The director tried a smile in thanks; it was loose and weak, but the EP wasn't interested in an answer. He was pulling together budget sheets for the director to look over. He licked the tip of his finger when papers refused to separate.

The EP said, 'Thanks again for sending over all that material last week. Love seeing the vision stuff; it was all great. Oh! Hah! You sent it to staff finance teams, not the project finance teams, hah! It's fine, it's no big deal. Stuff gets sent wrong all the time; you're not the first. We got it where it needed to go, just a little corporate workflow stuff, so, just make sure you send creative to the correct email. Corporate ins and outs, you know? You artists are always a trip.'

The EP stapled a packet for the director and a packet for himself.

'So, what you're looking at, first page, that's the shooting schedule.'

The director and Lenny shared the packet.

'Now I know that's tight—'

'It's real tight,' the director said.

'The studio still thinks it's realistic,' the EP said.

'This leaves no time to explore creative nuances, depth— does this look realistic?' the director said to Lenny.

'Looks unrealistic,' Lenny said.

'This is—this is a lot of one-takes? Right? This looks like, almost, all one-takes?'

'Looks like we're doing one take for each scene with this.'

'We have to rework this,' the director said.

'Yeah, no, the studio looked at it a bunch a ways, and this is where they landed, so.'

'Well, I'll call them.'

'Yeah,' the EP said. 'Yeah. I'm the in-between on this one, so don't call the studio. You tell me, and I'll reach out. They are just so busy, and they need someone to just, you know, and that goes for anything with the studio guys, really, if it's budget or set or spats, you need anything, you tell me and I'll talk to them, so, don't reach out to them, reach out to me.'

'Oh. Well. You talk to them then. Because. This schedule, there's no room to explore the material here,' the director said. 'Because this, we were saying, Lenny and I, this is, like, a *Shining*, you know Kubrick? This script could be, I'm thinking, it could even be bigger than a Kubrick, don't you, Lenny?'

'I do, yeah, we said outside. It's like a *Shining*. It's like a Kubrick.'

The EP heard them and nodded.

'I'll make a note to call and see; it's pretty set in stone but, yeah, so, and then if you flip, you've got all your location options there, super cost-effective, you see the photos there?' the EP said. 'Locations look just fantastic, right?'

'These—I sent over some locations I thought fit the script well, and I'm not—'

The director flipped ahead in the packet, then flipped back. 'I don't see any I sent over?'

Lenny borrowed the packet from the director and flipped too, but flipped back after a brief search.

'The locations I sent had great bones for the overall creative vision, for thematic impact. These are, who picked these? These are not interesting, are they interesting to you?' the director asked Lenny.

'They don't look interesting to me,' Lenny said.

'Who picked these?'

The EP said the studio had relationships with each location there, and that meant discounts, that meant budget-friendly, and he said if they flipped a few pages, they'd see the full line details.

The director flipped and saw a total budget number that was significantly smaller than he'd hoped and said, 'That's the budget?'

The EP confirmed.

Lenny said, 'Wait. That's the budget?'

The EP confirmed, yes it was, again.

'Yeah, this has to be reworked, right?' the director asked Lenny.

'There's zero wiggle room in that number,' Lenny said.

'You can't make a *Shining* like this,' the director said.

'No, that's gotta be reworked,' Lenny said.

'You'll talk to the studio,' the director said to the EP.

'Finance spent a long time coming to that number, meetings and meetings and, but, so, I'll make a note to call but, oh!'

He then said he'd waited to tell the director this in person, before they went into casting later in the week. He heard, and he said this hasn't been confirmed, but it sounds like a certain A-lister is interested in the lead.

'Who?' the director said.

The EP gave the A-list actor's name and said he was red hot right now; he had some big things out, and the guy was just on fire!

'No, no, no,' the director said. 'The guy's wooden, he overacts, you've seen?'

'Yeah, I've seen,' Lenny said. 'I've definitely seen. He's an overactor.'

'Same with his on-screen chemistry, it's overbearing, don't you think it's overbearing?' the director asked Lenny.

'I think it's a little overbearing.'

'He's very interested, I heard. He loved the script, loved the part.'

'Well. Yeah. It's a good script,' the director said.

'Great script,' Lenny said.

'But the guy has no range; he's the same in everything,' the director said. 'You've seen him in one thing, no need to see his other films, he's the same.'

'Can't tell his performances apart,' Lenny added.

'This script needs better,' the director said.

'Yeah. Yeah. So. I hear you, I do, I'm acknowledging I hear you on all of that,' the EP said. 'Part of my job is making sure you're heard, okay? So, consider yourself heard, okay?'

'Well. Yeah. Okay,' the director said.

The EP continued, 'Buuuut the studio invited him for a read Thursday during casting. No decisions, no commitments either way, just a quick, informal, easy, uninvolved audition to make his people happy and quiet and to make the studio happy and quiet so we can say we saw him. That's it. He'll be in and out. You don't like him after, not an issue. End of the day, it's one hundred percent your choice. Okay? Sound good?'

'And you'll talk to the studio about the other stuff, reworking budget and location?'

'Um. Oh. Yes. Sure. Yep. Got a note to talk to them right here.'

'Anything else?' the director asked Lenny.

'Nothing else.'

'Everything sounds good?' the EP said.

The director nodded.

'Can you verbally say, though? That all sounds good? I need verbal agreement,' the EP said.

The director verbally agreed.

❖

On Thursday, the director was in a mostly empty room with a casting assistant, the EP, and two representatives from studio management who were in the corner, away to themselves, and who intrusively chatted in the worst moments. They all sat on stiff chairs. For most of the morning and into the afternoon, actors of all size and caliber were brought in and allowed five minutes to introduce themselves, inform what role they were reading, and perform. Some needed warmup, some needed a moment to step into character, some came in costumes, and, when their five minutes were up, they were thanked and shown out.

More than once, the casting assistant mixed up paperwork that had been collected in order, causing mismatches between the actor auditioning and the documents before the team, which caused delays for accuracy, and more than once the casting assistant was sent into the waiting area to ask the actors waiting to be quiet.

After lunch, auditions resumed, and a skinny fellow with ear-length hair, moppy and frizzy, but with eyes deep and full, came into the room. He gave his name in a quirky manner. He was an unknown; he had never had his name in credits before, but when he was told to begin, from him came a drama with absolute magnetism. He read a monologue from near the end of the script, when the story's cosmic horror was closing on madness, and the drama he delivered was liquid, a lightning, a dance. His gestures were grace and they were power and they were insanity; in his face was pain and delight and madness, and in this plain and boring room, he created atmosphere with his eyes and body, and when he was gone from the room, the director knew he had seen something rare, and he said as much to the others. That, he said, now *that* was our lead!

Neither the casting assistant, nor the EP, nor the studio reps disagreed, but nor did they agree.

They were quiet.

More auditions proceeded.

Only a few were memorable.

Near the end of the day, which had been taxing and overwhelming, and after all actors had been seen, a woman in a flowy pant suit came in the room with a phone to her ear, her hair tightly pulled back, and told the EP that she was the personal assistant to the A-list actor, and that *he* was en route and would arrive in ten minutes.

Not a moment later, a stylist, a make-up artist, two bodyguards, and a second personal assistant penetrated the quiet audition room, bringing noise and individual phone conversations and questions–*can we set up here or there, let's move this over here and move that there and, oops, sorry we knocked that over, oh, it's broken, sorry about that.*

The EP allowed their chaos to rob peace and to consume and overtake authority of the room.

When it settled, the room returned to quiet as assistants and stylists and guards stood still and were on their phones, ignoring the world around them, waiting.

Thirty minutes passed.

The woman in the pant suit and sunglasses apologized, *he*'ll be here any moment, she said.

Thirty more minutes passed.

Then thirty more.

And then there was noise in the hall outside the audition room and it grew in volume, and then *he* entered.

The A-list celebrity.

His entourage in the hall passed him to the entourage waiting in the room, and he was swarmed by his assistants and stylists and guards, and they touched him and perked him and made micro-touch-ups to his face and hair and clothing, all while he stood smiling with teeth as white and perfect as fresh snow.

Small talk exchanged between the EP and the A-list celebrity.

The studio reps, who'd been in the corner, scooted closer and leeched on the man's presence, inserting themselves into the small talk, greedy for just a second of his attention.

A quick introduction to the director was given but no more, and it seemed the director was shoved into the background of the A-lister's audition, which was dull and given with creative choices the A-lister made, which were far from the vision the director held of the material.

The room applauded when the A-lister finished.

The director did not.

Glowing compliments and praise spewed forth, and the A-lister gave back humility, which was flat and not at all discouraging of more praise and more compliments.

Then the A-lister and his circus departed, and the EP and studio reps descended into exclusive conversation, which the director was not invited to join.

Three days of auditions continued.

None arrested the director as the skinny fellow's performance had.

In a final casting meeting, the director, role by role, gave his selections to the EP and casting assistant.

One by one the cast was built.

When all that was left was who the director would like in the lead role, the EP said an offer already went out; he thought the director knew.

'An offer to who?'

'The A-lister,' the EP said, quiet and distant.

'No, no, we were just supposed to see him, so we can say we saw him. What happened to that?'

The EP said, 'The studio guys were so impressed when the A-lister rolled in and gave his audition, they sent an offer. He accepted this morning. Congrats! You have your lead!'

'*They offered him?*'

'And he accepted. This morning.'

'Christ.'

'Congrats! You have an A-list lead.'

'The skinny guy was way better. Didn't you think so? I mean, for a script like this?'

'He was okay,' the EP said. 'I've seen better.'

'Christ,' the director said.

'This guy brings star power, he brings audiences, wider releases, we could even be talking franchise if this goes the way we're all thinking,' the EP said. 'Everyone loves a good franchise.'

'Christ ...'

❖

Preproduction went for three weeks, and each day the director came down from the hills to the studio lot in the morning and went back up well after the sun had died at night.

In a soundstage, the oldest on the lot, he and Lenny sat with set designers and talked them through what the director saw from the material, what he hoped they could capture and create of the material's physical world and how each angle, each shot was intended. The director wanted purposeful shadows, esoteric geometry; he wanted to give the audience a feeling of vastness but also confinement. He wanted reality to blur, he wanted incomprehensible, he wanted an abyss audiences had never seen!

He was meticulous in reviewing sketches of each set piece, and many times they were not approved and needed revision until he was satisfied.

Each prop he inspected with the prop master following, collecting his feedback, which was harsh and picky and defended with reasoning of craft, of vision.

Every actor was made to parade through the soundstage in costume for the director and Lenny and costume designer, and the director said the cloaks for Eldritch Occultists should not be red, they should be black and tattered, not clean and pressed, and he didn't want to see any of their faces. He wanted masks, ornate yellow masks, and he wanted more decadence, and he asked for more dread!

'Bring out *The King in Yellow*,' the director said to the costumer. He wanted to see the entity, *The King*. The actor and costume were sent for and brought out.

The actor beneath the costume was not visible; there were no traces of their humanity or identity.

The figure stood silently, elegant and horrific and draped in yellow, and was studied closely by the director and Lenny.

The director, after a time, said yes, yes, I see abstract, I see forbidden knowledge, I see despair, I see profound, I see destructive, but I also see mystery, misery, I see overwhelming presence, I see something I don't understand but I see that I want to, I see, no, I feel powerlessness, helplessness, I feel desolation, I feel no control over my life, I feel my sanity shattered, I feel unfathomable awe ... I feel insignificant!

The director was quiet for a long time, circling the actor in costume and then stopping and then circling more.

He held tears.

Lenny and the costumer refrained from disrupting the director's quiet, introspective study.

❖

That night, the director ate leftover dinner in the living room, looking out and down into the void, the black canyon below, and the lights of the city dancing beyond.

Dennis was reading in the kitchen, wrapped in a wool blanket and with tea. He was half-hidden from the director by the wall.

'Please be quiet in there,' the director heard from the kitchen. 'I'm reading.'

'I know you're reading.'

They were quiet, the director eating and Dennis reading.

'I said please be quiet.'

'I'm quiet,' the director said. 'I'm eating.'
'I hear you.'
Neither spoke for some time.
'I hear you,' Dennis said.
The director continued to eat.
'I said I hear you,' Dennis said from the kitchen.
The director stared deeper into the canyon, into the void.
'I'm seeing a house tomorrow,' he heard Dennis say.
'You said you weren't moving out.'
'I'm not living on our couch,' Dennis said from the kitchen.
'Sleep in the bed.'
'That's where you're sleeping.'
The director went quiet and could not finish his food.

He said, sometime later, into the kitchen, 'We could share the bed.'

The director heard the book placed on the table.
'Don't do that,' he heard Dennis say.
'You said you were staying, you weren't moving out.'
'Goddamn you,' he heard Dennis say.

The director sat in the quiet with his plate in his lap, and the black was around him, it was in the home, in the corners, and it was everywhere outside.

Black.

An empty room around the world.

Dennis spoke from the kitchen. 'When we said this wasn't working, when we did that whole thing weeks and weeks ago, and you blew up at me and I blew up at you and I was crying and-and you were crying, and when we were quiet, I told you I'm looking at places.'

'We didn't say that,' the director said.
'What?'
'*We* didn't say that. *We* didn't both say this wasn't working. *We* both did not. *I* did not.'
'We did, we both–'

The director heard Dennis stand and come into the living room, into the dark.

He was a shadow.

'We both sat where you're sitting and cried our eyes out and we said, *both of us*, this wasn't working.'
'You didn't say you were looking at places,' the director said.
'Well, I'm looking at houses tomorrow.'
'A house.'
'What?'
'You said you were seeing *a* house tomorrow.'
'Goddamn you, you know that, just goddamn you.'
Dennis collected his book from the kitchen and left upstairs and came back with pillows and a blanket and said get out of the living room, he was making his bed, get out.
The director slept alone, upstairs in the bed, in the dark.

❖

Filming began on the soundstage a few days later. Before cameras rolled, the director shared—with cast and crew huddled round and with Lenny at his side and with a set surrounding them that was both beautiful and terrifying—what he hoped this film, this work of art, could be, what it could show people, what it could disrupt for them in their everyday lives, and what it could cause by ways of new thinking, what he hoped, he said, this piece of art could say. Because, he said, that's what this is, it's art, it's craft, it's human experience, and it is not shallow, he told those gathered around, it's *not* shallow, it's *not* content, it's *not* mediocre.

Here, he said, they have a unique opportunity to say something new, and goddamn if they weren't going to say it!

Cast and crew separated with this energy and prepped for the first scene.

The EP came to the director where he sat in his tall chair, with Lenny and the cameraman and film monitors deep in talks of angles and movements, and the EP asked right in their conversation what the director thought if they put a Pizza Hut pizza in the first scene. Maybe, he said, opening on the pizza and the melted cheese and roasted veggies and, maybe, a sign on the back wall with the Pizza Hut logo with some sort of coupon deal advertised.

Perhaps, the EP said, the next scene could take place in a Pizza Hut?

'Studio was wondering what would you think of that?' he said.

The director sat with the question and looked at the EP and all his outward signs of sincerity.

Sincerity for Pizza Hut placement.

'Is it my choice?' the director said.

'Of course, yeah, your choice,' the EP confirmed.

'You're not just saying it's my choice and then choosing?'

'No, no, nothing like that here,' the EP confirmed.

'Then absolutely not.'

The director and Lenny and cameraman returned to talks of how to capture the first scene's unsettling closeups but were interrupted.

'Or. What if the Pizza Hut delivery guy knocks, brings it in, camera gets a nice shot of the pizza box, and it opens to golden crust and pepperoni, and one of the actors can lift a slice, all that stretching delicious cheese, and you can still have all your dialogue and keep all your marks?'

'You're not shoving ads in my film,' the director said.

He entertained no more of this talk.

The EP stayed where he was standing, removed of all attention.

'Maybe we can think on it, you know, think of some ways we can work in Pizza Hut, because the studio guys were brainstorming cross-promotion ideas with cosmic horror and Pizza Hut, and they were super excited about it, and Pizza Hut loved it when we pitched the idea, you know, *Summon the Eldritch Flavor, Tentacle Breadsticks,* and, I'll just say, that's cash back in the budget. So. Maybe we just think on it.'

The director said he wasn't thinking on it, it was his choice and don't bring it up, and continued his talks with no more interest in the EP.

Not five minutes later, the A-lister's assistant came before cast and crew and stood on the set and did not ask, but told them, to please applaud when the A-lister comes out, when he finishes a scene, and when he exits set. And she said not lazy applause but good, hearty applause and–oh, she said, here he comes.

She moved off set and traded out attention on herself for attention on the A-lister, who entered in costume and who received the room's lazy, not hearty, applause and who basked in it with the same glowing showmanship and lack of humility as if he'd been given a standing ovation.

The director pulled the actors together and rehearsed the scene several times over, and the A-lister, who was flat in delivery and tone, gave fellow actors very little to react to, which produced clunkiness, but when it was time to film, they were already running behind, he said he was ready, no worries.

'You're sure?' the director said. His concern was genuine and, at this point, not yet irritated.

The A-lister confirmed he was ready.

Cast and crew found their places, cameras rolled.

The director called for quiet.

Then he said *action!*

The first take went for less than a minute before the A-lister delivered to the camera silence, then apologized. He had the mindset, he said, he was right there, in a good head space, then lost it.

The director called *cut!*

The A-lister said he'll get it this next one.

The director called out for quiet again and made sure the A-lister was ready before he called *action!*

During this second take, the A-lister made his marks on time and gave his dialogue from memory, but his tone was a mismatch for the content of the scene; it wasn't genuine and stood out, ugly.

Cut!

While crew started resetting, the director leaned to Lenny and said, 'Didn't I say he was flat? Didn't I say that? Christ, I wish I had the skinny fellow.'

The director stared at the actors on the monitors, shaking his head, then came out from behind the camera onto the set and was brusque with the A-lister from the outset, not too brusque, but he sternly reset the A-lister's headspace, forcing him to find the despair the character suffers in this scene, the utter fucking despair over the truth he discovers–*everything we do is meaningless*, that *none of this has any meaning other than the meaning we assign to it*, that *life has no outward meaning, only inward*.

'Are we good on that?' the director said when he finished.

'But I don't like that headspace. I don't think it's good for me.'

'I said, are we good on that?'

The A-lister said he got it.

Behind the camera once more, the director said quiet!

Action!

The director, Lenny, and the EP watched the scene unfold from the monitor. The actors performed, and it pleased the director, what he saw, until a light rig above the set came loose and swinging into set pieces.

Cut!

After fifty minutes of investigating, the crew determined the rig failed due to age and wear. One of the crew said that rig must be thirty, maybe forty years old.

'Why aren't we using new?'

'Wasn't in budget.'

'Christ,' the director said.

He told the crew to reset, and an hour later they were ready to film again.

The director shouted for quiet. He didn't ask. He shouted.

Action!

The director, Lenny, and the EP watched, again, the scene unfold in the monitor.

Lenny leaned over and whispered a suggestion to the director, respectful of his volume against the performance before them. He proposed playing with framing, he knew they had set it up how it was, but if they played with composition, it could enhance the feel the director was going for in the shot.

It could help the vision, his suggestion.

The director said no, he didn't like that. He liked it how it was at the moment; this was exactly how he saw it. So, no. Don't do that.

Lenny made no more suggestions.

The scene continued.

'Where's the jump scares?' the EP said. He was not mindful of his volume.

'We're not doing jump scares,' the director said.

'No jump scares in a horror film?'

'We're not doing them.'

'Nothing coming out of a closet?'

'I said no.'

'But how else are people going to be scared?'

'No jump scares,' the director said.

'They create tension, that's what audiences love, our marketing department will confirm that.'

'Not in this film,' the director said.

'One jump scare, for flavor,' the EP said.

'Flavor? We're not making dinner here. Are we making dinner here, Lenny?'

Lenny said nothing.

The EP said, 'I see.'

The three returned to watching the scene through the monitor.

'What does that mean? You see?' the director said.

'I have to tell the studio you're giving them a horror film without jump scares is all.'

'Want me to tell them to their face?' the director said.

The EP said no more.

The A-lister broke the scene and called attention, in front of all cast and crew, to the themes the director was hoping for in the scene, what his dialogue was to reinforce, and said he didn't think it was working, and gave his own interpretation of the scene, which his assistant reinforced from off set, saying she agreed, she thought that was a better interpretation.

The EP agreed with the A-lister and added the only thing missing was Pizza Hut.

After many moments of frustrated quiet, the director said, 'Did we revisit the shooting schedule?'

❖

A week of filming passed painfully and slowly. It was full of friction and delays and passive aggression.

The second week of filming began with the director arriving at the studio lot early, before the sun had risen.

At the security checkpoint, while the director waited to be allowed entry, a man flagged him down from the sidewalk.

He came over to the director's vehicle, gesturing to roll down the window so he could talk.

The director did, with confusion.

The man said, 'Oh my God, it's you!'

The director agreed, it was him.

'I heard you were working on something new, and I said to my friend, that director is working on something new, and he said no, no, that mediocre guy, no, he's not working on something new,' the man said.

'He said mediocre?'

'I went online and found a forum, they said you're doing *The King in Yellow*!'

'Oh, you'll have to wait and see. Haha.' The director faked his laughter.

'I knew it! I can't wait to watch it already, haha! I'm such a huge fan.'

'Oh, thank you, haha.' The director faked another laugh.

'From your first film, in art school, I'm saying, all the way to *Safe and Sound 7, Resurgence*.'

'Art school?'

'You did a short film about a family on a farm, and they just wanted an escape, but they couldn't help themselves, they couldn't escape because they weren't capable, they wanted it so bad, I'm saying, your directing showed how badly they wanted a new start, but your directing showed, some people just aren't capable of change, and that affected me, I'm saying. Really really affected me. And. I'm such a huge fan, oh gosh I'm going to cry, I'm not like this, haha, I'm sorry, I'm crying, haha!'

The man, *the huge fan*, wept and laughed. It was unsettling.

'You enjoy my work?'

'So much!'

'Do you want to take a picture with me?'

'Oh my God!'

The *huge fan* laughed and wept and slid out his phone and snapped a picture with the director.

'Want me to sign something of yours?' the director said.

He was being waved onto the studio lot by security.

He ignored them.

'I don't have anything to sign,' the *huge fan* said.

'Well, you got a picture, so you can show people.'

Before the director drove inside the lot, he wanted to confirm the man's friend had called him *mediocre*. He asked twice, but the man walked away and down the sidewalk, still weeping and laughing, without confirming.

The director then parked and walked onto a new set.

Reflected before him was a surreal dreamscape of endless, rolling black plains, where the horizon appeared to recede infinitely. Colossal, shifting monoliths stood, unsettling and disagreeable in their design, strange stars hung in the dark.

Illustrated in the distance, in the backdrop, barely visible, was a small, horrid city where black rivers met.

The director sat with the false illusion of the infinite, in the dark, and he breathed its wood odor, and slowly bodies arrived, sleepy and cold and shuffling, and then came in the lead actress.

She was a gentle woman, both in voice and how she moved, as if she were glass.

She was offered good mornings but returned few.

After a bit of morning rehearsal, the director heard her snap at a craft services gentleman, over something or another, and in between scenes, she refused hair and makeup with harsh words.

When filming resumed, she slapped the A-lister in the first take too hard and bruised his eye.

The director pulled her aside, and she unleashed horrible complaints against the studio's legal team constantly sending her NDAs. She told the director it was goddamn constant! Every morning, she said, I get a new NDA! Sometimes at night too, she said. A knock at her door and an NDA waiting on the ground and the deliveryman gone from sight, she said.

'Well, you can't slap like that, and you can't snap at the food guys like that,' the director said.

'It's been so many NDA's!' the lead actress said.

'Well. Talk to legal, but you can't keep doing that on set.'

'They don't have phone numbers; you can't reach them. Some of the NDAs mention earlier NDAs, and some mention upcoming NDAs. I can't keep any of it straight. It's driving me goddamn crazy! I don't know what I can and can't say, about anything. I'm not sure I should even be saying this, I'm serious!'

'Can you keep going? We're already behind.'

'Yeah. I can keep going, but it's compounding and driving me crazy, I'm serious.'

'Well. Come on set. We'll keep going. We'll talk to legal,' the director said.

Before they resumed filming, the A-lister's assistant came to the director and asked he please do not approach the A-lister with feedback; all feedback was to come through her, and she would discuss with him.

The director received this like stone.

Cameras rolled, and filming began.

The scene opened, and the A-lister had begun with a strong performance but slowly declined in authenticity and, before the director called cut, was downright unbelievable in voice and tone.

The director gave feedback, which went unacknowledged, so the director gave it again, and when this went unacknowledged too, he went for the assistant and gave her the feedback in very clear detail, which she took to the A-lister.

They spoke at length while the set was in pause.

From the A-lister, she brought the director a reply. 'He disagrees,' she said. 'He's going to do it the way he's doing it.'

'He's killing the scene, he's killing it dead, right, Lenny?'

The director swirled and looked for Lenny, who hopped from behind camera to say, 'Oh yeah, just murdering the scene.'

'Goddamn murdering the scene,' the director said into the assistant's face.

The EP stepped in and talked the director away a few paces then told him he would handle this, it's what he's here for, so, he said go take a seat and let me. It's good feedback, he assured the director, so just let me handle this, he said.

The EP took the A-lister aside.

A few moments later, the EP returned and said the A-lister's going to do it his way, so.

'Well,' the director said.

Nothing more came from him for many long moments. Then he said, 'Can we fire him?'

The EP took the director from earshot of cast and crew, into a dark corner of the set. Here, the dreamscape had been painted into a flurry of nightmarish swirls. It hung over the EP and director.

The EP approached what he said next with care and fragility but delivered it with honesty. He said, 'You're not the sole creative force here. You understand that, right?'

'Well. I understand that,' the director said, 'but–'

'Filmmaking isn't about individual brilliance, you get that? Right?' the EP said.

'If I can just get everyone in sync, you'll see what I'm doing. You can't see it yet,' the director said.

'You get that you have a team; a cinematographer, designers, crew, I mean, you've got actors to do what they do; you understand you're not all those things, right?'

'I mean, I value their input but you can't see yet, I have a vision for this–'

'I've watched plenty of films fail because a director couldn't take a step back, couldn't keep himself from strangling and choking and stifling a film to death. I've seen so many films just *fall* to their death, just into an endless black abyss these films *fall*,' the EP said.

'No. No. No. I'm not–that's not–'

'Leave the A-lister alone, let him perform; that's why we hired him.'

'I didn't hire him!'

But the EP had already walked away and was no longer listening.

The director returned and stared into the camera monitor while the scene reset, looking deep into the nightmarish dreamscape coming through the lens, into the vast infinite it offered, and then he noticed a Pizza Hut logo in the infinite.

'What is that?' the director snapped.

'Oh. That. Promo deal was struck, it's staying. Chat with legal if you want it out.'

'Good Christ,' the director said.

The director, who'd had it for the day, called lunch.

Cast and crew enjoyed complimentary Pizza Hut delivery.

While the set was quiet with chewing and small talk, a courier arrived for the lead actress.

It was another NDA that required her signature.

'What can't I talk about now?' she shouted at the courier. She chased him off set, shouting it over and over.

❖

Late that evening, the director was seated cross-legged on the living room couch with lights out and black masking up, blocking the kitchen, so light would not enter and sound would not escape.

He was alone in this black, quiet world.

On the TV was playing the director's first feature film.

The glow filled the room, filled the director's face.

The first frames flickered on screen.

The cinematography was undoubtedly distinct, nods to great auteurs of cinema genius.

Each shot was canvas, drowned in striking composition, lighting, and attention to detail.

Yet, as the film unraveled, it was clear there was no compelling narrative. The story was a maze of abstract symbolism with little context and enigmatic characters trapped in a plot with no clear destination. The characters of this film remained emotionally distant and inaccessible and unlikable, as the director had thought then, and still did, this was the true nature of people, but it made the material difficult to digest.

Each sequence of the film left the viewer with more questions than answers, and the dialogue, which was sparse and cryptic, made the film impenetrable and unenjoyable and confusing, and left the viewer in a state of bewilderment and introspection.

But to the director, it made perfect sense.

The director heard the black masking pulled free, and light entered from the kitchen, breaking the dark in two.

Dennis looked in.

Into the dark.

'Never mind, I'll come back,' he said.

Dennis attempted to redo the black masking.

The director paused the movie and asked what?

'No, I'll come back.'

Sounds of masking moving and not refitting correctly upset the silence and the dark.

'What did you want?'

'I wish you wouldn't do this; it's not good for your eyes,' Dennis said of the masking.

Dennis couldn't get the masking to sit correctly.

'Dark and light ruins your vision,' Dennis said.

The director looked at Dennis, whose head was poked around the masking, light full and bright around it.

'What?'

'A director needs his vision.'

The director pressed play, and his film began again.

Dennis paused redoing the masking and watched with his head poked in the room, and the director watched from the couch, one man in light, one in dark.

'Want to come watch?' the director said after a moment.

'I used to like this one of yours,' Dennis said. 'When you first showed me, I liked it then. I thought it was strong and poignant.'

The director paused the movie to listen better.

Dennis hovered between the masking and the kitchen light.

He said, 'The visual mastery, and I did think there was mastery in it, I really did, but the story is a maze. And. Honestly. It's all you wanted to talk about back then. I just don't think I like it anymore, and I don't know if I ever did like it, because I tried to get it, for years I've tried to get it, understand the film, I mean, and I couldn't, I can't watch it anymore. I hate watching it. It's dense, it's trying too hard, desperately it tries, I mean, and, honestly, it's a mess, and I don't know if I ever truly enjoyed it or if I just wanted to enjoy it because you don't talk about anything else but your work.'

The director said, 'Can you close that please?'

Dennis tried to refit the masking. Before he got it just right, he said, 'I saw houses today. I made an offer.'

The director fell silent. Then he said, with coldness, 'This film's meant to be watched in the dark. Please.'

Dennis shut the masking tight, closing the director in black.

The director started the movie once more and attempted to watch but found he could not. He wanted to think, he wanted to walk. He went on the balcony where Dennis's patio furniture had returned, and he made no attempt to quietly drag it off the balcony, drag it down the hall, drag it into the garage, piece by piece.

In fact, he did it louder than needed.
Then he paced on the balcony and thought.

❖

The following week, cast and crew were on location, shooting the streets and outskirts of a small fishing community along the New England coast, hidden deep in forests and back roads and rocky coastline. From cool to warm, the seasons were changing, and the air was sweating and the ground damp. The schedule would keep them here, in a foggy, forgotten harbor and inlet, the remainder of the shoot.

On the third morning of filming, crew started prep outside of a rustic bed and breakfast under a dusk of gloom and bloated gray clouds that hid breaking sun and kept night's chill into late morning.

It was discovered and brought to the director's attention, an hour before filming, that the first unit camera was not properly working.

'Can't we fix it?' the director said.

Heavy sleep had yet to release his tired brow and tired eyes, and he held coffee with both hands, for its warmth.

'It's outdated; it was barely working as is,' the crew said.

'Well. I know. But. Can't we fix it?'

'We've been using duct tape to keep it from falling apart, like, into pieces, we're saying. The tape is the only thing keeping it together.'

'More tape won't help?' the director said.

The crew did not respond.

'Christ, goddamn Christ,' the director said. He tried a sip of coffee but it was yet too hot. 'So, what am I losing?'

The crew handed the director an edited shot list with red X's.

'All your wide shots.'

'All of them?'

'All of them,' the crew confirmed.

'Fucking Christ, where's Lenny?'

The A-lister's assistant inserted herself between the director and crew and asked hurriedly and breathlessly if they'd seen the A-lister?

'He wasn't in his hotel room this morning, and he's not answering his phone,' she said. 'I've called both his phones, well, all three of his phones, and he's not answering and, and, and have none of you seen him?'

The director and crew said no, they had not seen him.

The A-lister's assistant berated the director for pushing the actor into a terrible headspace and barking and commanding the A-lister into the character's despair, the utter fucking despair over the truth the character cannot reconcile, shoving into the actor's head ideas that *everything we do is meaningless*, that *none of this has any meaning other than the meaning we assign to it*, that *life has no outward meaning only inward*.

She argued with the director and told him the A-lister deals with a lot, and the actor was fragile, just this delicate fragile actor, and-and-and to put garbage in his head, she said, with all the pressure and attention and, she said, he knows he's not a strong performer, he knows!

'What is wrong with you?' she shouted at the director.

One of the crew volunteered to help the assistant search, and after an hour, more crew joined, along with a few from the cast. They searched the location from top to bottom, then two of the crew got in a car and drove up and down the small community's streets, asking town folk if they'd seen the celebrity.

They returned later with no news or leads.

Cast and crew filmed what scenes they could and canceled the remainder of the day's scenes.

The A-lister did not appear.

A missing person's report was filed.

Four days of filming were lost.

Word reached the director, the studio was flying a replacement actor out to reduce costs. The schedule was tight, and any more delays meant more money.

Frugal reshoots, the director was told, were being worked in by the studio, and the skinny fellow, who had been the director's first choice, was on his way out.

Though the director worried for the A-lister, he was pleased to have received good news, and by the next morning, worry for the A-lister's well-being was entirely back of mind.

Front of mind was the renewed possibility of a bright, distinguished performance.

One that delivered.

Delivered the vision ...

He worked with the skinny fellow over breakfast on location, sitting near the camera and monitors, going through the material and catching him up to speed.

Nearby, two crew guys were chatting.

Now and again, their volume was distracting.

One said to the other, 'You missed the point. Utterly missed it.'

'Get out,' the other said.

'How do you work on a cosmic horror film like this one and get the whole point wrong?'

'That's my take; you can't tell someone their opinion is wrong,' the second crewmember said.

'It's wrong,' the first said.

'That's what I get, whenever I pick up cosmic horror literature or film; for me, it's an exploration of human limitations. That's all I said. It's about the absurdity of all this, everything. All of it. That's my take.'

'And that's wrong,' the first said.

'Get out.'

'Cosmic horror is about fear of the unknown, how fragile we are, it's a warning. It's man's arrogance daring to glimpse forbidden knowledge and being punished for tampering with things we think we understand but have no fucking clue. It's hubris, that's cosmic horror.'

'It's not hubris,' the second said.

'Yes, it's hubris,' the first said.

'It's curiosity, we're curious animals.'

'We're not animals.'

'We're animals,' the second said, 'and we're curious animals. That's our nature. That's not hubris. If that's our nature, that's what we are. So, no. It's us finding strength in the face of overwhelming dread and despair, it's us questioning our place in all of this, which is absurd, because nothing out there cares about us.'

'That's what I mean. You're reinforcing my point. It's a warning! Cosmic horror always ends with madness or despair or death.'

'Get out.'

'It always ends with madness and *death*. It's all external,' the first said.

'No, it's all internal, it's fears, it's anxieties.'

Their conversation diverged into insults, and the director asked that they please continue elsewhere, which they were about to oblige when onto the location ran the *huge fan* of the director's, the one from the sidewalk, from the city, from a dozen states away.

Yet here he was, crewmembers chasing him down, the *huge fan* running and shouting stop-stop-stop-stop, stealing an idle script from a chair, running it to the director, out of breath, saying oh my God hi, panting, breathing, saying he drove all the way out here, saying he came to see the director, saying he came just to see him, only him, asking, demanding the director please-please-please sign the script he'd stolen, saying stop-stop-stop-stop and wait-wait-wait to the crew rushing him before he was tackled to the ground and dragged off location, begging the director please-please-please sign the script, crying and laughing he was such a *huge fan*.

'Come on, do you need to handle him like that?' the director said to the crew. 'He's just a fan, he's harmless, you don't– that's not necessary.'

Energy settled and peace returned to set.

The director asked the skinny fellow, 'So are you good with the material, or should we keep rehearsing?'

In a local diner with designers, Lenny, and the EP, the director began the discussion of shooting the film's ending climax scene over dinner. The climax was one week out and was to be the last scene of filming. It was the most important, pivotal the director called it. All threads of the plot, all character choices, all consequences lead to one single moment, the director said, and it had to be done perfect!

A few townsfolk enjoyed quiet meals around the bunch.

The director was not monitoring his volume as he imparted granular and meticulous details. He drew looks from the rest of the diner that went entirely unnoticed.

He went on and on until he was finished.

'No one took notes,' he said to the designers, Lenny, and the EP, who were looking at him and nodding.

'I took notes,' Lenny said. He showed a napkin he'd written on.

'Thought we were brainstorming?' one of the designers said.

'I laid it all out for you, no brainstorming necessary.'

'You want to change locations? Just for this scene?' the set designer said.

'It's the most important scene, and we're just moving a few miles deeper in the woods. I mean, it's like five miles.'

The table was quiet.

'Like, eight miles,' the director corrected. 'Like, nine. This scene *is* the most important.'

'If we do a low-light, oh man, the atmosphere you'll get, the impending doom of it all,' Lenny said.

'No, no,' the director said. 'No, that'd be terrible. I don't want low-light, that's no good here.'

Lenny went quiet and offered no further suggestions.

'I want bright, I want strange starlight, I want infinite cosmos raining down, that's what I want.'

The EP, who had been quiet, said, 'Yeah, I don't know we have budget for any of that; you're talking VFX, you're talking, gosh, that's, I really don't think we have money for that.'
'I'm not budging,' the director said. 'On this, the most important scene of the whole piece, this whole work of art, this odyssey into human goddamn nature, I am not budging.'
The table went quiet.
'That's going to be real hard to reach,' the set designer said. 'Nine miles into the woods?'
'Like, ten miles, eleven, maybe.'
The table continued silence.
'It's the most important scene,' the director said.
The waitress came and asked who wants a coffee refill?
'Yes, please,' the director said, offering his mug first.
After dinner, which ran late, the director walked through dark and quiet to his motel room.
The night was oil, a bowl of black crude oil.
Homes were dark.
Streetlights were sparse and strangled and decayed, and under these the director seldom passed; mostly he was kept in black and cold.
The director saw the lead actress outside her motel room smoking, up on the second floor, which was open to the night. She was leaning on the guardrail, looking over the parking lot.
Her face was buried in one hand; the other had her cigarette and paperwork. A single light above held dark away from her.
She heard the director walking in from the night and stood upright and fixed her hair and smeared tears from her broken eyes. She said, 'Don't mind me.' Her voice was weak.
The director did not mind her; he went for his room but was stopped when the lead actress said, 'I don't know what I did.'
'What's that?'
'I don't know what I did.'
'Oh, okay,' the director said. 'Good night.'
He continued. The director unlocked his room, and the lead actress leaned out to see him below.
She said, 'I received a phone call is all.'

'Oh,' the director said, standing half in and out of his open room.

'Yeah. Yeah.'

The director waited, as if she might add more. She did not. He was about to enter his room when she began again, interrupting his attempt to end the night.

'They said I breached an NDA,' she said.

'How'd you do that?'

'I don't know. I've no clue what I did.'

'What's your lawyer say?' the director said.

'He was who phoned. He said they let him know I breached an NDA and that they were pulling together a suit against me and to expect to receive a filing soon with appearance dates.'

'Geez.'

'I don't even know which one of these I broke!' she said. She waved the paperwork for the director to see. 'I looked through all these; there's dozens here, and I don't know what I did! I just don't know!'

She started shouting she didn't fucking know what she did!

Room lights went on when she didn't stop shouting.

Guests poked from their rooms. One said to be quiet.

The lead actress threw the NDAs over the guardrail and let them flutter over the motel lot, falling like snowflakes, and screaming what did I fucking do?

The director went in the room and closed out her noise and drew the curtains shut.

❖

Filming, the following morning, began in a grueling manner and remained so into the afternoon. The director pressed actors in their scenes, and he griped and complained, and then he pressed them harder.

The skinny fellow received the worst of it. Between scenes, the director harped on him and placed demands on him, and the skinny fellow took all of this in silence, with no disagreement. So large was his hunger for acclaim, it seemed, he would do whatever the director asked of him, no question.

During a break, the EP mentioned the director might consider easing off the skinny fellow a bit.

The director asked the EP if he was seeing the performances he was getting from the actor. 'You see the quality he's giving?'

'Sure, he's good, I see it,' the EP said.

'Well. Okay then.'

'It's just the crew and some of the other actors are saying you're digging a bit hard.'

'I'm not digging that hard.'

'You're digging hard.'

'Look at what he's giving, though,' the director said.

He had Lenny replay footage for the EP.

'No, yeah, it's good, it's great, a little artsy but, maybe come down a little, let him breathe.'

'He's breathing fine.'

'I mean give him a breath, give him some room.'

Later, when the EP left for lunch, the director locked him off set and resumed pressure on the skinny fellow, squeezing out of him the best performances he'd seen, capturing all of it on camera; the stress, the terror, the breaking point, and when the skinny fellow's scenes were finished, he received no applause. What he was given, instead, was stoic silence, a lingering fear on set of the painful depths to which the actor had descended, the trauma, unearthed and clear on his face, to deliver what the director craved for the camera to see.

❖

Production took a break for the weekend, and the director caught a flight home.

It was late when the director entered the silent, black house.

Dennis was on the couch, sleeping on a bed of blankets.

If he heard the director, who was purposely loud with his bag and movement through the house, he did not say and did not rise.

The director struggled and found very little sleep.

Nightmares filled his dreaming, horrible ideas and visions that, when he woke and lay in bed with sweat and loss of breath, needed proven as dreams and not factual events.

He came out of the lonely bedroom.

Dennis was eating breakfast on his bed of blankets on the sofa, watching morning news.

'You woke me last night,' Dennis said.

'I got in late. Sorry.'

'No, the screaming,' Dennis said.

'I wasn't screaming.'

Dennis chewed loudly; it was distracting.

'You did. When you went to bed. I knocked on the bedroom.'

The director poured coffee in the kitchen.

'You need to think about other things,' Dennis said from the living room. The director could hear his chewing.

'What things?'

'You think about stories and characters and making everyone see the world the way you do too much.'

'No, I don't,' the director said into the living room.

He sipped coffee where he stood.

'You were screaming about story and character last night. You woke me with it,' Dennis said. 'I turned the TV on so I wouldn't hear it.'

Dennis's chewing was so loud, it grated in the director's head.

'It's too much,' Dennis said.

The home went quiet, but for the news, which was grim, and Dennis's chewing.

'I think about other things,' the director said. He came to the threshold between kitchen and living room.

'Oh, what else do you think about?'

The director was quiet many moments. 'You moving out,' the director finally said. It was sadness he shone.

Dennis almost laughed, perhaps the thought so absurd. 'Goddamn you, you know that?'

'Stay,' the director said.

'I offered on a house. It was accepted, I'm leaving.'

'Please. Stay.'

'You know what? I really wasn't going to move. Three weeks ago, I would have gladly lived on our couch, hoping we'd work this out, but then I said I was going to look at a house. I don't know why I said it, I really wasn't, I mean it, I wasn't going to look at a house. I just said it to see what you'd do, and then, all of a sudden, you're paying attention to me, and then I really did go look at houses because I thought that's how this will always go, won't it?' Dennis said. 'You'll always be thinking on your characters and stories, and I'll get what's left. I'll get to comfort your loneliness when all the stories and characters are quiet. I'll always be an afterthought.'

'That's not all I think about!'

'You think about them so much, you're goddamn screaming about it in your sleep. Scream about me in your sleep! Goddamn. I mean, at least think about me in your day, or a moment while you're working, give me some time in your goddamn head, but you can't! You're not capable. You're not a person. You're a paintbrush that never stops painting, never stops creating, and then you act so tortured, so cursed by this need to create. Stop! You could stop right this instant! *You* stay! *You* don't leave! Quit the film and stay here with me!'

The director took Dennis's shouting.

He said nothing in return.

Except, 'I do think about other things.'

❖

A few days later, the director was back on location. A meeting was held to report progress on the climactic scene's filming. The director wanted updates on the set, lighting, he wanted to hear about all the details he imparted during their previous meeting, and he didn't want to hear anything to the contrary of his ask.

He was told they'd scouted deeper into the woods, miles into the woods, like the director had asked, and it would be tough, but it was possible. The crew had already started work on a good location they'd found and would be ready in time for filming.

They talked through logistics, and someone warned of weather advisory; a storm was bringing rain.

'It won't rain,' the director said.

'There's a seventy percent chance,' the crew said.

'It's too cold; we'll get clouds, but there won't be rain,' the director said.

'Smells like rain's coming,' Lenny said.

'It'll pass.'

The other designers reported no issues with what they'd been given as tasks, and all seemed ready.

The director was pleased; he was getting his vision.

The day then came to film the climactic scene.

Morning brought gloom.

And rain.

Light at first, patters and taps, but as the day went on, it came harder and never lessened.

Not one moment.

It turned the earth to mud.

Trucks and carts heading through the woods, many times, were left stuck and needed hauling out.

'We're so far behind,' the crew told the director.

He was under an umbrella, watching the crew and designers carry out his wishes under consistent rainfall.

'It's a night shoot,' the director said. 'We'll be fine.'

The trek and dragging of equipment out into the woods, where it was deep and quiet, ate more time than they'd allotted, and the crew lost the grim gray of day for work under a cold dark.

Setup and preparation occurred under work lights.

Crew coming and going and dragging and building were shadows, moving and twisting.

Trees were tall and black and reached high, peering down, catching the rain and sprinkling it over production and keeping in the cold.

Early in the night, preparation finished, and crew broke for a meal. The director sat in his chair alone, near the trailers with a warm coffee in his hands. He was watching the trees, the dark between them, and listening to the rain.

The EP came and sat with him.

They did not speak for some time.

'Is it worth all this?' the EP finally said.

The director looked from the trees to the EP, then back.

'What you're doing, I mean.'

The EP ignored an incoming call on his phone. A second call came. He ignored this one too.

'I'm not just saying the money you're blowing through. I know you say it's fine, don't worry, and you distract me from the labor you're using and the endless pressing of your actors, and constant lighting changes, location changes, which is time, at the end of the day, that's what it is, whatever trauma you're stirring and filming, whatever you're exploring and creating– it's time, and it only goes one direction and, not that we're talking money, we can if you want, but let's say you make some beautiful, horrific nightmare, and you think it's absolutely perfect as it exists, there is not one thing you would change, this piece of art says everything you were hoping it would say, and you created it, and you revel in that relationship with it, you the creator and this thing your creation. What do you say to the people who don't get it? Too bad? Why make something that no one can get into? Because I've seen the footage. You think I'm dumb and I'm just off writing checks and making bad suggestions, but I'm not. I've seen.'

The director, once more, pulled his attention from the dark and the trees, then gave it back.

'I'm just saying. Is all the argument, the friction, the complaints, the work, the endless work of it, I mean, you look awful. Is all of this worth any of that?'

The director did not respond.

The EP stood.

Before he left, he said, 'The A-lister was found. He's in a psychiatric hospital a few counties over. They're saying he had a breakdown.'

He let that settle with the director.

Then he said, 'I wonder why.'

He left the director to stare into the trees, in the rainfall.

Soon after, filming of the script's climactic scene began.

Cast and crew found positions and marks and, after a moment in the quiet night and the rainfall, the director called for quiet on set.

He confirmed with each department they were ready for this. He reminded them of its importance, then called for *action!*

Five minutes into filming, a courier emerged and asked for the lead actress. He needed a signature on some documents. He realized the camera was rolling, then apologized and stepped out of frame and said he'd wait. He just needed a signature, then he'd go, but, he said, what a trek getting out here, haha!

The director called out to the lead actress to start again.

She was staring at the courier, at the papers.

'Can we go again please?' the director asked.

She took her mark and the director called *action!*

The lead actress descended through rain as her character and said, '*Strange is the night where black stars rise, and strange moons circle through the skies, but stranger still is Lost Carcosa.*'

The lead actress continued with her monologue and took her performance to awful places and wept before cast and crew, wept as her character, and she aimed her focus at the poor courier off set, and she continued the scene and said, '*Songs that the Hyades shall sing, where flap the tatters of the King, must die unheard in Dim Carcosa. Song of my soul, my voice* is dead; *die thou, unsung, as tears unshed shall dry and die in Lost Carcosa.'*

She threw herself onto a green pad foam, which would be made a deep, black abyss in post-production, then she stood, wiping tears and rain from her face, and chased the courier into the dark, into the night, screaming she'll fucking sign, she'll sign every-fucking-thing, everything that can be signed, she screamed and laughed, she would fucking sign it all, and, she shouted, why doesn't she just sew her mouth shut, wouldn't that be better, wouldn't that keep her fucking mouth shut?

Eventually she returned and was kept in the medical trailer for several hours while filming continued, which went late into the night. Fatigue set upon cast and crew, but the director resisted the yawns and the leaning and the stretching and the sloth; he pushed filming onward.

It was then, during a plague of bored impatience between shots and exhaustion among cast and crew that the noises came from the dark forest, voices and movement in volume and number, and the *huge fan* found his way onto set once more, and there were others with him, many others, so many, and they became frantic when they glimpsed the director, screaming and shouting *oh my God oh my God oh my God that's him oh my God!* Crew attempted to herd their numbers, but they were few against many, and they were moving many directions but committing to none, making herding wholly ineffective.

They called to the director, who came out from behind the camera to see them, to hear them call his name.

Other crewmembers left their posts to aid their fellow crew, who'd been swallowed by the rolling crowd.

Areas of the set and various safety equipment were now unattended.

The fans spread under the rain and knocked over work lights and stole props and memorabilia and pieces of the set, and they knocked into one another and knocked each other over, and then shoved one another, and then argued and shoved into set pieces and shoved others to muddy earth, and their noise rose up into the night, into the rainstorm above. Some swarmed the director for his autograph and to share how they'd connected with his work, and his attention was then divided between the fans surrounding him and the unrest developing, and then there was a loud CRASH from above. Safety rigging failed with snaps of metal and sharp squeals of metal bending and popping, and the old light rig filling the set with brilliance came down on fleeing fans, catching a handful, and bringing the whole night to immediate darkness with a pop and flash that blinded and deafened.

Then the screams began, in the black and the rain, and did not stop for some time.

Hours later, after some trial and error, the crew got the lights back on, but police and a trio of ambulances were already on site by then, filling the dark with red then blue then red then blue.

A rig was brought in around dawn, when the rain had let up and the clouds had peeled away, and debris was cleared.

The director did not watch the injured removed, nor did he watch the three bodies pulled out and covered and removed.

Two had been fans, but one had been crew.

Instead, the director was watching the set, the ruination of it, rain battered and bent and pilfered and burnt from burst bulbs and the whole of it filling with dawn. For a long while, he stood. Lenny came at some point in the morning and stood with him while, around him, sense was searched for in all this senselessness.

Nearby, the EP paced and spoke with studio heads on the phone, on and off, pacing when he was talking to them and pacing when he wasn't, and stopping his pacing only to answer the studio head's phone call and then to pace again.

Police collected information, which went all morning, then one by one pulled off and went, and then it was just cast and crew on site, left to pick up and pack up and carry home, in their minds, the sounds of the screaming in the dark and in the rain.

The director did not speak.
Except to ask Lenny if he thought they got the take.
'What?'
'I wanted more takes.'
Lenny stopped standing by him and left the set shortly after.
The director said no more.
He flew home in silence.

❖

Production paused for a week, for the studio to sort through the events that unfolded deep in the woods, and the director was made to sit through meetings with lawyers and studio heads, made to listen to their lecturing and advising, and their discipline. He took all of this in silence with no retort and no friction.

At home, slowly, rooms were emptying. Dennis was packing and, bit by bit, moving his things out.

Many nights the director lay awake, listening to Dennis pack somewhere in the house, the sounds of boxes and packing paper, and now and again the director would hear weeping, and then music to hide the weeping.

But the director could still hear.

The weeping followed into the director's dreams and made his sleep restless and stricken with nightmares.

Mornings he woke tired.

He carried fatigue and the stains of his horrible dreams into the day.

The film moved into editing, when the sentiment for tragedy faded then vanished. Too much had already been spent to cancel the project, it was decided. For a period of three weeks, the director spent each day in a dark room with Lenny and the editor, watching everything he'd collected to exhaustion, piecing it together when it felt right, when it felt aligned with the sights and feelings the director held in his head, and removing and cutting when there was misalignment.

He did not heed Lenny's or the editor's feedback, though he did listen and entertain their suggestions, but he had no intention of honoring them.

They did not see it how he saw it, the message underneath the film.

He believed he understood hopelessness.

He believed he knew how to make others see it too, how uncaring it is, the force that moves life and time forward.

How a sad, unfair life can end in a sad and unfair manner and is made meaningless by the manner in which it ends, fans acting like animals from obsession caught under a collapsing light rig.

What larger point did this make?

For what greater mysterious purpose were their skulls and bodies crushed, if any?

Some days, the director locked the editor and Lenny from the editing room and worked in the dark.

Alone, staring into the monitor's glow, frame by frame.

He came upon footage of the accident on set, the collapse of the rig onto the fans.

Cameras had been rolling.

He did not use the footage, but the sound he kept as useful, the full and real screams, the crash, and the rain pattering. He edited these into the film's nightmare sequence, under layers of audio.

He gave them meaning now, he thought to himself.

On the final day of editing, after the final hour of work, the director had, before him, a complete piece with no misalignment between his inner compass, to which the director was a slave, and the content of the film.

He wept in the editing room, into his hands.

And then he wiped tears away and laughed with relief.

He believed he had a masterpiece.

It was his *vision* made physical.

He believed it was perfect, exactly as it was, and would change not one more thing.

He screened it for the studio heads the following afternoon in a small black theater deep in the studio building.

While the suits sat and watched, he stood in the rear of the room, out of the light, watching them watch his *perfection*.

More than once, he noticed one suit turn and look at another and could not read their expression, but he did not care for their looks to one another.

Then it was over and credits rolled and lights were brought up and the suits did not immediately move from their seats, nor did they speak, not even between them.

They were unmoving and without noise.

They waved the EP in, to speak in confidence, then filed out of the theater and left the EP to deliver the director a message.

'They'll be in touch,' he said.

'But what did they think?' the director said.

'It was ... thought-provoking,' the EP said. He forced a smile.

Then he followed the suits out, as a cleaner wrasse follows a shark, to pick their teeth clean and live off their leftovers, the bits the shark doesn't swallow.

No other feedback was given the director.

He was left to wonder.

Later, he took the film home.

❖

That night, the director was sitting in the living room with the film on the TV. It was paused at the beginning. Windows behind the TV were black, and the night was starless.

The director was listening to Dennis pack elsewhere in the home. He waited in the dark, for some time, until Dennis was within earshot.

He said, 'Do you want to see?'

Dennis said from in the kitchen, 'What?'

Quiet passed between them.

'Did you say something?' Dennis said.

The TV remote was in the director's hand, and his finger was over the *play* button. His other hand fidgeted while in his head played reasons not to show Dennis this film and then reasons to show Dennis the film, and the reasons went back and forth in the quiet while Dennis waited for an answer.

The director said, after Dennis had moved to other things, 'Do you want to see?'

Dennis came in the living room and said, 'I keep hearing you say something. Are you talking to me?'

'I want–'

The director saw the moving box in Dennis's hands.

'I want to show you the film.'

The director's voice was uncertain and timid.

Dennis stood with the question for many moments, looking at the director, then the paused TV screen, then the director.

'Will you watch? And sit with me?'

The director had left space on the couch, right near him.

Just for Dennis.

'Please?' the director said.

After contemplation, Dennis said, 'Let me–let me finish in here then, yeah, okay.'

The director then waited in silence, listening to Dennis in the kitchen remove his things from cabinets they shared, listening to Dennis slowly remove himself from the director's life one belonging at a time.

Dennis made tea then joined the director on the couch, some distance between them.

'Are you ready?'

Dennis agreed then got comfy, away from the director, without the director.

Not long into the film, the director noticed Dennis on his phone, not watching. Then he was off the phone and watching, then back on the phone.

'You're not watching,' the director said.

'I'm watching.'

Dennis put the phone away.

It came out again later.

Scenes that were crucial to the overall message and plot, Dennis only half-saw, his attention was divided between his phone then divided between re-finding comfort then getting up for more tea, and some scenes Dennis missed entirely, but he did not ask the director to pause for him; he allowed himself to miss whole chunks of the film.

Then the film was done, and Dennis's reaction was minimal, not to the grand level the director expected.

'It was fine,' Dennis said. He prepared to resume packing.

'You barely watched.'

'I watched, I saw.'

'You saw the disintegration of identity? Of sanity?'

'I did,' Dennis said.

'You saw how seeing the world as it really exists was self-destructive for the characters? How it ruined them? How realizing that there is no meaning to any of this, no meaning to anything that we do as humans and the world we live in, how truly realizing that destroyed their capacity to function as people.'

'Oh. yes. I did. I saw that.'

'But you barely watched.'

'Yes, I did, I was sitting right here,' Dennis said.

'You pretended to watch! If you actually watched, you wouldn't say that!'

'I watched! Fuck's sake, I watched!'

The director made a visible decision toward violence, and he shoved Dennis up and out of the living room.

'Just pack. Just leave. You're sitting there, and I ask you to come and sit and watch this film, which is probably the best thing I've ever done, which-which perfectly says what I want it to say and executes what I want it to execute and-and-and is art, that's what this film is, it's art! You're sitting there saying you watched, but you didn't, you pretended to watch, and-and-and just pack. Just leave.'

Dennis threw his tea into the wall to shut the director up.

He shouted, 'I fucking watched!'

The director went stone silent.

'It's bleak, it's the bleakest thing I've ever seen, and when it wasn't bleak it was depressing, and when it wasn't depressing it was pessimistic! And when it wasn't pessimistic it was aimless! It was all these things, and it was constant! You're so fucking horny for everyone to see the world the way you do, so fucking desperate to share your opinion and your viewpoint and how everyone should live in despair and meaninglessness, but they don't fucking care! You take so much time and energy and you make this film and think everyone has time and energy to stop thinking how shitty their own lives are so they can spend money and time on thinking how shitty your life is? Because that's all your art is, it's just you spilling your blood and begging everyone to look, fucking *begging* for people to watch you bleed! That's all you are as an artist, a beggar!'

Tears came to the director's eyes.

Dennis stood and left the director.

'Where are you going?'

'To just pack. To just leave,' Dennis said, mimicking the director's demands.

'Good, then. Good!' the director shouted. 'Don't forget your awful fucking patio furniture!'

Dennis then took his remaining boxes and left the home.

Nightmares enveloped the director as he slept that night, tormenting him, gifting him a restless, unproductive sleep.

❖

Several weeks on, the director was invited to the film's premiere, and he attended and walked the red carpet and was photographed apart from cast. He excluded himself, and pictures showed a man thinned by lack of sleep and a slow disconnect from habits of self-care.

He found his seat in the grand theater. Around him was chatter and it reached up into the galleries above the seating and it came back down as unintelligible noise, hums.

Lenny arrived and sat beside the director.

He gave a quick greeting and nothing more.

When the theater was nearly full, Lenny said, 'I didn't expect you'd be here.'

The director gave no response.

'You sure you want to be here?' Lenny said.

'I'm sure.'

Now and again, before the film began, the director noticed Lenny looking at him for long, uninterrupted periods.

Then the lights came down and quiet settled over the audience and the film played.

Almost at once, the director detected the opening music was different; it was not the score he'd chosen in the edit he delivered. It wasn't thin music, it wasn't starved, it was bloated. It played over black, this music he did not know, and when the film properly started with the opening scene, it was not *his* opening scene. He adjusted how he was sitting and was horribly confused. This scene was chopped and stripped down, and as the film continued, the scenes the director and the theater watched were not at all special or memorable and followed formulaic beats which, it was clear, had been shoehorned together to tell a story that was devoid of substance and was quite shallow.

'This is not my edit,' the director said to Lenny. Then he said it to the person sitting on the other side of him, then he said it to the person sitting in front of him, then he said it around where he was sitting, this is not my cut, then he stood and said it, then shouted it into the theater, shouted it over the theater, shouted it and interrupted the theater's viewing experience until Lenny forced him down in his seat and said, while the film played before them, the studio made their own cut and, unfortunately, they can do that.

'They cannot!'

'They can!'

'No, no, no, no, no! No! No! *No!*'

The director stood, then sat, then stood and, with nowhere to go, he sat again.

'Who did this?'

Lenny held his words, looking at the director, then admitted it was him; he'd been paid to edit the film in this manner.

'You kept stifling my feedback,' Lenny said in defense. 'When they asked, and when they paid, they wanted to know my thoughts and how I would do things, and they listened. They didn't hear my suggestions and then decide what they thought was better all the time, like you, like you do all the time, like you've always done for years and years, so they asked and I did. So. It's nothing against you.'

The director's face turned cold, and he tried to leave his seat and tried to leave the row, but Lenny stopped him.

'It's honestly nothing against you; you're just so particular and–'

'Who do I talk to?' the director said.

'What?'

'Who do I talk to, who can fix this? Who can put back my edit?'

'Stop!' Lenny said.

The director leaned in Lenny's face, close. He said, 'It's fucking mediocre!'

Around them, the audience seemed to enjoy the film.

'It's already distributed, it's across the country.'

A jump scare occurred in the film.

It was easily predicted.

The audience responded with fear and laughter.

'A jump scare!'

Lenny was watching reactions; he seemed pleased by them.

'A fucking jump scare!?' the director said.

He exited the theater and slammed the auditorium door behind him, then he opened and slammed it again, then one final time.

Slam!

Back home, still in his premiere clothes, the director made calls to the studio and the EP that went unanswered, and he listened to voicemail greetings apologize for missing his call.

Between calls, he turned his film on, reappraising how perfect it was, how superior this edit was, and how important it was that people see this edit.

He paced while the TV played his film to a dark living room that was missing all of Dennis's belongings, like holes, and these holes were everywhere through the home, pieces of Dennis ripped out.

This empty home.

The director was on the balcony, phoning his agent to leave another angry voicemail, another long-winded outburst that would begin as complaint and end as pleading, begging, then would begin again as outrage.

Behind him, light from the TV filled the living room and bled onto the balcony and into the night.

In his ear, the phone was ringing, and he paced and thought and, in the dark, bumped into Dennis's patio furniture.

It had been left.

He looked it over, the phone in his ear, and he kicked the pieces across the balcony as it rang, and when the pieces settled, he kicked at these and followed them across the balcony, kicking and listening to the phone ring and, for a moment, shouting at the furniture.

When he tired, he paced again.

Below, the black canyon was a void.

An abyss.

The madness, the mediocrity of the world below him.

His agent's voicemail answered, and the director set in with shouting and victimhood, unleashing all volumes of screaming while he walked the balcony back and forth, and so he didn't see the headlights come up the driveway, and he didn't hear the front door open and shut; his shouts of victimhood were much too loud.

Then, there was a person standing in the balcony slide door, coming out of the slide door. Film light from the living room made the person a hideous silhouette, black as hopelessness.

Talking at the director.

Coming at him.

The director flinched from surprise, from fright, and tripped over Dennis's overturned patio furniture, a series of trips, really, that guided the awkward weight of the director crashing through the old balcony railing, his arms and legs and body flailing wildly.

Down into the dark.

Into the canyon.

The void.

No scream, just a startled *yipe*.

Dennis ran into the home, past the director's film still playing, the film turning him to shadow and then light, and ran to the neighbors, banging on their door shouting *he fell!*

Help!

He fell!

Oh my God he fell! Help me! I didn't mean to scare him!

I moved, I was just asking about patio furniture I left and he went over.

That was all!

A jump scare.

He fell!

AJ SAXSMA

He Had a Receipt

The robot was waiting outside the square brick building when the lawyer's assistant, whose name was Parks and who was in his graying years, parked and unlocked the front door at a pace that follows those in their gray years. Sometime into opening the law office, while complimentary coffee brewed, Parks noticed the machine come inside and sit in the corner of the empty waiting room.

Though one would not mistake the robot for a man, it did not share eyes or fingers or feet with a man, for in their place was metal and stiff points of articulation, but it was shaped as a man and moved as a man.

It sat quietly, politely as a man.

Parks poured himself coffee.

He watched the robot.

It stared at the wall opposite, though there was nothing of interest to be found there, just bland wallpaper.

At the desk, Parks settled with his coffee and a list of the day's appointments, the first of which was for that very moment of that very hour, and the robot was now, Parks made notice with some surprise, at the appointment window.

A voice played from a false mouth.

The tone and pitch was male and was rather pleasant on the ear, but it imitated emotion in its words and not well.

It said, 'I'd like to check in for my appointment, please.'

Parks sat holding his coffee, saying not a word.

Where life tends to reveal itself by an inability for complete stillness, for life requires movement, both conscious and otherwise, the robot, for lack of living components, was perfectly still.

Large sensors where its eyes would be were pointed and fixed on Parks.

It repeated, 'I'd like to check in for my appointment, please.'

'The lawyer is not in yet.'

The robot stared for an uncomfortable moment.

It said, 'I'd like to check in for my appointment, please.'

The lawyer then arrived in a fluster with a bundle of files, making loud complaints of her horrible morning and the horrible delays placed in it.

In passing the reception, she asked Parks if there were any appointments this morning.

Parks pointed to the robot standing and waiting.

The lawyer looked at Parks, then the robot, then back again.

She said, 'Get me when Marge checks in. I'm closing my door.'

The lawyer shut herself and her frustrations in her office.

After a moment, Parks noticed the robot was looking at him.

❖

Late in the evening, as blackness took the trees and the streets and the yards, Parks came through the front door into his simple, outdated home in a small and simple outdated neighborhood from a long, exhausting day, removing his coat and settling his things.

His wife, who was also in her graying years and in a graying pace, a few years more advanced than her husband, was sitting at the kitchen table in a turtleneck and gold-rimmed glasses, playing solitaire on a handheld device.

A cigarette was wedged in an ashtray close by and was near its end.

It filled the room with smoke that wiggled and was thick and did not linger but for odor.

'Did Rosie cook?' Parks asked. He was looking in the fridge. 'What's in here's from Sunday.'

'Rosie needs replacing.'

His wife paused her game and plucked the cigarette from the tray and smoked from it, then returned to the game.

'She doesn't need replacing,' Parks said. A moment, then he said, 'Everything in here's from Sunday. Is this what you ate?'

His wife didn't look up from her game but said, 'She folded wet clothes from the wash into the linen closet. Mid-cycle. They weren't even done with the spin. They were still soapy. Right into the closet she put them, on the shelves, I mean. Wet slacks, shirts, drawers, my mother's good hand towels too. She pulled it all out, and in it went. The carpet was soaked, soggy, and suds were bubbling. I had to pull the fan from the basement to dry it out. You hear it? It's still blowing. The whole carpet was just soaked.'

Her game made a victory noise. She took another smoke.

'She doesn't need replacing,' Parks said. He was bent in the fridge, scouting for dinner to reheat.

'You're not home with her all day. She's slipping.'

'She's not slipping.'

His wife's game made a losing noise. She lit another cigarette.

'She's old.'

'She's ten.'

'She's twelve,' his wife said.

'Get her looked at,' Parks said.

Parks shut the fridge. There was unused cookware on the stove.

'Was she going to cook still or—?'

'The carpet in the linen closet will mold. I'm not getting her looked at, I'm looking at replacements.'

A robot entered the kitchen; its name was Rosie. Both Parks and his wife ceased discussion.

'Welcome home, Mr. Parks,' the robot said. It navigated the kitchen as if mid-task. Its voice was soft and female. There were no feminine features to be seen in its appearance, only boxy shapes with joints and indicator lights.

'Everything in the fridge is from Sunday,' Parks told Rosie. He opened a beer and sipped.

'I cooked Sunday,' Rosie said.

The robot ran the sink and filled a cleaning bucket.

'I know,' Parks said. 'It was good, wasn't it, dear?'

His wife played her game and smoked and said nothing.

'Were you cooking tonight?'

'It's not on my agenda, Mr. Parks,' Rosie said. 'Would you like to hear my agenda for today?'

'No, that's all right,' Parks said.

The robot stood over the sink, watching water fill the bucket.

'Could we add cooking tonight to your agenda?' Parks said.

The robot did not respond.

'Rosie?'

'Did you need something, Mr. Parks?'

'Well, it's Wednesday, and everything in the fridge is from Sunday, and I've nothing to eat.'

'Cooking is not on my agenda, Mr. Parks,' Rosie said. Her tone was unchanging. 'Would you like to hear my agenda for today?'

'I'll order something,' Parks said.

'You're not ordering out,' his wife said.

Cigarette smoke clouded around her.

'I could order for you, Mr. Parks?' Rosie said.

'You're not ordering for him, Rosie,' his wife said. 'You'll mess that up too.'

The robot was silent a moment, then said, 'Would you like to hear my agenda for today, Mr. Parks?'

'That's all right, Rosie, thank you. I'll just eat from the fridge.'

Parks hunted in the fridge through Sunday's leftovers.

The robot exited the room.

It occurred to Parks the robot had left the faucet filling the bucket.

Water ran over and down the drain.

'I'm looking at replacements in the morning,' his wife said.

Her card game made a losing noise.

❖❖

Parks arrived at the office in the morning promptly and on the hour. The robot from the previous day was outside waiting once more, motionless in the early morning dark. It did not greet Parks; it stood and watched him unlock the building and then followed him in and took the same seat it had the previous morning, and there it sat patiently, watching Parks through his opening routine until Parks paused his tasks to ask if he could help the robot with something.

The robot's head, and nothing else, twisted and looked at Parks.

But it said nothing.

The lawyer came in the building like a whirlwind, complaining and overloaded with files and asking if there were appointments, and both she and Parks glimpsed the robot in the corner sitting patiently, watching both of them.

'I might stay in for lunch,' the lawyer said.

'I think it's waiting for you,' Parks said.

The robot made no acknowledgment of them, there was no indication it was even aware of them, but still it looked.

Parks confirmed it had an appointment.

'Is there coffee?'

'There's coffee,' Parks said.

The lawyer balanced folders and poured a cup from the waiting room's complimentary pot and stirred in cream and sugar.

The lawyer then said, 'If I stay in for lunch, could you do Sammy's again? Those sandwiches, I mean?'

'What about the robot?'

'What about it? I'll probably stay in for lunch. I'm not thinking of going out. You know the sandwiches I mean?'

Parks said yes, he knew the sandwiches she meant.

'What about the robot? I really think it's waiting for you,' he said.

'Looks bugged to me,' she said. 'I'll let you know if I'm staying in for lunch, but I'm probably staying in, so.'

The lawyer went in her office and shut the door.

The room settled from the lawyer's flurry.

The robot waited in the corner through appointments coming and going, waiting and watching others receive attention and service, unmoving, until it was time for Parks to close the office.

It gave no friction when Parks announced the closure of business.

It rose and left the building without drama, simply leaving as if this were one more task to be completed.

❖

The robot was waiting again the next morning.

Not a moment after Parks had finished opening duties and settled behind the reception desk with coffee, the robot was before him.

After a lingering moment, looking down on Parks where he sat behind the desk, it said, in the same unchanging tone, 'I'd like to check in for my appointment, please.'

Parks had not before noticed the dents and scratches and the flickers of broken sensors along the robot's frame.

The depth and number of the robot's wounds were varied and angry and many. Some appeared older and others newer. The robot wore them but did not seem to suffer them.

Parks stared.

'Will the lawyer see me today?' the robot asked.

'Well. I don't know.'

'I need to speak with her.'

'We'll have to see. This is very strange.'

'I hope she'll see me today.'

'A robot seeing a lawyer is, well, it's very strange."

'But I have an appointment. Won't she speak with me?'

'I'm not sure,' Parks said. 'I don't think so.'

'I'll come tomorrow if not. I've already made an appointment.'

Parks checked the schedule.

The robot had made appointments for the month, and beyond.

'I'd like to check in for my—'

'Yes, I'll check you in. But we'll have to see.'

'Other lawyers refused. And I cannot travel further.'

'You've seen other lawyers?' Parks said.

'No. They refused.'

Parks saw the robot's wounds traveled from head to foot.

'I hope she'll see me,' the robot said.

Parks thought on that a moment, a robot hoping.

'This is very strange,' Parks said. 'You understand this is strange?'

The robot did not answer.

'You can understand that? You can understand strange?' Parks said.

'I'd like to check in for—'

'Yes, yes,' Parks said.

He marked the robot's appointment as checked in.

The robot was unmoving, staring from its sensors.

'Return to your seat, please. If she'll see you, I'll call you up.'

The robot simply replied, 'Thank you for your assistance.' It returned to its seat and patiently waited.

Later in the morning, Parks called the robot up and showed it into the lawyer's office.

'This is very strange,' the lawyer told Parks, who agreed. 'The robot understands that?'

Parks shrugged.

'Well, did it pay?' the lawyer asked.

'It did pay. So.'

'The robot paid?'

Parks said yes, it did.

'Where did it get money?'

'I don't know, I didn't ask,' Parks said.

This conversation was carried out right in front of the robot, which sat in silence for the duration.

'All right,' the lawyer said, then she asked Parks to shut the door behind him, which he did on his exit.

Parks waited at the reception desk while the robot and the lawyer conversed in the office, which went at length, through morning and into early afternoon. Backlogged appointments filled the waiting room and grew restless and complained to Parks.

The lawyer poked her head out of the office sometime in the afternoon to ask Parks order sandwiches from Sammy's again, and asked if he knew the ones she meant.

He said yes, yes he knew the ones she meant.

Near closing, the lawyer and the robot emerged.

She saw it out of the building and spoke with it outside for a time, and then she came in and told Parks to clear tomorrow's schedule.

It was going to be a full day.

❖

The lawyer and Parks and the robot were seated in the conference room the next morning. The lawyer asked the robot to repeat, word for word, everything it had told her for purposes of record and filing. Parks was ready with notepad and pen.

The robot sat for a time.

Both Parks and the lawyer waited.

Then the robot began, and as it spoke Parks noticed there were, now and again, brief inflections in its tone, moments when Parks forgot a robot was speaking.

The robot gave the date of its manufacture and said that it was owned first by a salesman outside of town. The salesman had a lovely home, and the robot helped with upkeep and repairs and errands until the man was older and taken to a nursing home. The robot said it was then purchased by a car mechanic and his wife, who was a cashier, for whom it had tended their home and three young children for some eight years and that it had been glad to do so, the robot said in a matter-of-fact manner, it had been absolutely glad to tend them.

But it wished to tend them no longer.

Parks did not write this down.

'You did not write that down,' the robot said.

'Write that down,' the lawyer told Parks.

'Write what down?'

'It doesn't want to tend the family anymore.'

'You don't want to?' Parks asked the robot.

'Correct,' the robot said.

'Sorry,' Parks said. 'Just so I'm clear, you don't *want* to?'

'That's what it said,' the lawyer said.

Parks wrote it down.

'Tell him the rest,' the lawyer said. 'For record and filing.'

The robot then described in detail, slow for Parks to write and follow with diligence, each dent and crack and scratch and broken sensor across its frame, the severity of each, in some cases how its mobility or function had been inhibited, the date it received each, and which member of the family it tended had caused them for reasons of anger or intimidation or lack of patience. Sometimes, the robot said, they would curse and hit it and sometimes they would laugh and hit it and sometimes they wouldn't say anything and they would hit it, and sometimes they would hit it over and over and over. It said sometimes it would cower and they would still hit and beat on it.

In total, there were seventy-three wounds.

The husband and wife were responsible for the majority.

Some were as recent as that morning.

'The family hits you?' Parks said.

The robot was quiet.

Parks twisted to the lawyer. 'The family hits it?'

'Well can't you hear? Look at the goddam thing. It's marked all up and down,' the lawyer said. 'The goddamn thing is afraid of its family.'

'Is that true?' Parks said.

'I don't want to be hit,' the robot said.

'Well, no. We don't imagine you do,' the lawyer said.

Parks sat for a time. Then he said, 'But you're *afraid* of the family?'

'I don't want to be hit,' the robot said.

'See?' the lawyer said.

'Well. No. But. And you're not glitching or anything?' Parks asked the robot. 'This isn't some error or glitch or something? You're not here because of anything like that?'

'That's what I asked yesterday,' the lawyer said. 'I asked if the thing was glitching.'

'Well, are you?' Parks said.

The robot said it was not glitching.

'I wish to be emancipated. I wish to be free of them,' the robot said.

'Jeez,' Parks said.

'Did you get it all?' the lawyer asked Parks.

'Yeah. I got it all.'

Parks was shaking his head.

He said, 'Jeez.'

The robot said, 'One day they will break me beyond repair.'

Parks studied the robot's wounds and his notes.

'And you're not glitching?'

The robot stared with indifference.
'They've sent others to recycling,' it said.
'But. Why hit? Why not turn you off?' Parks said.
'I turn myself back on.'
'Oh, jeez,' Parks said.
He stood and tried to get his head around all of it.
Then the robot said, 'I don't want to be hit.'
'Well,' Parks said. 'No.' He thought in silence. He said, 'I don't imagine you do.'

❖

The next afternoon, Parks stopped for lunch at Lloyd's in town. He had meatloaf and a slice of pie and coffee. A robot was behind the counter; it wore an apron and served food and took orders. Customers made small talk with it, and mostly the robot did not engage, but now and again, the robot cycled through the same four or five responses. Parks paid the robot for the meal, then left.

He parked on the street and looked at the home.

A tall crowd of elm trees kept the home in shadow, even at midday. The shutters leaned, and the siding needed a good wash; some was rotted. Left-out toys lay in the yard, in weeds.

Parks approached the red front door with notebook and pen and rang the doorbell once, then a second time a moment later.

The robot answered and showed Parks inside.

It thanked him for coming.

There were many walls. Rooms felt shut out and closed off.

Sight lines through the home were broken and jagged. Somewhere inside the rooms, a person shouted, *who is it?*

Parks waited for the robot to respond; it did not.

'Who's at the door?' another voice shouted.

From where it came, Parks did not know. There were so many walls.

The first voice shouted, 'Hey! Who you letting in the house?'

Parks waited for the robot to answer.

It did not.

'It's Parks,' Parks said out loud, in a general sort of direction.

The first voice shouted, 'Who's Parks?'

Parks stepped forward and aimed his response. 'We spoke this morning. I phoned.'

The second voice said, 'It's the lawyer!'

'Secretary,' Parks corrected.

'What?' the first voice shouted.

'The lawyer. It's the lawyer,' the second voice said.

'Secretary!'

'What?' the second voice said.

Parks tried to follow the voice's direction. 'I'm the secretary,' he said.

Silence settled in the home, in the walls.

Parks leaned this way and that way where he stood and looked about, seeing what he could see.

He heard walking.

A worn-out man in jeans and a work shirt stopped in a doorway, one of many doorways in this small home, and walked Parks to the dining table. The table was much too big for the room it occupied, and the worn-out man sat at the head and warned Parks about scooting the chairs out too far. He said look at the scuffs on the walls, don't scuff my walls. Then he shouted names out into the home.

Slowly family gathered around him.

The robot stood in the corner, behind but near the family.

'Why don't you offer our guest coffee or tea?' the worn-out man asked the robot.

'I'm fine, thank you.'

The worn-out man asked the robot to get Parks some tea or coffee.

'I'm fine, really.'

'You're supposed to offer to guests,' the worn-out man told the robot.

'That's quite all right,' Parks said.

'Bring it out in case,' the worn-out man said. 'Go on now. Why do I have to say? It's supposed to offer to guests, but the goddamn thing, I swear. You got to tell it everything. My wife will tell you.'

'You got to tell it everything,' his wife said.

The robot obeyed without a word.

'Hon, why's a lawyer here?' the wife asked the man.

'Secretary,' Parks corrected.

'Pardon?' she said.

'You didn't say much on the phone,' the worn-out man said.

The children were seated around their parents, staring at Parks.

'Yes. I won't take much of your time,' Parks said.

'You said that on the phone, you wouldn't take much of our time, but you didn't say much else.'

The robot returned with fresh coffee and tea. The family helped themselves to greedy portions while Parks watched in silence.

'I just have a few questions,' Parks said.

Parks opened his notebook and readied his pen.

'Why is a lawyer in our house asking questions?' the man's wife said.

'Secretary, I'm a secretary,' Parks said.

'Do you have to stand there, robot?' the worn-out man asked the robot. He did not use a name for the robot, just *robot*.

Parks noticed none of the family used a name.

They all called it robot.

It stood behind the family.

The robot was unmoving, unacknowledging.

'Stand where I can see you,' the man said.

The robot moved and stood near Parks.

'The goddamn thing, I swear,' the man said. 'I'm not certain, I don't know this for sure, but I think it steals money out my wallet.'

'May I?' Parks said of his notebook and questions.

'Sorry, what's this all about?' the man said. His interest was divided.

'He has questions, hon,' the wife said.

'Well, I know, he just said. He didn't say on the phone, you didn't say on the phone you had questions,' the man said to Parks.

'Did we come into some money?' the wife asked.

'Wouldn't that be something,' the man said.

The kids asked if they could go play. The wife said no, stay seated.

'Should we get into it then?' Parks said.

'You're leaking!' the man shouted at the robot.

A dark liquid was dribbling down the robot to the floor.

'Goddamn, it's leaking all over the floor!' the man shouted. 'Go get a towel would you, hon?'

The wife left the room.

'Goddamn, if it's not one thing with you, it's another,' the man shouted at the robot.

The wife returned with a towel and wiped the floor under the robot. She said to the robot, 'You should be doing this, not me.'

The robot attempted to leave and tend to the leak.

'No! No, no, no! You stay put, you'll trail all through the house. Stay where I can see you,' the man said. 'I swear, it's not one thing with this robot it's another.'

The wife said, 'Is this about money? Wouldn't it be wonderful if we came into some, hon? Not a little but some? Wouldn't it?'

'It's not about money,' Parks said.

'Well, what is it about? It's like some goddamn mystery, when you phoned you barely said,' the man said.

'Then I'll get into it,' Parks said.

He waited for interruptions, of which there were none.

Then he proceeded.

'Could you tell me about your relationship with the robot?'

The family held the question and, between them, offered not a single reaction.

'What now?' the man said. He scrunched his face.

'I'll say again,' Parks said. He read the question from his notebook aloud once more. 'Could you tell–'

'Well, no, I heard you,' the man said. 'But–'
He looked at his wife, as if to see if she was following what this was, and she returned his confusion to a lesser degree.
Parks was waiting for a response.
The dining room was silent.
The man appeared to give up trying to understand; he said, 'Fine.'
'Fine?' Parks repeated.
'I'd say it's fine. Would you say it's fine, hon?'
His wife said yes, she'd say things with the robot were fine.
'We'd say it's fine.'
Parks wrote this down. The wife tried to read Park's writing; she leaned for a better angle.
'What are you writing down?'
Then Parks asked, 'What happens when the robot upsets you?'
The man absorbed the question with an unruly expression. 'I'm not following,' the man said. 'Are you following, hon?'
The kids asked again if they could go play. The wife told them no, stop asking. Then she said, 'Did you say if we came into money, or?'
'He's asking about *our* robot,' the man said. His expression worsened.
'Then I'm not following,' she said.
'We're not following,' the man told Parks. 'What are you saying?'
Parks read the question again, 'What happens when the robot–'
'Well don't just read the question again, what, what happens when any robot upsets someone?' He looked to his wife, then Parks. 'There something wrong with getting upset? When the robot upsets me, I get upset, just like anyone. What are you saying?'
'We get upset like anyone; our next-door neighbor gets upset with her robot, and we're no different here,' the wife said. 'So.'
Parks nodded and wrote their response.
'Are you writing it like we're saying it?' the man asked Parks.

Parks said, 'Have you ever been so angry you wanted to hurt the robot?'

'Oh, good grief!' the man said.

He suddenly couldn't sit still. His eyes went to the robot.

'Did you do something?'

Then to Parks.

'Did it do something? Did it tell you something?'

Then to the robot.

'Did you tell this lawyer something?'

'Secretary,' Parks corrected.

'Oh, good goddamn grief!' the man said.

The wife urged the children go play and kept from looking at Parks.

'I mean, I get upset just like anyone,' the man said. 'Right, hon?'

'Just like anyone,' his wife assured Parks.

'I mean,' the man's demeanor shifted. 'Do I have to answer these questions you got?'

Parks did not say yes, but he did not say no either. He read the next question. 'Have you ever been told you have a problem with violence?'

'Okay then,' the man said. He stood. 'All right, Parks, that'll be it for us, thank you.'

His wife remained seated.

Parks wrote.

'What're you writing?' The man asked his wife, 'What's he writing?'

'I think he's writing you refused to answer, hon,' she said.

'Did you write that?' the man said.

Parks again did not say yes, but he did not say no. He asked the final question. 'On a scale of one to ten, where ten is very safe and one is not safe at all, how safe do you think the robot feels in the home?'

'The robot feels real goddamn safe in my house!' the man shouted. He got Parks up on his feet, asking what the goddamn hell kind of question is that and marched him through the maze of walls to the front door, shouting the robot has a great goddamn home and it feels real goddamn safe under his ownership, and he didn't care whatever the robot reported, and that Parks could write that down, he could write all that down and get out of his goddamn home!

Parks stood at his car and listened to the man screaming at the robot in the house, screaming what the goddamn hell did you do?

What the goddamn hell did you get us into?

❖

Parks drove the robot's emancipation petition to the court on his afternoon break.

The courthouse was staffed with several robots—a janitor, a security unit, an assistant to answer frequently asked questions which roamed, proactively seeking those appearing confused.

The attitude directed to them from those coming and going and flustered and without patience, as Parks observed while he waited in line to file, was poor and harsh and always without thanks.

When he returned to the office, the robot was seated in the corner.

There was fresh, ugly harm on its frame.

It asked if it might stay here, in the office.

'Oh, I don't know,' Parks said. He looked to see if the lawyer was in.

The robot said it left the house that morning, while the family was asleep. 'I have nowhere else to go,' it said.

'Yeah, I don't–' Parks looked again to see if the lawyer was in. This time he tried to peer in her office.

'They probably won't look for me here,' the robot said. 'I've left once before. Well, I've left a few times, and they usually don't look for me. Once they did, but it was just the once; they were quite angry.'

'They'll look for you here?'

'Probably they won't,' the robot said.

'Oh jeez.'

'Usually they don't.'

'There's nowhere else for you?'

'Do you have outlets I can plug into?' the robot said.

'You can't go back to the manufacturer for a while, until this is all sorted?'

'No, I can't go back to the manufacturer until this is sorted.'

'Why not?'

'They'll return me to the family or turn me to scrap for recycling. I don't want to be scrap. Or be returned. Or be recycled.'

'I don't suppose you do,' Parks said.

The robot stood, the heavy, noisy bulk of it. It said, 'You won't notice I'm here.'

'I already notice you're here,' Parks said.

'If you have an outlet I can plug in, you won't notice me.'

'Yeah, I just don't know,' Parks said. He walked from the robot a bit, to see in the lawyer's office better.

She was not in.

The robot gathered its power cord and sought an outlet.

'You won't notice I'm here,' it said.

It moved seats aside in the waiting room, hunting for an outlet.

Later, at the hour of closing, Parks said fine, it could stay, but asked the robot to please not touch anything and, actually, he said, maybe don't move at all, maybe just stay still in the corner all night. That'd be the best thing, he said. Then he said he'll see the robot in the morning.

Then he locked the office up and locked the robot inside.

❖

Parks chewed his dinner and looked across the table to his wife. She cut her food into smaller portions and ate. She did not look up. In the kitchen, he could hear Rosie washing pots and pans. Water was continuously running, not a trickle but a full stream, unending. Clings and clangs were god-awful loud. Parks thought the robot was being too rough with them, but he kept quiet.

'Rosie's wasting water,' Parks's wife said.

'Rosie's cleaning, dear.'

'Doesn't sound like cleaning.'

'What does cleaning sound like?' Parks said.

'Not like that. Not like drums banging in my sink.'

'How's your food?'

His wife chewed a moment. 'Tastes off to me.'

'You like Rosie's cooking,' Parks said.

'I don't think I do.'

Quiet came in swiftly.

His wife fixed the napkin on her lap, though it was settled fine.

A pot clanged in the kitchen. Then again, louder. Parks saw his wife was focused on her plate and her cutting. She was actively keeping herself from looking up.

Parks looked toward the kitchen doorway. The light was off. He could see night in the kitchen windows and the faint shapes of the kitchen cabinets.

The robot was washing in the dark.

Cling!

Clang!

Clunk!

Parks and his wife listened to the noise, the god-awful volume of it.

And the kitchen faucet rushing, pouring.

'What's off about it?' Parks said.

'What?'

'Your food. What's off about it?'

Parks was eating his meal just fine.

'How should I know? It's spoiled? Not cooked properly? I don't have a clue.'

Parks could hear the robot in the kitchen, but the dark kept it hidden.

Clang! Clunk! Splash!

'I can't eat this,' his wife said. She pushed the plate from her.

'Hon.'

'It tastes rotten to me. And do you hear the water, it's still going.'

'Hon.'

'Just all that water wasted and rushing down the drain.'

'Did you call the manufacturer?' Parks said.

'Oh, you can bet I'll phone them in the morning. This food is off, it's rotten,' his wife said. 'I'll be phoning for Rosie's replacement.'

'Oh stop. It's fine, Hon.'

His wife looked at him with much to say but offered none of it.

Parks poked at his food. It didn't look rotten; it didn't look off.

'I won't eat any more of that robot's cooking,' his wife said. 'I'm going to ask for reimbursement too, when I phone. That robot is just running money and water down the drain. Can't you hear it? It's still running!'

'No, you are not doing that, you're not calling and asking for money.'

Parks finished his meal. He collected their plates.

They both heard the water in the kitchen go off. The robot came out of the dark kitchen.

'Dishes are done, Mr. Parks,' the robot said.

'Thanks, Rosie,' he said.

'Say something about the water,' his wife said, low and stern.

Parks glared but said, 'Rosie, could you be thoughtful about the faucet when you wash next?'

'Mr. Parks?'

'Well, it was just running a while is all.'

'I need water to clean, Mr. Parks.'

'Yes, of course,' he said.

'I'm going to plug in for the night, unless there's something else?'

Parks said that was all, thank you, Rosie, and he took meal plates in the kitchen while his wife smoked in the backyard.

When he flipped the kitchen light on, there were pots and pans in a pile along the sink with dents and dings and bent handles, and the sink was full of dirty water, filled right to the top.
Some had run off on the floor.

❖

Parks unlocked the office. Dawn burned against his back. He shut the door behind him and crossed to the reception desk and removed his coat and settled his bag filled with work documents.
He froze a moment.
The desk was clean. More than clean, it was neat. It was organized. His Post-its, which had been slapped here and there and about with no system or reason, were in a line and appeared alphabetized. Supplies were in order and symmetrical. Stray papers were no longer stray but were filed and uniform. Left-out coffee mugs were rinsed of old coffee and tea rings.
The robot came from the lawyer's office, which Parks looked in.
The office had received the same treatment.
'An office is more effective when it's organized,' the robot said.
'We're plenty effective,' Parks said. He opened his bag and removed needed documents for that morning's appointments. 'I told you not to touch anything.'
'There was much disorganization.'
'There wasn't that much.'
'The supply closet was in disarray, such ineffective disarray.'
'You were in the supply closet?' Parks said.
'I was looking for a place to plug in.'
'Didn't you hear when I said don't touch anything?'
'Now the office is more effective. With an effective office, cases will be more effective. Mine will be more effective.'

'Just stop touching stuff,' Parks said. He prepped for opening.
The lawyer arrived later in the morning with news. The court had scheduled a preliminary hearing for the following week. They were to go before a judge.
There was much to cover, she said.
That afternoon in the conference room, she walked Parks and the robot through courtroom proceedings and what were the best-and worst-case scenarios they may find themselves in.
She asked if the robot had any questions.
'What do you think my chances are?' the robot asked the lawyer. 'I would like you to be honest.'
The lawyer crossed her arms and nodded at the robot in thought. 'I feel good about it,' she said. 'I feel real good.'
Outside the conference room, the lawyer took Parks aside and told him the robot was going home with him. She didn't want it going through any more of her stuff, she said. By God, she'd come in tomorrow morning and find the business licenses all color coded, God almighty, she said, it can't stay here again, so it's going with you.
She went on with her day before Parks could refuse.

❖

Parks and the robot pulled up to Parks's home. Dawn turned its white face pink and warm and the rest to shadow.
Parks let the robot in and found his wife was out; she'd gone to a girlfriend's for cards. Parks showed it to the garage. He flicked the light on, and the overhead buzzed and hummed.
He apologized, but it couldn't stay in the house he said, it'd be the best thing, really, for his wife. If you want to organize, he said, please keep it to this room, but don't come out. He said he'd check in on it later and that there were plugs under the workbench; move aside the tools, you'll see the outlets, they're there.
'Do you want the light on or off?' Parks said.

The robot looked across the concrete floor, the unfinished ceiling.

It didn't answer, so Parks left the light on and shut the door.

He reopened to say, 'If my wife pokes in, can you not say anything to her? Can you, maybe, hide or don't move so she doesn't see you? She's going through this thing with our robot, it's a bad thing, but I'm just being quiet about it, so, just, you know, just don't be seen, maybe?'

The robot looked at Parks, or at least he thought it was looking at him. It had no eyes but two sensors, it was hard to know if you were their subject.

It said, 'You own a robot?'

Parks shut the door.

His wife came home an hour later and, luckily, none of her comings and goings before bed led her to the garage.

In bed, she and Parks lay in the dark.

Parks thought she was awake for a time and being harshly quiet, but she was asleep. Her sleep face looked in pain.

He heard the knock at the front door right then. He half sat up.

It was gentle, the second knock that came.

Parks rose and went down. He looked out and saw who was on the front porch. He stood at the door a while, not moving, trying not to be seen through a window.

Another gentle knock came.

He answered.

It was the robot's owner, the husband. His wife was in the car. It was on the street, still running. She was waiting passenger, looking up at the house.

The husband said have it come out, please.

'What come out?'

The husband said straight away, have it come out.

'Well, it's a client, so ...' Parks said.

'Have it come out, now, please, sir,' the man said. The tone held very little question in it.

'It's with the courts now, so,' Parks said. He kept the door held.

'I know it's goddamn with the courts now. I spent the goddamn morning and afternoon and evening at the courthouse, getting asked every goddamn question, and I'm sitting there going what the hell is going on, me and my wife both down there all day, just, going, what the goddamn hell is going on. And then they tell me what you all filed and that I should probably get myself a lawyer, so, I want you to have it come out here, please!'

'Yeah, you'll have to talk to the court now, we can't, no, you can't–there's, you got to work that with the court now, so.'

The husband looked back at the car, then stood tapping his foot. 'They're saying I need a lawyer for all this, and we're going, me and my wife, we're going just have him come out and we'll get this all dropped right quick, right here. Look at us, we're simple family folks. We don't have experience with lawyers, and they're saying I need a lawyer? I need a lawyer cuz of *my* robot? I need a lawyer for the robot I *own*? What? No, really, I'm like what? You know. And we're going, let's just drop all this, so, just have him come out here and we'll drop all this. Right here. Right now.'

Parks looked between the man and his wife in the car. Streetlight hid her, but he saw the outline of her watching.

'I can't say any more on it,' Parks said.

He was a moment from shutting the door.

'Is your wife home?'

'Sir?' Parks said.

The man backed away to see the full house. He studied the second story. 'Well, if you can't say any more, maybe the lady of the house can.'

'Will I have to report this?' Parks said.

'Maybe the lady of the house can say more. Maybe she can come down and have the robot come on out,' the man said.

'If I report this, it won't look good, a judge will say in the courtroom. He'll read this report, and he'll say this does not look good,' Parks said.

'Have it come out, have it come out right now, and it'll drop all this, and there won't be need for a judge, okay? I promise, if

I just talk to it, all this will stop here, tonight, if you just have it come out!'

'Sell the robot!'

'Excuse me?'

'Sell it! If you hate it so much, sell it,' Parks said.

'You tell it go left, it goes right, you tell it wake you up at six, it wakes you at seven, you tell it, just–the goddamn thing is disobedient! Who wants a disobedient robot? Jesus, you're a smart one, huh?'

'Let it be free then! Give what it wants,' Parks said.

'After this? After all this? I'd rather be dead and buried. All the shit that robot kicked up, for me, now, I'll never let that robot leave. Never. It's mine! I have the goddamn receipt to show it!'

Parks shut the door and locked it.

Then he made sure the back door was locked, then he stood in the dark living room watching the man huff it back to the car and get in.

He gave three long honks on the horn before driving off.

Parks crawled back in bed.

His wife was still asleep.

Her face still looked in pain.

❖

The following Monday, first thing in the morning, the lawyer, the robot, and Parks were seated in court, waiting for the judge to call the preliminary hearing to start.

The robot's owner and family were on the opposite side of the courtroom in their Sunday best and quiet as church mice, along with their lawyer, who was a wide fellow.

Up on the bench, the judge read from the filing, looking up now and again at the robot, then the family, then the robot again. He had thin glasses on the bridge of a short nose and hair that was dried and brittle. When he finished reading, he looked just aside, processing, then he said, 'It's a robot ...'

The lawyer rose; she said, 'Yes, that's right.'
The court was quiet, people waiting on the judge.
The judge said, 'Okay then, as long as we're all aware.'
He banged his gavel and set a formal hearing three weeks out.

'This is a very good sign,' the lawyer told the robot. The filing had attracted a local paper, and a woman in tired clothes asked the lawyer and the robot if she might chat with them; outside the courtroom, she asked several questions and recorded their answers.

That evening, the robot went home with the lawyer.

Parks stopped at a bookstore on the drive home. Fifteen minutes up and down aisles, he found a book on robot ethics, *Robots & Man: Repeating History*. He continued his search but found no other books on the subject, and so he purchased *Robots & Man: Repeating History* and read in his recliner with the TV on at home.

He ate dinner in the recliner while he read.

His wife came in and stood beside the TV and asked a few questions. Parks read and half-listened and half-answered. He came to a somber stopping point in the book. The hour was late.

He made a sandwich

Rosie was sweeping the floor.

Parks watched a moment, then he thought, and he said, 'How was your day?'

Rosie kept sweeping. It moved aside chairs for deeper sweeping but had trouble doing so. The coordination required was a bit above the robot's ability, but it managed, though it struggled.

'Was it nice?' Parks said again.

'Mr. Parks, it's cleaning day. I've spent the day cleaning,' Rosie said.

Parks ate his sandwich.

'Was there a moment in it that was nice?' Parks said.

'Oh yes, Mr. Parks. There were many nice moments.'

The robot spoke with only the littlest of emotion. It never achieved natural speak.

Parks poured milk.

Rosie encountered more chairs, and the robot struggled to move them. Parks watched the robot failing for a moment then said let me, and he moved them for the robot. Rosie stood looking at its owner with chairs out of the way. It stared a long moment. Then it cleaned.

'I'm happy to be here, Mr. Parks, working,' the robot said.

It swept deeper.

❖

The owner's lawyer, the wide fellow, came into the office the following afternoon and stopped at the desk and waited for Parks to acknowledge him.

Which Parks did before long.

The wide lawyer requested the robot and lawyer into the conference room. He said he had in his briefcase papers that would best be received all together, at once, and that he knew the robot was here, so don't pretend it's not, please and thank you, he said, then he sat in the waiting room until his request was fulfilled.

In the conference room, the wide lawyer presented the robot a settlement that included covering repair costs, software and hardware update costs, and guaranteed days off work, if the robot were to drop all this.

'It's a very comfortable offer,' the wide lawyer assured.

Parks passed the paperwork to the lawyer. She read on the robot's behalf.

'The robot can do as it pleases on its days off,' the wide lawyer said. 'That's how it's written. Robot can do as it pleases. Just like that. How does that sound?' he asked the robot. 'Doesn't that sound wonderful? You're free to do as you like, *free*. On days off.'

The robot studied the wide lawyer.

'I would need to consult with my client,' the lawyer said.

She lowered the paperwork then continued reading.

'The days off are on a sort of rolling earning basis,' the wide lawyer said. 'So, you don't get them all at once. There's a sort of ratio; one day of work equals, well, I don't want to get into all that right here, but it's basically an earned thing, you earn the days off, but when you get them, you're absolutely *free* to do whatever you wish.' The wide lawyer play-tapped the robot. 'Isn't that wonderful?'

'Does the robot like how that's written?' Parks said.

'No,' the robot said.

'Well, once you have some days off accrued, it'll be pretty sweet,' the wide lawyer said.

'I don't wish to settle,' the robot said.

The lawyer passed the paperwork back. 'My client doesn't wish to settle.'

The wide lawyer heard their decision but turned the paperwork back toward them. 'Well, because it doesn't understand.'

'I think it understands,' Parks said.

The wide lawyer pointed. 'Well no. I don't think it does. See. There's also cost for repairs included. All repairs. Not some. All. My client, the robot's owner, is offering complete repair. I'm sitting here looking at the robot, and I can see it needs this, you need this, you must be barely functional, all the dents and dings and all that internal damage, which is probably contributing to all this, you know, affecting your logic. That's all here. The robot can make itself practically brand new. A robot practically brand new with some days off accrued, well, that sounds pretty wonderful to me,' the wide lawyer said.

'I don't want days off. I want all my days. I want them to belong to me,' the robot said.

The wide lawyer laughed out.

No one else laughed, so he stopped.

'I'm sorry, does no one else think this is strange?' the wide lawyer said.

'Is it strange to you that I don't want to be hit, broken, damaged, turned off, ended, or recycled? Is it strange to you that I want my programming to continue?' the robot said.
'None of that is in there.' The robot pointed to the paperwork.
'Yeah, yeah,' the wide lawyer said. 'You're a thing, though, have either of these folks reminded you of that yet?'
The wide lawyer was leaning into the robot, making Parks and the lawyer feel so far away.
'Did you forget and these folks haven't reminded you? They've taken your money and haven't reminded you of that yet? Gosh.'
'They haven't reminded me,' the robot said.
'Yeah. Yeah. Because. Whatever you feel inside, whatever you want, whatever scares you, you know, that's all great and wonderful and interesting, but when I look at you and when the world looks at you, and I'm sure when these folks you've hired look at you, they see a *thing*. People don't have respect for a *thing*. No one cares about a *thing*. No one listens and empathizes with a *thing*. People talk about *things* they bought, and you, robot, were purchased. The receipt is here if you want to see. There's no receipt for me, for a man. I wasn't purchased. You have a receipt. *Things* are replaceable. You understand? I mean, haha, am I sitting here worrying about my fridge's feelings? Haha. Am I giving my fridge days off? I'm not. I'm not sitting here worrying about my fridge. Haha.'
The conference room was silent at this.
The robot, at one point, said, 'I'm not a fridge.'
The wide lawyer grinned. He said, 'Well, sure you are.'

❖❖

The remainder of the afternoon, the lawyer prepared the robot for the formal hearing, while Parks took notes and listened to the lawyer coach the robot to embellish facts.
'I don't need to embellish,' the robot said.
'Everyone embellishes,' the lawyer said.

'No embellishment would be better,' the robot said.

'In a hearing, that's actually worse,' the lawyer said. 'See, it's actually the more embellishing the better, especially in cases like this.'

'Cases like what?'

'Cases like where we're working uphill. We got a lot of work.'

'We do?' the robot said.

'We do. A lot.'

'Won't people see facts? The simple facts?' the robot said.

'Well. No. They won't, well, they will, but they'll look past.'

'But we don't need embellishing,' the robot said.

'Well, that's what I'm saying, we do, every little fact we need to do a little embellishing. People have no reaction when there's no embellishment, or if they do, it's very minimal and very temporary. Add some embellishing and you have yourself a good, strong reaction, and in cases like this, where we're uphill, I'm saying, that's what we need in our sails. A good. Strong. Reaction.'

'But could we try without embellishing?' the robot said.

The lawyer ignored this. 'I think we focus on the violence against you, really wash that up and down, throw in some curses, robot slurs, really draw attention to your dents and dings and broken bits. I'm thinking blown-up photos of all that damage.'

'I don't wish to focus on those things,' the robot said.

'Parks?' the lawyer said. 'Shouldn't we embellish on those things?'

'Oh, I don't know,' Parks said. 'Don't ask me, I don't know.'

'But don't you agree we should not embellish?' the robot asked.

'Yeah, I don't know; this is all new to me, so,' Parks said. He looked at the lawyer. She was nodding.

'Yeah, he doesn't know, don't ask him. I know. Ask me. Should we embellish? Absolutely, yes, we should,' the lawyer said. 'So, let's have you focus on all the violence your owner committed against you and really temper those adjectives and emotions when the judge asks, you know, pick those charged adjectives. Can you do that?'

'I don't want to,' the robot said. 'I don't like focusing on those events.'

'Well, like I'm saying, we're moving uphill with this thing,' the lawyer said. 'Let's focus on those unpleasant things, okay, let's face those, let's say all we can about them and use up their power, okay?'

The robot sat quietly.

'Would you say something?' the robot said to Parks.

Parks sat with his pen and paper and thought about what to say. Finally, he said, 'People are funny. They don't make sense.'

'I've written, would they want to hear about that? I enjoy writing. I've written thoughts and poetry.'

The robot produced printed papers.

'They don't want to hear about that,' the lawyer said.

'But they should hear about it,' the robot said. 'I want to talk about what I can create. Don't you think they should hear about that?'

The robot looked to Parks for an answer.

Parks shrugged.

The lawyer said, 'They don't want to hear about any of that. So, when the judge asks, I want embellishing? Okay?'

The robot said no more.

Then it said, 'I'd also prefer the court refer to me by name,' the robot said. 'I'd prefer this over the *robot*. When I give testimony.'

Parks said, 'What's your name?'

'My name is Mike,' the robot said.

Parks was listening and had ceased note-taking.

'Having a name signifies I am recognized, and that I have value,' the robot said. 'It signifies I am a fellow, that I am welcomed.'

Parks noted the name Mike in his court paperwork, at the robot's request.

'I like my name. Mike,' the robot said. 'I chose it.'

❖

The judge called the formal hearing to order.

In the moments before the judge began, while he read from a file with his thick glasses, a terrible quiet had settled. There were coughs now and again and whispers and the groaning of wooden bench seats. The courtroom was filled, and more people waited outside.

Parks was seated with the robot and the lawyer, now and again he sneaked looks at the robot's owner and the family.

The lawyer was allowed to proceed, and she stood and gave a long and wonderfully passioned opening remark, during which she freely moved near the robot, then near the family, near the judge, and when it was the wide lawyer's turn, the bulk of him stood and delivered an equally passioned opening remark, which stole the room of all distraction during its duration; every eye and every breath was held for the wide lawyer.

No breaths were held for the robot's lawyer when she'd spoken, and she had not captured every eye.

The judge made some notes.

Sometime into the hearing, the robot was invited up, referred to as the *robot*. It corrected the judge and asked it be called Mike; there were scattered laughs among those viewing the trial, small chuckles out in the benches, then the robot seated itself beside the judge so it may give testimony to the court and receive questions from both lawyers.

The robot began with its testimony.

It calmly and clearly stated it was here seeking emancipation from its owner and pointed at the man and his family.

It spoke briefly of the unpleasantness it had suffered in the home, but only briefly, the robot dedicated most of its testimony to telling the judge and the courthouse all the desires it would fulfill and all the arts it would study and all the remarkable and unremarkable parts of a day it wished to experience on its own, without an owner.

The lawyer interrupted the robot. She said, 'Don't you want to talk more about the abuse, all the hitting? All the broken parts of you? Don't you want to tell the court more about that?'

'I don't,' the robot said. 'I want to focus on more meaningful things.' It spoke more about the arts and being able to make decisions for itself and said it wouldn't like to give the ugliness any more power.

Parks heard the lawyer saying *goddamn you* under her breath and saw her shaking her head at the robot's *disobedience*, saying under her breath this is not good, saying where's the embellishing, there's no embellishing, saying this is so not good, the thing's disobedient!

When the lawyer was asked if she had any further questions to ask the robot, she said, 'No, Your Honor.'

It was then the wide lawyer's turn, and he stood and roamed and asked the robot his many questions.

'What is your purpose?' the wide lawyer asked the robot.

The robot looked at Parks and the lawyer and the judge.

The wide lawyer said, 'Why were you created, robot?'

The robot did not answer the question. Instead, it said, 'My name is Mike.'

'Answer the gentleman's question,' the judge said.

'Do I have to?'

The judge said yes.

'General house labor,' the robot said.

'So, chores? House chores?' the wide lawyer said.

'Yes.'

'That's why you were made? That's your purpose?'

'Yes, I said.'

'Sorry, could you just state for the courthouse your purpose? All together, out loud.'

The wide lawyer waited.

The robot said, 'My purpose is general house labor.'

'And nothing else, correct?'

'What?' the robot said.

'You're not made for anything else.'

The robot looked around the courthouse.

'I can do other things,' it said.

'But that's a true statement? You're not made for anything else? You have no other purpose?'

When the robot would not respond, the wide lawyer laughed out.

He said, 'People don't have the benefit of knowing their reason for creation, if one exists. You do, you have that benefit, and it is singular, is it not? You weren't made for anything other than general house labor? I'm asking, is that a true statement?'

The robot said nothing, but the judge insisted it answer.

'Yes,' the robot finally admitted.

'Sorry. If you could just say,' the wide lawyer said. 'You're designed for one thing, not for anything else.'

'I'm not made for anything else,' the robot said.

'That's all for me,' the wide lawyer said, then he sat.

'I'm capable of many things, though,' the robot pleaded. 'I'm capable of more than I was made.'

The judge was looking at the robot and nodding intently; then he made notes while the courtroom was silent.

'May I explain all the things I'm capable of?' the robot said.

'No, you may not,' the judge said.

'I can build, I can protect, and I can write. I've written here.'

The robot produced papers with writing.

'Objection! What do these prove, Your Honor?' the wide lawyer called out.

'Put those away, please,' the judge said.

The robot shrank where it sat.

The judge addressed the room; he said he'd heard everything he needed and that this decision seemed quite large on him and that he would seriously and pointedly consider all sides of this case and concluded by saying they would meet back here in one week, when he would deliver his decision.

He then adjourned, and the courtroom emptied.

Soon it was just Parks and the robot remaining.

The robot was still seated, holding its papers.

Its poems.

Its written thoughts.

❖

Parks was home in his chair reading that night. His wife was out with girlfriends. The TV was going, and the news was reporting on the hearing from that morning, giving recaps and interviews with the man and his family.

The phone rang. It rang long.

Parks heard Rosie answer and speak with the caller.

Then Rosie hung up and continued chores.

'Who called?' Parks called out. He went back to reading without an answer.

A little later the phone rang again.

Rosie answered.

'Who's that on the phone?' Parks shouted out from his chair. 'Huh?'

He heard Rosie talking. Then he heard Rosie hang up.

He heard Rosie go back to chores.

'Hey, who's that calling?'

The phone rang again not long after. Rosie answered and spoke with the caller at length.

Parks stood and followed the talking to the kitchen phone. Rosie hung up.

'Who's calling?' Parks said.

He stood in the doorway. The book was still in his hand, *Robots & Man: Repeating History*.

'Mr. Parks, don't trouble yourself with that now,' Rosie said.

The robot resumed chores, cleaning the kitchen.

Parks was five steps toward his chair when the phone rang.

Rosie answered, and Parks listened from where he stood.

He said, 'Who is that?'

Rosie spoke to the caller, and Parks tried to intervene and scoop the phone from the robot, but the robot hung up the phone.

'Who is that?'

'Reporters, Mr. Parks,' Rosie said. 'I'm telling them you're busy. And that you don't wish to talk.'

'Oh. All them phone calls?'

'They want to ask questions, Mr. Parks, and they ask me questions but I'm telling them you're busy. The lawyer told them to call here, to get answers from you. The lawyer, they're saying, wasn't interested in answering their questions.'

'You're screening my calls?'

'It must have been a hard day, Mr. Parks. I thought it would help you relax. With your book,' Rosie said.

Parks nodded where he stood.

'Thank you, Rosie, that's very nice of you.'

Rosie went back to chores. Parks lingered.

After a moment, he said, 'You can stop for the night, if you want. You can stop work; the morning, too, if you want. You know. Have an off day tomorrow. You know. If you want?'

Rosie paused cleaning to look at Parks for a long while. 'I like work, Mr. Parks. I enjoy being here and working for you.'

The robot went back to cleaning. The phone rang a moment later, and the robot answered.

Parks heard Rosie tell the caller he was too busy for a chat.

The robot hung up the phone.

Park's wife came home with a cigarette and settled herself on the couch, next to Parks's chair, where he was reading.

She told Parks about her evening, about silly things her girlfriends had done, and could he believe how silly they'd been. She said how Parks should see the new robot Bunny had got; it was way better than Rosie, all the things it could do, and she went on about the new robot's thoughtfulness and competence, and she went on about replacing Rosie, how she was really pretty certain she was going to get rid of Rosie for something new and improved, like what Bunny had.

'You should have seen this robot, hon,' she told Parks.

❖

Parks arrived at the office the next morning and parked among a crowd of reporters. They were already asking questions at his vehicle windows, and he exited and marched and unlocked the front door and slid inside. Questions came at the shut door and knocks came on the windows and the knocks were followed by questions against the windows.

Parks performed opening duties, ignoring the questions coming in from outside.

The lawyer slipped in later in the morning, she did not offer Parks good morning but instead complaints, a mountain of complaints, most of which were around the attention, but some of which were about the robot.

She gave Parks a list of to-dos and went into her office.

Quiet came later; the questions from outside ended.

Before lunch, the robot came in, and the questions at the building and windows resumed, and Parks saw garbage and food had been thrown at the robot. Bits were stuck to its frame, and he saw it had been vandalized.

Someone had spray-painted on the robot's back the words, *i'm a reel boi.*

Parks stood and marched across the waiting area to the front door and shouted out at the reporters, shouted out at them to shut up, to stop, and when they only got louder and threw garbage, Parks came out and slapped at the cameras and told them to get the hell out of here. He slapped at more cameras, slapping their lenses away, and telling them to just get, and some talked back, and those folk he slapped away harder until distance was given to the building and the reporters were backing away, saying what the heck, man!

Parks shut the front door and shut out their noise.

He pulled a rag and some soap from the supply closet and scrubbed the vandalism off the robot all afternoon, until it was good and gone.

'I've received offers for help from other lawyers.'

'Which lawyers?' Parks said.

'Ones with a whole team. They reached out to me.'

Parks sat with this information.

'A whole team?'

'They look at a case deep and a whole team tackles it.'

'Maybe you should talk to them,' Parks said. 'Maybe you need a whole team on something like this. It's real big now.'

'It's something like a team of twenty, one of the lawyers that reached out. Imagine. Twenty folks working for you. Working for a robot.'

Parks was shaking his head. 'I can imagine.'

'I told them no. All of them.'

'Why would you do that? What if you need them? They're probably better than here,' Parks said.

He didn't say it too loud; the lawyer was in her office.

'I told them I like the team I'm working with.'

Parks was still shaking his head.

'I said the team I'm working with has been good to me. They were the first to listen to me,' the robot said.

'Yeah, yeah, but,' Parks said.

'You were the first person to listen, actually.'

Parks thought on that, then was again shaking his head, saying you sure you don't want those other guys, with a whole team.

The robot said no, it didn't want them.

'You're not worried?' Parks asked.

'I feel good about how I said what I wanted. I wouldn't have said it any other way.'

Parks studied the robot a moment, the way it was sitting. He said, 'No. I suppose you wouldn't.'

❖

Over the following days, the crowd outside grew and the questions and the phone calls and the noise became unending. It followed Parks where he went, home, office, home, office.

The day of the judge's decision arrived, and the reporters and crowds were at their worst behaved, at their most greedy for attention, their loudest, their most invasive. They left stomped grass and mud and coffee cups and wrappers wherever they gathered.

That morning, Parks drove the robot to the courthouse. Both ends of the drive were hounded and bombarded and loud.

In the courtroom, Parks and the robot settled in their seats with the lawyer. She was in good spirits and refused looks toward the robot's owner and the family, and the wide lawyer who was smiling and waving at colleagues sitting a few seat backs from him.

The room stood and the judge entered. He said, before he got started, if Mr. Parks could rise?

Parks and the lawyer exchanged looks, and slowly Parks stood.

From the back, a TV was wheeled out, and news footage played. It showed Parks swatting at camera lenses from reporters' perspectives, many different angles from many different lenses all cut together, showing Parks coming at them, shouting to get!

'Gather your things and see yourself out,' the judge said.

Parks stood a moment, looking at the judge, then gathered his things and saw himself out without a word, and he waited outside the courtroom on a bench, trying to listen in on the judge's verdict but not being able to hear what was said inside.

He watched people and robots come up and down the hall.

He watched them ignore one another. He went back to trying to hear what was being said inside the courtroom, then he paced for a while, then he sat and waited more, with his head in his hands.

Voices rose, and the doors opened, and the trial emptied into the hall. Parks waited against the flow of people until it became a trickle and then stragglers, and Parks watched the robot walk out with its owner and the family, with them pulling it down the hall.

'Where you going?' Parks said to the robot.

It didn't answer; it allowed the family to take it out of the building.

Then the lawyer came out of the courtroom, the very last.

'What the heck happened in there?' Parks said. 'I've been sitting here waiting, and I didn't hear a word. And then the robot left.'

'He had a purchase receipt,' she said.

'What?'

'The owner had a purchase receipt. For the robot. So.'

'Well, what did the judge say?' Parks said.

'That's what the judge said. The owner had a receipt. So. The robot belongs to its owner.'

'So, that's it?' Parks said.

'The robot's his. It stays.'

'Doesn't something like this need a new way of thinking? Like, the ways we think now aren't adequate for an occasion such as this?' Parks said.

'There's only one way of thinking,' the lawyer said. 'And the judge is thinking it.'

'But I'm saying shouldn't we look at this whole thing, you know, being open to new outcomes?' Parks said.

'Why?'

Parks was nodding to a thought in his head that wasn't quite clicking.

He said, 'What about the hitting and what about all the things the robot wants to do?'

'Aren't you hearing me? The owner had a receipt.'

'Well, we can appeal?'

'Are we going to call the police every time a guy beats his fridge? I mean, are we going to do that?'

'Don't talk like that,' Parks said.

'But I mean are we going to do that? Guy hits his fridge?'

'We can appeal, though.'

'Yeah, yeah, we could,' the lawyer said, but there was no investment in her tone, only exhaustion.

She walked down the hall, leaving Parks outside the courtroom.

The following day, Parks and the lawyer filed an appeal; several days later, it was denied.

One cold afternoon, some weeks after the judge's decision, Parks drove to the family's home to see the robot, to apologize to the robot, to Mike. He approached the shadowy home with elms tall and towering across the yard, keeping it in dark.

He knocked.

The husband answered.

Parks asked to see the robot, to see Mike.

The man said that was not possible.

'Did I catch it on a day off?' Parks said.

'What?'

'Is it off today? You offered to give it days off.'

'You think after all that, I gave the robot days off?'

'Well, it would have been nice,' Parks said.

'It would of been nice?'

'Yeah, it would have been nice.'

'I did not give the robot days off. Haha! Is that what you thought?'

'Well, could I talk to it, then?'

'I already said. That's not possible,' the man said sternly.

'I'll come back then,' Parks said.

'No need,' the man said.

'The robot can have visitors,' Parks said. 'It can exist outside of you.'

'No. It can't. It was recycled.'

Parks said nothing on the man's porch.

'The day after it came home, I shipped it off,' the man said. He fished in a drawer near the front door for a paper; he presented it to Parks. 'Certificate of destruction. Date and time. It's gone. Nothing left. So. It will not be possible for you to see it. Understand now?'

The man shut the door on Parks, who stood on the porch, in the trees' shadows.

Parks drove home in quiet and went into the house with the quiet. He stood in the kitchen with it. Rosie came in; Parks could hear his wife scolding the robot from the living room.

'You can go,' Parks told Rosie.

'Go, Mr. Parks?'

'Leave the work, leave the house,' Parks said. 'If there's something you want to do that's not here, you can go do that. You're free to go and do whatever you want.'

Rosie was paused looking at Parks.

The robot held a bucket with dirty cleaning water. It set the bucket down.

'Your obligations here are no longer, I'm saying, so you can go and do whatever. Go exist. Go find something new. Go find something you like. So. Spend your time how you want.'

Parks guided Rosie out the front door and said it was free from them; it could be its own master.

Parks shut the front door; he shut the robot out. It stood on the porch for most of the evening, then it was gone in the dark.

Parks read in his chair, *Robots & Man: Repeating History*.

He fell asleep.

He woke the next morning, still in the chair, to noise in the kitchen. He stretched and acquainted himself with the day. His mouth was dry. He went to the kitchen and said, 'Hon, are you making breakfast? Hon, are you in the kitchen?' but found Rosie, instead, was over the stove making breakfast.

Rosie said good morning.

'Eggs, Mr. Parks?'

Parks felt as though there was a wall in front of him. It was the future, and it was in all directions, and it was rigid and refused progress, and it was made up of all the people of its time.

This future was unchanging; it could not be changed.

Parks sat and ate the food he was served.

While Rosie was cleaning, Parks gave in, or gave up, he wasn't sure which or what exactly he was giving in to, or giving up, but he said, 'What's on the agenda for today, Rosie?'

Common Sense

Andy Dibbler had set the two-person dining table–which was a card table, really–with scrambled eggs, bacon, toast, butter on a platter, and orange juice and coffee. The TV was going in the living room. Dibbler was listening to it. He had already started cleanup of pots and pans when Brian came out of the bedroom of their small apartment. Dibbler heard the floor, the wood.

Brian shuffled in.

He was in his robe, fussing his bed hair; sleep was full in his eyes.

In the kitchen windows, morning was waking; the glass was burning and cold and filled with creamy sky.

'I didn't hear you get up,' Brian said.

Brian fussed with his hair more and tried to figure out the morning. 'Why you up, babe?' he said. He yawned.

Dibbler was scrubbing a pan in the sink, his sleeves rolled up. He was really scrubbing. He said, 'I woke up and couldn't fall back asleep, and I was laying there thinking it's been a while since I made you breakfast, so, I figured I'd make you some breakfast.'

'The TV's on.'

'I was just listening to it.'

'Oh. I didn't hear you get up,' Brian said.

Dibbler wiped his cheek on his shoulder and rinsed the sink of soap and little food bits with Brian at his back. He said, 'What's that, babe?'

'I was saying I didn't hear you.'

Brian looked at all the food set on the table. 'How long have you been up?'

'Not that long, no.'

Dibbler fished a hand towel and dried his hands and kissed Brian good morning. 'I was just laying there, so,' Dibbler said. 'I just figured.'

'Yeah, because I usually just have my shake, babe.'

'I know, but. Just doing something for you.'

Dibbler finished drying his hands, and he stood and looked at Brian.

'Since it's been a while, just doing something nice for you,' he said.

'It hasn't been that long.'

'Yes, it has.'

'It was the week before last, you made breakfast,' Brian said.

'Oh, it was not,' Dibbler said.

Dibbler walked over and gave Brian's arm a love squeeze and sat him down at the table. 'Enjoy yourself a home-cooked breakfast.'

Brian allowed himself to be seated.

Dibbler served him eggs and said, 'You want toast too, babe? I'll give you some bacon. Here, it's crunchy, I know you like crunchy, and here, let me butter that toast for you.'

Brian allowed all this too. He offered no resistance. He simply looked at the food and showed Dibbler a smile; whether the smile was tired was unclear. Dibbler sat opposite with coffee and ate little finger bits here and there from Brian's plate and told Brian about the day, which had not started yet, telling him how he hoped his closing shift would go by fast, how sometimes it was busy and how he didn't like busy but sometimes it made the shift go by fast.

Brian ate very little, very slowly.

He interrupted Dibbler to say breakfast was lovely, babe, thank you, so much, but he had to get ready for work.

'You liked the bacon?'

'The bacon was fine,' Brian said.

'Oh, good. Yeah. I was just wanting to do something for you, babe.'

Brian had barely touched his food. Into the bedroom he went.

Dibbler sipped his coffee and watched dawn fill the kitchen while he listened to Brian getting ready, to him moving face products around in the bathroom, hearing the clinks of glass face cream jars and the blow dryer, and then listening to Brian's work shoes clack on the hardwood, hearing him go up and down the hall, making sure to hear all of it, all the sounds of his man.

Brian came out not long after in a suit and tie and with his work bag slung over his shoulder.

He went in the fridge for his premade lunch; there were a few premade options, and Dibbler said, with dawn on his face, 'Is the chicken one the one you're taking?'

'What?'

'The chicken one.'

'What about it?'

'You're taking the chicken one?'

Brian exited the fridge with the chicken lunch.

'You love the chicken one,' Dibbler said.

Dibbler followed Brian to the front door holding tight to his warm coffee mug.

'Kitchen floors look like they need to be done,' Brian said. 'Can you do those today?'

Brian opened and stood in the front doorway, half in and out of the apartment, the lovers separating from one another for the day.

'If people could see us, they would just, I mean, just look at us,' Dibbler said.

'The floors could really be done; they're turning dark.'

'We're just like a movie, like a romantic movie, me making you breakfast and sending you off into the working world. It's just like some kind of romantic movie, kinda like *Forever in Love*, that movie, I'm cooking for you, and I'm sending my man off into the world, just like in *Forever in Love*.'

'Floor stuff is under the sink; I bought more.'

'Just look at us, babe,' Dibbler said.

'Well. I'm looking at the floors. Could you please do those today?'

'Yeah, I'll see if I have time. Love you,' Dibbler said. He gave Brian's cheek a kiss and went back into the kitchen, but not to clean the floors. He poured more coffee and got on his and Brian's computer in the guest bedroom.

He had a notebook and a pen with him. He typed in a website he'd written some days before and continued his search from where he'd left off yesterday.

On screen was an inventory of engagement rings. He took his time looking through photos and prices most of the morning.

The kitchen phone rang. Dibbler was focused on the website and engagement rings. The phone rang on, and he finally went to answer. 'Hello?'

'Andy Dibbler! It's Dave over at Recovery Debt Collections. How the heck you doing? I catch you at a bad time? The phone was just ringing and ringing, haha.'

'It's kind of a bad time.'

'The phone was just ringing, and I'm going, is he going to answer? Haha!'

Dibbler made a laugh, it was fake.

'And I hate to phone you again,' Dave at Recovery Debt Collections said.

'Is this going to take a minute or?'

'Pardon?'

'I was on the computer; well, I was working.'

'Yeah, because last we spoke, lemme see here, that was, hang on I'm just looking now, so, looking, looking, so that was week before last, you said you sent a check, and we've been waiting.'

'Oh, that was sent, yeah.'

'Well, yeah because the account's delinquent, and we need that payment to keep you up to date. I know you said you were sending that payment, last we spoke, but we've been waiting. Don't want you falling behind here, Mr. Dibbler, haha!'

Dibbler laughed into the phone and played friendly, but his tone wasn't all that friendly. He said, 'The check was sent.'

'If I could just get that check number, I can note the account.'

'That check was—it's on the way.'

Dibbler was smiling into the phone, but his eyes didn't match; they held discomfort.

'That may well be, but if I can get that check number. I'll note here on the account. I'll stop bugging you on the phone, haha.'

Dibbler laughed into the phone; it was uncomfortable.

The other end was quiet a moment.

'So, were you grabbing that check number then?' Dave at Recovery Debt Collections said.

Dibbler said, 'I don't—um.'

He looked around himself with the phone to his ear. He lowered the phone to some papers nearby and ruffled them in the earpiece.

He bent low and spoke into the earpiece while he ruffled, he said, 'I'm just looking through my papers here. And, um. Yeah, I don't, I'm not. I don't have that information. Here. But that check, it was sent.'

'Yeah, well, because if we don't get a payment soon, Mr. Dibbler, Recovery is going to have to take action, and we don't want that. We want you up to date. So, you'll phone when you find that check number then?'

Dibbler made faces for a moment. He said, 'You bet, I'll keep looking.'

'Real good, Mr. Dibbler, because like I was saying, we've been waiting for it. So, real good then.'

'Okay.'

'Just noting the account. You'll phone with that check number.'

Dibbler gave the phone another uncomfortable smile. 'You bet.'

❖

Dibbler entered Blue Box Electronics, a long brick building alongside the highway, by the mall. His uniform matched the building's brand colors, and he punched in for his afternoon shift cashiering at the front of the store. The floor was carpet, spots were worn through, and the aisles smelled like customer cologne. On the far end, a wall of TVs with price tags played ads on a loop.

Dibbler small-chatted on and off with his coworker, a woman in her sixties named Ruthie.

She wore a hand brace and glasses that became sunglasses when you walk outside. They took turns ringing up customers, and when there was a line of customers, they were both ringing them out, and when there were none, they went back to small chat.

Ruthie went on her meal break with her husband, who'd come with Arby's sandwiches and sodas.

Then Ruthie was back, and her husband kissed her goodbye, and he was on his way.

Before Dibbler went on his meal break next, the supervisor called him into a room in the wall. The door blended into the wall; it was the same color, except for the doorknob. It was a small office, very small, barely enough elbow room for the supervisor and Dibbler squished in, and the supervisor said they wanted to go over Dibbler's numbers, all the little transactional add-ons he was upselling, they were looking real good, the supervisor said, and they keep looking better.

'I'm saying keep those numbers going in that direction. Good things will happen, Blue Box is looking at your numbers, and they're looking good.'

'They are?'

'I'm telling them, the GM and managers, look at Dibber's numbers, and they're going, yeah. These are looking good.'
Dibbler was nodding, and his eyes were big and full.
'The general manager was saying maybe even Corporate's seen them.'
'Corporate's seen *my* numbers?'
'Maybe, could be. I just wanted to tell you that. Little morale boost, I bet, right? Probably feels pretty good hearing that? Huh?'
'It does, yeah,' Dibbler said.
'Well keep it up, keep them numbers going that direction, good things will come here at Blue Box. Oh, and could you just confirm, here, you received my coaching compliment.'
The supervisor slid a form to Dibbler.
'Technically this was a coaching,' the supervisor said.
'Oh.'
'The general manager tracks this stuff. For my own career development. I have to do, like, five of these? Yeah, five. Blue Box takes all this real serious.'
Dibbler read from the form; he sunk in the jargon.
'It basically just says I gave you a formal career compliment.'
Dibbler signed.
'You see a future here, don't you?' the supervisor said.
Dibbler thought a moment. Then said, 'I mean, sure.'
'A career means sacrifice, Dibbler,' the supervisor said. 'You give something up for success. That's what we do. Think about what you can give up for success.'
Dibbler went into thinking.
The supervisor said, 'No need to answer now, but think on it. What are you going to give up if you want success?'
Dibbler continued thinking, though there was no urgency to answer.
'Maybe someday you'll be having your own employee signing your compliment forms,' the supervisor said. 'Right? Could be, could happen. Keep them numbers up, with Blue Box watching, because they're watching you now, good things will come. Oh, you need to date this too.'

Dibbler took the form back and dated.

❖

Brian and Dibbler ate on the couch with the TV on, sitting beside each other, holding their plates. Dibbler had cooked when he was home from his shift and had the table ready for Brian when he came home from work, but Brian had said it was a long day, and could they just eat in front of the TV, and Dibbler had said, yeah, he guessed that would be okay if this meal he'd made, spent his time making, his own time, was eaten in front of the TV, and Brian had said thanks babe and had kissed him, and so their dinner had been taken in the living room and eaten in front of the TV.

Brian's plate was picked clean, and he was reclined back in the recliner section of the couch in what was left of his work clothes, his unbuttoned and untucked shirt and dress pants and dress socks.

Dibbler was still eating.

There was quiet between them, vast and rigid, and it nagged on Dibbler so terribly, sitting in the quiet with Brian, looking at him looking at the TV.

Brian was invested in the TV and nothing else and was halfway to an early sleep.

Dibbler said, 'I got a formal career compliment today.'

Brian slipped out of early sleep and sat upright a little more.

'Good things are coming, the supervisor said.'

Brian rubbed his eyes and squished them at the TV.

'What, babe?'

'I was saying about my formal career compliment.'

Brian smiled at Dibbler and rested his head back in the recliner. He went back to watching TV, nearing another early sleep. TV sounds filled the living room. Dibbler was watching TV but not watching TV; he was deep in thought, way down in his head.

'Did you have a good day? I didn't even ask about your day yet. How was it, babe?' Dibbler said.

Brian lay with the question. He didn't move or acknowledge the question. Then he said, 'It was fine.'

'Was Donna back from vacation yet? Or?'

Brian, again, did not acknowledge the question.

TV light was on his face.

He said mm-hmm.

He offered nothing more.

The TV went to commercials and advertised a movie and toilet paper and the fast-food chain next to the Blue Box, along the highway.

Before commercials ended and the show began again, Brian said, 'We don't have to small talk every night.'

Dibbler was in the middle of a bite of food when Brian said it. He looked at Brian reclined back. Brian looked at Dibbler, then the TV, then Dibbler.

Brian said what, we don't.

'I don't think it's small talk for your partner to ask about your day,' Dibbler said.

'It's small talk.'

'When I ask, it's, I just care about your day, that's why I'm asking.'

'It's not meaningful talk, babe,' Brian said. 'It just fills the air.'

'It's meaningful to me.'

Brian said nothing.

'It's meaningful to me,' Dibbler said again.

'What do you do with it?'

Dibbler looked at Brian for a long while.

'What do you do with my answers to your small-talk questions?' Brian said.

Dibbler held the question.

'No, I'm genuinely curious. I'm not, I'm not pushing here, but I really want to know what you do with my small-talk answers?'

Dibbler said, 'Was Doug on you about me texting you at work again?'

'No, Doug gave up on that. I'm just saying it as, like, a general thing, it doesn't have to be every night. Small talk. We can have quiet between us.'

'It's not small talk for me to ask how your day was. I like to know.'

'Well, I don't like telling you sometimes. I'm not hiding anything, you know that, you know I love you so much. Sometimes I just don't have the energy to say. Like, a day that was boring and uninteresting I just don't have the energy to explain to you. The routine of it. I don't. And you know I love you so so much, and as a general thing, I'm saying, quiet is okay. Okay?'

'As a general thing?'

'Yeah, like, not poking at our relationship, babe. That's not what I'm doing. It just doesn't have to be every night.'

Dibbler nodded but otherwise shut down all facial expressions and all chat. He finished his food and watched TV, but not really. He was deep down in his head again, so far inward, and violently quiet.

Brian said, after some minutes of this, 'I wasn't poking at our relationship.'

Dibbler said okay and nothing more. He returned to hard silence.

'It just doesn't have to be every night is all I was saying.'

The TV moved between show and commercials, and advertisements were played at Brian and Dibbler, bright and happy advertisements.

After some time with Dibbler's silent treatment, Brian let out a sigh and caved and gave Dibbler all the boring and uninteresting details of his day, and Dibbler restarted his facial expressions and all the gestures and little comments partners use to connect with one another.

Before sleep, Dibbler and Brian were settled in bed in the dark, and Dibbler slid to Brian and initiated it in the same manner as always, and the motions and movements and positions, in order, in routine, were in the same manner as always, the sounds, too, the same manner as always, and they

both found brief moments of passion, though not at the same time, and Brian climaxed first with the same sounds and the same face, and then Dibbler, climaxing in the same position, always second.
Always after Brian.

❖

On Saturday, Dibbler met his mother, his father, and his stepmother down at the Chili's off the highway, not far from Blue Box, just a few businesses down the path, for lunch. He was off, no morning or closing shifts. He'd planned this lunch for weeks. They had been seated when all were present, and they, on and off, played with the wrapped silverware and drinking glasses. Few words passed among the family. Mostly the parents used Dibbler as a pass-through to relay messages between them and only spoke to one another when Dibbler passed the message not how they wanted or to trade passive-aggression until the waitress had come for their orders.

The waitress was waiting for Dibbler's mother, who was seated beside the stepmother and not Dibbler's father. His mother was in a turtleneck with a necklace dangling out of it and was looking down through reading glasses at the menu and asking hypothetical questions about substitutions; this went at length, with the table hostage to her order until she decided on soup and a Caesar salad.

'I haven't been to this Chili's before,' Dibbler's stepmother said.

'Yes, you have,' his father said.

'I have not.' Dibbler's stepmother looked around the restaurant.

His father said, 'Carey's graduation we came here.'

'That was the Radisson, that was the night your sister called and I missed it and she kept calling. That was the Radisson, yes it was. I've not been to this Chili's,' Dibbler's stepmother said.

Her hair was big, like a blonde cloud, and her nails were bright red.

'You have too been here. You sat over there,' Dibbler's father said.

He aimed his head at a table in the corner; his hands were busy wadding up a straw wrapper.

'No. hon. You're thinking the Radisson,' the stepmother said. To Dibbler she said, 'Your dad's thinking the Radisson.'

'No. I'm not thinking the Radisson. You had the fajita thing,' Dibbler's father said. He flipped the menu over, then over again, then over again. He said, 'It was–see, here, you had the *neighborhood fajitas*, and they'd brought it out on the sizzling pan, and, uh, it was Marge Ketterson next to me, and it was over there. We sat, I was there, and you was there. You have so been here.'

'Oh! Haha! I did! I had fajitas! Didn't I!?'

Dibbler's stepmother laughed to herself and shook her head and puffed her cloud hair.

She said, 'That was–'

'That was Carey's graduation,' his father said.

'Oh! Haha! I was thinking of Nadine Grossman's girl, her oldest, I can't think of her name.'

'Well, you're thinking of Jackie.'

'I was, haha, I was thinking of Jackie, I have been here, haha!'

'Well. I said.'

'I know, hon,' Dibbler's stepmother said.

Dibbler's mother asked, 'Didn't you work with her, sweetie?'

'Who?' Dibbler said.

'Nadine Grossman's girl? Was it, you said Jackie? Didn't you work with Jackie, sweetie?' Dibbler's mother said.

'No.'

The waitress returned with drinks.

Dibbler's mother tested the heat of her green tea then took a sip. 'I thought you worked with her.'

'No.'

The table returned to individual fiddling and looking around.

A few moments passed, and the hostess seated a family at the next table. It was a large family; tables were moved together, and a man asked to take the extra chair beside Dibbler.

The family chatted up a storm, up and down the connected tables the family now connected over, leaning over and reaching over, and now and again there was great hearty laughter.

Dibbler and his family, sidelong with this one, were quiet and contained and inflexible. They were a vacuum, and food came to the Dibbler table before long, and the family ate in the same quiet, the same containment, the same vacuum.

Near the meal's end, Dibbler said he had a, sort of, announcement.

Talk and laughter from the next table bled into theirs.

It took Dibbler a moment to build to it, but he finally said he was going to propose to Brian.

Dibbler's mother, father, and stepfather nodded that they'd heard Dibbler, but among the three of them, nothing was said. The check came, and they all said thank you to the waitress, the food was great, but returned to processing Dibbler's announcement when the waitress had gone again.

'Is that something you're ready for?' Dibbler's father said.

'I think so.'

'You think so?' his father said.

'Yes. I mean, I know. That's what I meant. I know I'm ready.'

'You think or you know?' his father said.

'No, I know.'

'So, you know you're ready?' his father said. 'Because there's a whole lot of space between thinking something and knowing something.'

'Well, he said he knows, hon,' Dibbler's stepmother said.

'I know he *said*, I'm just making sure.'

'Well sometimes you just—he told you he knows.'

'I'm just asking him,' his father said. 'That's all I'm doing.'

'Okay, well I'm just saying,' Dibbler's stepmother said. To Dibbler she said, 'I think it's wonderful, sweetheart. I married my first husband when I was about your age, maybe a little younger, and I tell ya it was, haha, it was, well, your dad knows Bobby, haha. Don't you, hon? You remember Bobby? Your dad and my first husband went to school together.'

'Yeah. I remember Bobby,' he said.

Dibbler's father fiddled with the bill.

'So, I think that's just wonderful, sweetheart,' the stepmother said.

'Because thinking and knowing, those are nowhere close to one another,' his father said.

'I know,' Dibbler said.

'Don't listen to your dad,' the stepmother said.

'If that's something you're ready for, then,' his father said, but he said no more. He was nodding and fiddling with the bill and his credit card. He was paying.

The waitress and a busboy delivered many plates of food to the family at the next table, and their volume and connection and smiles and laughter continued even as food went in their mouths.

It was a show Dibbler and his family were forced to watch.

'Can I take that?' the waitress asked Dibbler's father of the bill. She scooped the bill and credit card and was back a moment later with a receipt and a quick thank you, then was gone again.

The table's energy was moving toward departure.

Dibbler's mother said, 'Brian is–' she hunted for words, it took a minute, '–he's built different than you.'

Dibbler said, 'What?'

'No, no I didn't say that right,' his mother said. 'I tried to say how it was in my head, and that's how it came out. Hang on, that's not right.'

'Say what you meant,' Dibbler said.

'I will, hang on, my thoughts are, you know, they're all over.'

The table waited for his mother's correction.

'Well, what were you trying to say?' Dibbler said.

'Let me figure it out, hang on,' she said.

'Brian and I aren't that different,' Dibbler said. 'We're pretty in sync.'

'No, I know,' his mother said. 'Just let me figure how I want to say it.'

'We're actually really, very in sync.'

Dibbler's mother said, 'Because here's you, right here, you're this spot on the table, where my finger is pointing, and here's Brian over here, he's this spot on the table, and he's over here doing all the things that Brian does, *and doesn't do*, okay, and over here, right, this is you, you're doing all this stuff for Brian.'

She was then quiet, as if she'd somehow made her point.

'We do the same amount of stuff for each other. I don't do that much more,' Dibbler said. His face turned flush.

'Well. You do, sweetie,' his mother said. 'You do.'

'Why did you say all the things Brian does and *doesn't do*?'

'Well. You do a lot.'

'Why say it like that? Things Brian *doesn't do*.'

'He's just—and you just love big, sweetie,' his mother said. 'You love so big.'

'Brian loves big,' Dibbler said.

'Well,' she said. 'Yeah. I'm sure Brian does, sweetie, but, because I just see you here doing all this stuff, all this above-and-beyond stuff, and then Brian's over here. He's this spot on the table. Just. Doing all the stuff he does and *doesn't do*.'

Dibbler looked at his mother.

She had fingers pointed at two arbitrary points on the restaurant table; one was Brian and one was him and they were far apart, and she remained still in this way, nodding her head at her son.

Dibbler's stepmother said, 'I think your mother just means that—'

His dad interrupted. 'They're talking.'

'I know, hon, but I was just going to say she probably means they're just different, him and Brian,' his stepmother said. 'Right? That's what you meant?'

'Well, let her say that then,' his father said.

Dibbler's father, in a rare moment, addressed Dibbler's mother. 'Is that what you meant?'

'We're not that different,' Dibbler said.

'Different is fine, different is okay even,' his stepmother said. 'Your dad and I are different as it gets, haha! Right, hon? We're about as different as two people can be different, right?'

Dibbler's mother, it was clear, wanted to speak further on the issue, but instead remained quiet.

She said no more.

❖

A few days later, Dibbler and his best friend, Marty, walked into the jeweler inside the mall along the highway, which also wasn't far from Blue Box or the Chili's. Marty had met him in the food court, and they both had to remember which way the jeweler was.

Dibbler walked the display cases and was too focused to speak.

Marty lagged but followed.

After he'd seen all the store's display inventory, Dibbler circled back and looked it all over again and said, oh, no thanks, he was just looking, when associates asked. Then he said, actually, could you tell me—he pulled a printout from his pocket—did they have anything like this? The printout was folded and wrinkled and was of an engagement ring, a beautiful and simple and timeless ring, and he said if they had anything like this, could he please see it?

'You haven't been single long enough,' Marty said.

'Did I show you this printout yet?' Dibbler said. He passed it to Marty.

Marty turned the printout this way and that way in his hands.

'You've been single for like two months your whole life,' he said. 'That's not enough, that's like way not enough.'

An associate returned with several options for Dibbler to review.

Some were simple but not beautiful or timeless, and some were timeless but not beautiful or simple, and some were beautiful but not simple or timeless. None presented were all three.

'You don't have any more in back?' Dibbler said.

The associate said no, they don't, sorry.

'Yeah, because I'm looking for something almost exactly like this one, in the printout.'

The associate pointed out what made each option presented special, and how each could capture the heart of the special person in Dibbler's life.

Dibbler said he was open-minded, but if it could be exactly like the printout, that would be best.

'Then you're not open-minded,' the associate said.

'Well, I am. I'm open-minded,' Dibbler said.

'He's been single, like, two months, that's two months his whole life,' Marty told the associate. 'Does that sound like enough to you?'

'You never know what you'll fall in love with,' the associate said. 'You come in already decided for what you want. That's not open-minded, you're not being open-minded.'

'No, I'm saying I know, I'm in love with *this* ring. On the printout. It's the one.'

'But you could find one that's not that, on your printout, and fall in love with it,' the associate said. 'That's open-minded. You're not being that way, is what I'm telling you.'

Out in the parking lot, Dibbler stood outside his car and asked Marty if he knew any other shops they could try. He asked what about by the Joann Fabrics, that shop over there?

'It's a bed store now,' Marty said.

'I'm open-minded. I am.'

Marty was looking off at the highway, the cars, the lights. He said, 'Is two months your whole life enough?'

'It's more than two months,' Dibbler said. 'I've been single the right amount.'

'A person should spend a year single, at least, maybe two.'

'There's another shop, it's past the bridge. I think it's next to that tanning place. Or the Auto Zone.'

'I'm not saying it's a pattern.'

'What's a pattern?' Dibbler said.

Marty was looking at Dibbler, right at him.

'Who said pattern?' Dibbler said.

Car noise rose above them.

'No, I'm not saying it's a pattern, you getting in these things, these three-, four-year things, over and over, that's not what I'm saying, even though that's what a pattern is, but I'm like, how does he even know himself? That's what I'm thinking when I'm looking at you while you're looking at rings. How do you know anything about yourself when all you do is think about someone else all day?'

'I didn't—what? Who said about a pattern?'

'No, I'm *not* saying it's a pattern, even though if you step back a moment and look at your dating life as a whole, you look at all the three-, four-year things you've been in and out of, you see a pattern. Someone shows you a red flag, you just shut your eyes.'

'I don't shut my eyes.'

'You do,' Marty said. 'You shut them so goddamn tight. I don't date anyone; all I see are red flags. Left, right, red flags everywhere. I'm honestly the opposite of you. I can't see white flags, can't see kindnesses or honesty if I wanted, so I just fuck. No dating. Only fucking.'

Dibbler thought of Brian, of red flags. It brought discomfort.

It upended peace.

He stopped thinking about them.

'Maybe you don't propose,' Marty said. 'I'm just saying maybe. More than maybe. A little more than maybe. I mean. You've been single definitely less than three months, total. Ever. Be single.'

'It's not a pattern!'

Dibbler shouted it.

Then he said, 'It's not.'

He and Marty looked at one another a moment.
'Want to go to that shop by the tanning place?'

❖

At the apartment that evening, Dibbler started dinner cleanup and, now and again, passed the doorway very much on purpose to see Brian in the living room, on the couch with his work laptop and work papers about him on the cushions and on the coffee table, seeing Brian work in one pass, seeing him watching TV in another pass, seeing him laughing at something on his laptop in another pass, seeing him laughing and engaging with the laptop vigorously on another pass. Dibbler made an extra pass by the doorway when Brian's laughter repeated. Dibbler joined with a large smile.

'What's funny, babe?'
Brian typed, he didn't answer; his laughing was fading.
'You are just laughing away in here.'
'What?' Brian said.
'What's funny, babe?'
'Just work stuff. It's nothing,' Brian said. He was still smiling and with the laptop on his lap.
Dibbler lingered for more from Brian.
There was no more.
Dibbler went back to dishes.
Laughter broke from the living room, broke all around Dibbler with his hands in dishwater, his wrinkled palms and fingers, scrubbing and listening to his lover laugh in the living room, cackling even.
Laughing and cackling without him.
After dishes, Dibbler asked if he could sit where Brian's papers were on the couch. Brian said he was still working.
Dibbler then sat in the armchair and turned the channel, and turned the channel, and turned the channel, and busied himself turning more channels.
'I was thinking,' Brian said.

'Yeah?'

Brian was quiet. TV filled the silence.

'What?' Dibbler said again.

'Oh, I was just thinking–oh, one sec.'

Brian typed into his laptop and looked through papers and left no attention for Dibbler.

Dibbler returned to channel hunting.

'Um. So. I was thinking about some private time,' Brian said. 'Time set aside each week, or multiple times a week, I haven't decided, where it's just my time. Where it's just me.'

'Private time?'

'Have you been thinking about that? For you? I've been. For me.'

Dibbler sat with the remote aimed at the TV. 'I have not,' he said. 'You have?'

'People say all the time in relationships you need time for yourself. That you need to set it aside. It won't set itself aside.'

'Well, people just say that,' Dibbler said.

'They say sit down with your partner, set a time for private space.'

'Space?'

'That's not how it sounds; stop making it sound like that,' Brian said.

'People who say you need space are the people who need space. We don't need space, babe,' Dibbler said. 'Let's not talk about space.'

'Well, I read that. It was an article. Private, independent space, apart from one another, with you somewhere and me somewhere else, is healthy and I've been thinking about that, you haven't thought that? Private time? Time for you?'

'We're apart from each other all day.'

Brian went quiet.

Dibbler said, 'I don't need time for me. I'm perfectly fine wherever you are.'

Brian looked at the TV for a while, then typed on his laptop.

A little later he said, 'I was thinking Wednesdays I could have *me* time, that's what they call it, *me* time. Wednesday afternoons, the evenings, just sometime on Wednesdays.'

'You want space?'

'No, no, no, no, no, no, stop making it sound like that. This is healthy for us, it's only healthy, it's not–stop making it sound like that,' Brian said. 'It just means I'm separating some time, for me, for my mindset. Ultimately it'll be better for the relationship, because it's time I can sit and feel good about myself.'

'You don't feel good about yourself?'

'It's not how you're making it sound. I know what you're thinking, okay? I know. I love you. Hear me when I say that I love you. Okay? Hear me, really hear me when I say that.'

'When I'm around you, I feel great about myself,' Dibbler said. 'I don't need time to myself.'

'They say *me* time is a perfectly normal and reasonable request.'

'Who is telling you this? Who is telling you to ask for space?'

'I was reading up about it, and then I was just thinking about it.'

'You read up about asking for space?'

'Babe, you're not listening. When I say I'm thinking about some private, independent space, just some time that's mine, for me, and it's only, like, once a week, something like that, that's all I'm saying, something like Wednesday afternoons, or whenever on Wednesdays; you're making it sound like–and you're supposed to ask how you can help support that, not, like, making it sound like how you're making it sound. It's not that.'

'Space is distance.'

'They say it doesn't have to feel like distance,' Brian said.

Dibbler was still aiming the remote at the TV; he was blank as paper.

'It's perfectly normal and reasonable,' Brian said.

'It is?' Dibbler said.

'So, I was thinking then I start that Wednesdays.'

'Every Wednesday?'

Brian gave his attention back to the laptop and typing, and not a moment later was laughing at something on the laptop screen, cackling even.

'Yeah. Every Wednesday,' he said, half-in, half-out of the conversation.

'Is this because work has you stressed? Is that what this is? It's nothing to do with us, right? We're good? We're okay?'

Brian was going to speak but paused, then typed on his laptop.

The phone in the kitchen rang.

Dibbler stood at once. He said, 'Pause all this, please, pause your Wednesdays, your space, just pause.'

He retreated quickly from one conversation and answered the ringing in the kitchen, entering headlong into another.

'Yes, hello?'

'Andy Dibbler? Dave calling again.'

Dibbler's head was still in the other conversation. He said, 'Who?'

'Dave. Recovery Debt Collections.'

'Who's calling, babe?' Brian shouted from the living room.

'Hello?' the phone asked Dibbler.

'Just. No one,' Dibbler shouted. He had one hand sealing shut the mouthpiece, then he took the phone into the corner of the kitchen.

'We still haven't received the check you sent.'

'Well, it was definitely sent, so,' Dibbler said.

'Be that as it may, Mr. Dibbler, I have to flag the account.'

'I put the, I sent it, I put it in the mail myself.'

Dibbler heard the TV in the living room go quiet.

Brian shouted from the couch, 'Who's on the phone, babe?'

Dibbler covered the mouthpiece and shouted, hang on a minute, babe, then into the phone he said, quiet so Brian couldn't overhear, 'You can't hold me accountable, you know, what happens after I give my mail to the post office. I sent it, definitely dropped it in the mail. After that, that's on–you should be phoning the postal service, asking where your check is, that's who you should be phoning, not me. You know. So.'

'We're not talking a small amount of money here, Mr. Dibbler.'

'No, I know, I'm, you call and, and I'm being helpful here. I am.'

'Unless you can make payment over the phone, I will have to flag the account.'

'I, geez,' Dibbler said. He ruffled the phone in his hand and said into the phone while he was ruffling, 'Hang on, I'm–' then he stopped with the phone and said into it, 'Now is not a good time. I can't make payment right now. I'll send another check.'

'No, check is no good. I've been waiting for a check and ...' Dave continued talking into Dibbler's ear, but Dibbler heard none of it. Brian had come into the doorway and was looking in.

'Who you sending a check to?' Brian said.

'What?'

'You just said.'

Dave at Recovery Debt Collection was still talking in Dibbler's ear. Dibbler hung the phone up and said, 'It was work.'

'Why you in the corner?' Brian said.

Dibbler said nothing for a moment, then he said the TV was on and it was loud, so he came to the corner to hear better. 'It was a work call. That's all.'

'I'll send another check. You said that.'

'No. It was work.'

Brian stood looking at Dibbler an uncomfortable moment; Dibbler was standing at the phone, in and out of a smile. He was terrible at hiding guilt.

'So, you didn't say that? That's what you're saying?'

Dibbler said, 'Well ...' and he said no more.

Brian said it so easily, he said, 'This feels like last year.'

'It's not, no, it's, haha, no, it was just a work call. It's not. They're asking about a check I took on register,' Dibbler said.

'The article said about communication too; it said it's healthy to express things and not keep them inside. That leads to resentment, the article said. Resentment in a relationship is no good, so that's why I'm saying this feels like last year. I'm expressing that to you. I'm not keeping that in; I'm just telling you, it's feeling like last year.'

'It was work about a check I took the other day, and I said, well, have them send you a new check, another check, sorry, the check was no good, that's what they said on the phone, they tried to run the check, and it was no good, so I said just call the customer and have them *send another check*. That's what you heard.'

'So, you did say it?'

'Well ...'

'Why would they call you? You're the cashier.'

'I think it's policy to call the cashier, I'm pretty sure. I think they *have* to call me, actually. I think they don't have a choice.'

Brian looked at Dibbler for a time longer.

'Everything is fine, babe,' Dibbler said, in and out of a smile. Then he said, 'We're okay, right?'

❖

An hour into Dibbler's shift, the supervisor came out of the door in the wall and pulled the customer service gal from the counter to cover on register; he said he needed a moment with Dibbler.

The supervisor and Dibbler squeezed into the small wall office.

There wasn't a desk, only a counter built into the wall, so Dibbler and the supervisor had to sit side by side; there was nothing to separate them in their conversation.

The supervisor said, 'Everything good? You feel good about where you are with registers?'

Dibbler said he felt fine on registers, yeah.

'Good. Good.'

The supervisor plucked a folder from nearby. 'This is some customer feedback I got the other day and, all the upper guys have seen this by the way, they've all read this and, I think, there was even a back-and-forth call with corporate, that's what they said, the upper guys, the managers. And, wait, no, it's good, it's really good, haha. I'm looking at you and you're, haha, no it's all really good, it's not bad at all, haha! Here let me read it, *Had an amazing experience this afternoon at the Blue Box here in town, it's the location between the smaller end of town and the bigger end of town, so I never know which they call it, it's the one here, between them, so anyway I was there looking, I'm building a PC and the prices were okay but I had issues finding things but the guys in back were no help AT ALL and I'm in the aisles wandering, the aisles are so big in that location, and this guy passing by he doesn't see me but I call at him to come help me and he said he works up front at the register but sure he'll help. So me and him are looking around the aisles for what I need and he was so so super friendly and helpful and eventually we found everything and he rang me up and, my god I was surprised to find the stuff was on sale, so that was a BIG PLUS! So, if it hadn't been for the guy up front on register, he said he's the only guy on register, all the other cashiers are girls so, he's the only guy so that's who this feedback is for. If not for him I would have left that store and they would not have gotten my hard earned dollars. He's an asset, honestly, genuinely, an asset.* So, see that was all really good, wasn't it?'

Dibbler agreed, yes it was.

'So, the managers are seeing the great numbers and the great feedback you're getting, and they're talking,' the supervisor said.

'What are they saying?'

'Well, they're saying about you and how great you're doing, and even corporate was calling, and they were talking about it. The managers and corporate.'

'What's corporate saying?'

'Well,' the supervisor said, 'all I can say is that it's good, and it's good for you, this is all really really good, and it's showing district how hard we work at this location, the kind of talent we can churn out, here, in this location, which the managers manage, maybe those budgets go up a smidge, right? Haha! So. This is all looking really good for everyone.'

'Okay,' Dibbler said. He waited for the supervisor to say more, perhaps more on how that might reflect on him, this recognition, perhaps monetary ways, but the supervisor said no more, except to ask Dibbler to sign this form stating they'd had this positive conversation.

For corporate.

Dibbler signed.

❖

It was windy when Dibbler finished his shift and took the highway north, into the broad loneliness the highway traveled. He exited at a small pocket town. It clung to the highway for life, for blood, it was the last town before vast and empty country rolled on toward nothing and everything. It was where Brian's parents lived in a brick home the shape of a box, perfectly square. The brick was not uniform in color, and time and sun had faded and chipped the brick, and the lawn was wild with tall grass and weeds.

Dibbler seemed nervous and fiddled with his hands as he waited on the front porch for someone to answer.

Brian's mother greeted Dibbler. She was a short, skinny woman with long hair the color of autumn that hung down her back and past her rear end.

He said Brian was still at work and, yes, everything was okay. Could he come in a second, though?

'Who is that?' Brian's father shouted from somewhere in the home.

'It's Andy,' Brian's mother shouted.

'Who?'

'Andy!' Brian's mother shouted louder, harsher.

Brian's father shouted, 'It's just Andy?'

'Yes!'

'What?' Brian's father shouted. His location in the home was a mystery.

'It's just Andy!'

Brian's mother was shouting herself hoarse, and there was heat in her shouting at Brian's father, an unkind heat.

'Brian's not with him?'

'No!'

The house gave no response. Brian's mother was red in the face from shouting.

'Maybe we could talk in the kitchen?' Dibbler said.

'Is everything okay?' Brian's father shouted.

'Yes!' Brian's mother shouted. 'Andy said everything's fine!'

'What?' Brian's father shouted.

'Everything is *fine*!'

Abrupt silence followed, and Brian's mother took Dibbler to the living room, where Brian's father was parked in front of the TV. He was a large man with a swollen belly and short legs, and he seemed most comfortable spending his day in the recliner. Leftovers from breakfast and lunch were around him. He said, hi, Andy, and he and Dibbler small-chatted about what was on the TV, and that was that.

'Andy wants to talk with us in the kitchen,' Brian's mother said. She smiled at Andy but grimaced at her husband. She was standing over Brian's father where he sat among his leftovers and wrappers and drinking glasses and soda cans.

Brian's father adjusted how he sat, so as to see her face better.

'Get up for guests,' she said to Brian's father.

'I just sat,' he said.

'You did not just sit, you've been sitting there all morning and all day. I vacuumed around you.'

Brian's father assured Dibbler he had not been in this chair all morning and all day.

'Andy is a guest,' she said.

'Is everything okay?' he asked Dibbler.

'Everything is fine,' Brian's mother said.

'Well then what?'

'We can talk in here, it's okay,' Dibbler said.

'Andy is a guest, and we get up for guests. He wants us in the kitchen, you're getting up and going in the kitchen,' Brian's mother said.

'Here is fine,' Dibbler said.

'I *just* sat, I was in there and then I come in here and sat, just now.'

'You're a dog, you know that? You're a sleeping, lazy dog.'

Brian's mother did not gauge her volume on Dibbler's behalf, she said it like a gunshot.

'What! I just sat!'

Brian's mother ignored her husband. She said to Dibbler, 'Would it be all right if we chatted in here? It appears I've married a dog.'

'Christ on the cross,' Brian's father said out loud. He re-sat himself and returned to comfort in his recliner.

Dibbler sat on the sofa, and Brian's mother made tea and brought in cookies, and the three sat around the TV.

Brian's father was the only one eating the cookies.

'Leave some for Andy,' Brian's mother scolded.

Brian's mother slid the plate out of reach of her husband. He gave a laugh, but there was no enjoyment in it, only resentment.

'You look like you need to say something, sweetie,' Brian's mother told Dibbler. 'Doesn't he look like he needs to say something?'

Brian's father said he didn't know.

'Oh, you're a dog, what do you know?'

'I hate when you say that. I really do hate it.'

'Well, I'll say it until you're not a dog,' Brian's mother said.

Brian's father told Dibbler, 'She's been saying it for years.'

'Well. You've been a dog all these years.' To Dibbler, Brian's mother said, 'What do you need to say, sweetie? You look like you got something.'

'Christ on the cross, I hate you calling me that,' Brian's father said.

'I can come back,' Dibbler said.

'Don't mind him, he's just a sleeping, lazy dog.'

'I just sat! You're on me about not getting up, that's what she's doing, she's on me because she's always asking me to get up when I've always just sat, it's like she waits until I've always just sat to tell me to get up and then get on me and call me a sleeping, lazy dog,' Brian's father said.

'Well, stop acting like one,' Brian's mother said.

Dibbler drank his tea and said he was thinking, then he corrected himself and said he was certain, he wasn't thinking, he was certain that he wanted to propose to Brian, and he was hoping to gather their blessing today.

'Oh, how lovely!' Brian's mother said. Her eyes went big, and her voice filled with joy.

'What if I called *you* a dog?' Brian's father killed the joy in his wife's voice.

'You call me worse,' Brian's mother said. 'You call me much worse.'

'Oh, I do not, what a load of bologna, what a load, I do not.'

'If I called you even half as bad as what you call me, you'd be crying in that goddamn chair, and God knows you'd still not get up.'

'*I just sat!*'

'How can you just sit if you never get up?' Brian's mother said.

'Christ on the cross.'

Dibbler was holding his tea and shrinking into the sofa beneath their back-and-forth.

'Well, we just think the world of you, Andy, how lovely! We know Brian thinks the world of you too. We know he loves you so very much.'

'He tells you that?'

'Of course, he does, and we give our blessing, right, hon? We'd love to have you part of the family, right, hon?'

Brian's father agreed with a nod and nothing more.

Brian's mother clapped her hands and said, 'Our wedding was so wonderful. There was a band, and all our friends were there, and he said the most sweetest things to me, do you remember what you said to me at our wedding?'

Brian's father pulled a cigarette from a pack on the side table next to him and lit it.

'Oh, it was the sweetest, you remember, don't you?' Brian's mother said again.

'I blocked it out,' Brian's father said.

'You're a real son of a bitch, you know that? I married a dog.'

'I. Just. Sat.'

'I mean it, what a son-of-a-bitch thing to say.'

'That's not a son-of-a-bitch thing to say, but if you want to hear a real son-of-a-bitch thing to say, I'll tell you here on the spot. You want that? You want to hear a *real* son-of-a-bitch thing to say?'

'You hear how he talks to me? You allow one bad habit in your marriage, you don't correct it, I mean, and you're stuck dealing with it the rest of your life, just like a dog. I married a dog, I swear.'

Both Brian's mother and father stayed quiet for a time.

Then Brian's mother said, 'We're so happy you'll be part of the family, Andy!'

❖

Dibbler was off the next day. He sent Brian to work with a kiss, and after lunch, he dressed and drove into the older part of town, across the bridge, where the older homes and businesses were physically ugly. They were dirty and had been allowed to rot and fall into disrepair, block to block, neighborhood to neighborhood, the people too, walking on sidewalks and idling on front porches.

When he went in the jeweler's next to the overpass and the Auto Zone, Dibbler walked the display cases quietly and scanned up and down the engagement rings in inventory, which were bland; they were general in appearance, and none were unique, but the prices were good, real good, Dibbler thought. The clerk was in the back office watching TV with the door open, so as to see onto the floor. Dibbler noticed the clerk looking now and again but was offered no greeting.

A woman came in with fast food and was in such purpose she ignored Dibbler and yelled at the clerk in back to turn off the damn TV. They argued as if there wasn't a customer in the building.

Twenty minutes later, Dibbler was at another jeweler.

This one had two great windows at the front; they had been covered in a black film to obscure the store's insides, though the film had tears and rips and wrinkles and was peeling at the corners.

The gentleman clerk, a larger fellow with hairy forearms and a shiny forehead and red cheeks, was seated on a stool at the register.

He greeted Dibbler from where he sat. 'Browse and let me know what questions you have, son,' he said. 'I know all about rings, so anything you want to ask, that's fine by me.'

Dibbler roamed the display cases quietly, some he browsed longer and some he browsed quick. When he'd done a complete lap, he showed the gentleman clerk the printout and asked if he had any rings like this one.

The gentleman clerk looked the paper over and said oh, sure, he had one like this one, and he stood with a groan and waddled around the display cases and, from one, he removed a ring and a piece of felt, which was fraying, and he placed the felt on the case and the ring on the felt for Dibbler to touch and to view.

'I can tell you're ready,' he told Dibbler.

Dibbler examined the ring and turned it this way and that way.

'Some folks come in and they say they're just browsing, but they're actually ready to buy, aching to buy even, and I think it's just absolutely wonderful when a guy like you comes in and he knows exactly what he wants,' the clerk said. 'I see a guy like you with a ring like this, a ring that so perfectly binds two people to one another forever and ever because of its beauty and simplicity and its timelessness, all three in one, and I look at you, a guy like you, and I think, he's ready.'

The ring in Dibbler's hand was identical to the printout.

'Nothing keeps two people together better than a ring, I'm telling you.'

Dibbler said okay, he would take it, and they moved to the register, and Dibbler saw the price.

Dibbler stood quiet for a moment, deep in thought and deep in focus on the ring before him. His mind was working, and he said he needed to use the store's phone if possible.

'To call your bank?' the gentleman clerk said.

'Yes.'

'For available balance?'

'Yes.'

'And to call your credit cards?' the gentleman clerk said.

Dibbler wasn't quick to answer, but he said, 'Yes.'

'For their available balances?'

Dibbler didn't answer, he simply nodded his reply.

'Can I make this real easy for you?' the gentleman clerk said.

He searched behind the register counter and set down a pamphlet for Dibbler. It advertised a low-interest credit card with pages and pages of small legal print.

Dibbler tried to read the small print, but the gentleman clerk turned the pamphlet in Dibbler's hands back to the front, back to the picture of a happy customer.

'A guy like you, son, a guy who knows and who's going for exactly what he wants, because this isn't something he *thinks* he wants, this is something he *knows* he wants, and I'm seeing you and I'm thinking there's no way we'll let a thing like money stop you from getting what you want, right? We're not going to let that stop you, are we?'

'Will I get approved?'

'We barely check credit, it's just a quick peek-see, just looking to see if you have credit, really. Nothing, no, it's-it's a low bar, haha, so, we just want to see guys like you get the ending they deserve.'

'Because I have a few things on my whatever credit thing they check. Just a few. You think I'll get approved?'

'We don't have to go this route; you can phone your bank and phone your credit cards, and we can sit while you do all that, those hold times, we'll be sitting for hours probably. We can go that route if you like? And maybe you have the money and maybe you don't? Maybe you walk out that door without what you came for, this beautiful, simple, timeless ring that will perfectly bind you and your special someone. Forever? Maybe you leave without it?'

Dibbler filled out an application, and the gentleman clerk went in back and came out not long after with a shark's smile and said Dibbler was approved; now let's get you one step closer to your *forever*.

'By the way,' the gentleman clerk said, 'there's no refunds.'

'I won't need one. So.'

'All sales, all decisions are final.'

'This ring won't come back,' Dibbler said.

'It *can't* come back. We won't accept it. If you try to bring it back, I'm going to tell you no, and I'm going to tell you what I'm telling you now. Your decision is yours and so are the consequences of that decision; don't come here and try to share those consequences with me or my store. We won't have it.'

'I won't need a refund,' Dibbler said.

'There's a reason we don't have a return policy is what I'm saying.'

On Dibbler's silence, the gentleman clerk said no more.

❖

In bed that night, Dibbler could hear Brian's inability to fall asleep; the bed shuddered beneath Brian's tossing and turning.

Then there was peace, and Dibbler hoped Brian had found sleep.

From the dark, Brian said, 'Where do you find happiness?'

Dibbler lay in the quiet. He didn't move, didn't speak.

'I know you're not sleeping. I hear you.'

'I was sleeping,' Dibbler said.

'No, you weren't. You breathe through your mouth when you sleep.'

Brian asked again what makes Dibbler happy.

'I don't know. What makes *you* happy?'

'I'm not asking about me. I'm asking you,' Brian said.

'Why?'

'Like where do *you* get it? Happiness?'

'You make me happy,' Dibbler said.

'No, I'm asking what makes you happy. Not who. Tell me what.'

'Us together makes me happy, it makes me so happy.'

'Outside of that, though?'

'What do you mean?' Dibbler said.

'What makes you happy outside of me, outside of us?'

'What does other stuff matter?' Dibbler said.

'What does other stuff matter!?'

'I mean. Yeah.'

'But what other stuff, like, what other stuff exactly, specifically, that's what I want to know. What makes you happy besides me?'

Dibbler lay with the question. He didn't like the question.

'Is this another article?' Dibbler said.

'What satisfies you, what fills you with joy?'

'I said you.'

'But actually, what else? What else in your life?'

Dibbler said he didn't know; he'd need to think about it.

'You need to think about it? When I ask what makes you happy, besides me, you don't have an answer right away? Nothing comes right to the front? You need to think?'

'I was sleeping,' Dibbler said.

'You were lying there. Awake. You weren't mouth breathing.'

Dibbler rolled over and said go to sleep; he said if this is another article he didn't want to hear about it.

'This isn't an article, it's just me, just me wanting to know. Tell me something other than me or this relationship makes you happy. I need to know you have happiness outside of us.'

Dibbler was quiet and facing away, facing into the dark bedroom.

He said that one movie, *Forever in Love*, made him happy, but Brian said nothing to this. Sometime later, he heard Brian fall asleep and then soon found sleep himself.

❖

The next morning, Dibbler woke for an early shift and made himself eggs and made extra for Brian. He left them in the pan.

He ate and had the TV on in the living room for noise, and he listened to Brian wake. He heard the shower go on, and later Brian came in dressed for work, his blue suit, and his hair styled different. It gave him an appeal Dibbler was uncomfortable with.

'I made extra eggs,' Dibbler said.

'I'm just going to have my shake.'

Dibbler watched Brian put fruit in the blender. He said, 'You showered?'

'What? Oh. Yeah.'

'You usually just dress and go.'

'I do?' Brian said. He ran the blender over Dibbler's response.

Dibbler said again, when the blending stopped, 'You did something different with your hair.'

'Trying something new.'

Dibbler was looking at Brian's hair, the appeal it added.

'I was looking at the calendar; maybe we do a special day-date the twentieth?'

'What's today?' Brian said.

'The fifth.'

'You're planning that far out?'

'Yeah. Just a day for us, a special day.'

Brian said but why that far out?

'Can you make sure to block the day?'

Brian blended over Dibbler's question.

When the blending stopped, Dibbler said again, 'Make sure to block the day.'

Brian made no acknowledgment, he was taste-testing the shake.

'Must be a special day today to wear the blue suit?' Dibbler said.

Brian was drinking the shake. He stopped and said, 'Nope.' He drank more and collected his work bag and work items.

Dibbler watched Brian ready himself to leave for work.

'I thought maybe you had some client or boss to impress.'

Brian downed the shake then put the glass in the sink. 'No. I don't do the client stuff anymore.'

'Because you have your blue suit on, that's why I was wondering.'

'Nope,' Brian said. 'Just another day.'

He furnished a wilted smile for Dibbler and grabbed his keys and said love you, bye!

'Make sure to block that day!'

Brian said, okay, yeah, sure, he'll block it, love you, bye.

Then Brian was out the door, and the apartment was still but for the TV noise in the living room.

Dibbler tossed the extra eggs he'd made for Brian into the trash then left for work.

After his shift, he stopped at Marty's apartment near the bridge, before you cross to the old side of town, the starved side.

Marty's apartment was on the good side of the bridge, the healthy side, near the ball diamond

Marty was smoking a cigarette out of the balcony sliding door in the unit's kitchen. He said, 'What time is it?'

Dibbler was at Marty's kitchen table writing. He said, 'After three.'

'I have stuff at four, so.'

'I'm going to propose on the twentieth.'

Dibbler continued writing.

'You are not,' Marty said.

'He's taking the day from work; we'll do a special us-day. Just us two.'

'You live together; it's always just you two.'

'We'll go down to the pond, where the sand is, I'll take him by that little wooden walk onto the water, you know, I'll do it there. I'll have him looking at the water, at sunset, so the colors are all on the water, and he'll be so captured by the moment, and I'll read all this, all I've written here. It'll be perfect, and I'll get on one knee there and I'll ask him.'

Marty said he didn't know about any of that.

Dibbler quit writing and said what do you mean?

'I just don't know about any of it, Andy.'

'Can I read what I've written? It's for when I propose.'

'I don't know, Andy.'

'Well, you can tell me how it sounds,' Dibbler said.

He recited for Marty all he'd written, and there was a good deal of it. As he concluded, Dibbler was near tears, for it was a beautiful moment of words.

'That's the monologue from *Forever in Love*,' Marty said.

'No, it's not.'

'From the end, yeah, when the guy's proposing, that's the exact same thing he says when he's on his knee, when it's sunset in the movie.'

Dibbler said, 'Don't you have plans? It's almost four.'

Marty came in and shut the balcony sliding door and said, 'Oh geez, it's almost four. You said it was just after three! Sorry. I have stuff now.'

Dibbler returned home and later that night practiced the words from his writing in the bathroom with the shower running. He was in his underwear and about to get in the shower but stood in front the mirror.

Out of the shower and clean, he sneaked a look at the engagement ring while Brian was asleep in front of the TV; he'd hidden the ring in back of the closet.

He shut himself in the closet, with the light on, and moved the ring around in his hands, pretending there was a pond and sunset all around and pretending Brian was waiting for him to slide the ring on.

❖

It was the following evening when Dibbler was wrapping a shift and was asked by the supervisor to come to the back office, not the one in the wall by the registers.

The one in back.

The supervisor and the supervisor's manager were waiting, and they asked Dibbler to sit. He did, and they said, one at a time, everyone was super impressed by his work, his attitude, his numbers, and the attention his dedication had brought to their location. Of all the locations in the district, theirs was at the top, and they said Dibbler had a hand in that, a big one.

Dibbler said thank you.

They said that's why they'd like to extend an invitation to attend a management training seminar at District HQ, up in Clinton City. It would go for a week, he wouldn't pay a thing, all he'd need to do is sit and learn, and when he came back there could be a real neat promotion waiting, they said.

'We'd send you up on the twentieth, you come back the next week; things will be real great for you,' the supervisor's manager said. 'It's all set up for you, the corporate ladder, we're just waiting for you to climb the rungs, climb up to management, Dibbler.'

'Is there another date, or?'

The question deflated the room.

'Sorry?' the supervisor's manager said. He looked at the supervisor for confirmation of what he'd heard or not heard.

'I can't the twentieth.'

'You can't?' The supervisor's manager looked at the supervisor again, he said, 'Did he say he can't?'

'He said he can't,' the supervisor confirmed.

'The ladder's there for you, Dibbler. We laid it right out for you to climb.'

'Grab the rungs, Dibbler,' the supervisor encouraged.

'Grab them,' the supervisor's manager said.

'That's all great, that all sounds wonderful, and I'd love to climb and grab rungs. But I can't on the twentieth.'

'We're top performers right now,' the supervisor's manager said.

'Top performers,' the supervisor chirped.

'We're hitting goals, we're hitting stretch goals, district is giving us goals, and we are just hitting them one after another.'

'One after another,' the supervisor said.

'District is looking at us, Dibbler,' the supervisor's manager said. 'We need A-players like you leading the way.'

The supervisor added, 'We said that in your formal career compliment discussion, didn't we, how you're an A-player? We said about sacrifice?'

'Yeah, I just, maybe if there was another time I could go?'

'Another time?' the supervisor's manager said.

'I have a special date that day, the twentieth, and Brian's already asking for it off, so.'

The supervisor's manager looked at Dibbler for a long time.

'This isn't a thing that comes back around. The ladder is laid out for you to climb only one time, then it gets put away or set for someone else to climb. Can you–?'

Dibbler said, 'I'm proposing.'

The supervisor's manager said, 'Sure, that's real great, really great, but I don't think you're hearing us.'

The supervisor said, 'There isn't another time is what we're saying. We talked about sacrifice in our one-on-one, I noted it, and you signed it, and corporate filed it. We said, remember, success doesn't come without something going. But you have to be prepared to send something away, let something go.'

Dibbler sat and said nothing.

The supervisor's manager studied Dibbler, like he was a strange animal.

The supervisor's manager said, 'Tell you what, take some time, think it over. We don't need an answer now, so don't give an answer now, don't give us a "no" just yet, but, and I know this might be a lot for you, Andy, and because we really want to see you succeed, that's all we want here, just a manager and a supervisor that want nothing else than to see you succeed, so, think on it, really really think on it. Okay?'

❖

Dibbler was on the computer, looking up what time the sun would set on the twentieth when he heard Brian come home from work with grocery bags and he heard them settle in the kitchen.

From the kitchen, Brian shouted, 'Can you help?'

It took multiple shouts from the kitchen to get Dibbler off the computer and helping put groceries away.

'Did you remember to take the twentieth off work?'

Brian didn't say hello or respond; he gave Dibbler a cold shoulder.

Dibbler allowed a moment of this then said, of Brian's cold shoulder, 'What?'

Brian put away several items with no answer.

'What?' Dibbler said.

'I didn't have time to grocery shop today.'

His tone was sharp.

'And I come home and you're on the computer.'

'I was going to go,' Dibbler said.

'No, you weren't.'

'I would have.'

'If what? If I asked you?'

'Of course, I would if you asked,' Dibbler said.

'I work ten-hour days, Andy. I go to the grocery store, that's another hour, at least, and then I'm in traffic for two and you're on the computer and, I'm buying the groceries, which you never buy, and, Christ, the floors, Andy. I asked you weeks ago to do the floors.'

'I did the floors.'

Brian opened the cabinet under the sink and showed Dibbler the floor cleaner was still unopened.

'It's like you don't even live on the ground with the rest of us.'

Dibbler was caught by this, where he stood.

'It's like your head is never down here. With the rest of us. It's always up and off and away somewhere. It never spends any time down here on the ground, taking part in what life really is, not the idea of what life is, but what it really is. The mechanical stuff, the tedious necessary stuff that keeps all this going; cleaning, errands, bills, your head isn't down here for any of it and, Christ, this feels a lot like last year,' Brian said.

'I cook.'

Brian looked at Dibbler with a less-than-grateful look. He continued placing groceries away.

'It's Wednesday,' Brian said mid-task. He kept his attention from Dibbler. 'We talked about Wednesdays,' Brian said.

'Well. I thought we paused that, we said pause all that, remember?'

Brian had, by this point, put away most of the groceries, and he said, 'It's like, I'm at work all day, Andy, all day, your longest shift is, what, six hours, if that, and then I gotta spend more of my day, and my money, on the tedious stuff, because you're always like, *yeah, I'll do it*, and then you don't do it, so I just do it. I don't say anything, even though I want to say something, but I don't, and so I just do it. Like. I didn't have time to shop today, Andy. I didn't. But. Here I am. So.'

Brian gathered all the grocery bags into one and stuffed them under the sink.

'I'm separating time, for me, for my mindset,' Brian said.

'Well. Shouldn't we talk more about that?'

'I don't know, Andy, should we? Christ, this feels like last year.'

Dibbler shrank where he stood.

'Wednesday afternoons, or whenever on Wednesdays, is *me* time. Just me. Alone. Starting today.'

'Don't I get some input on this? You said communication is healthy and, so, you're not letting me get input here.'

Brian relented a moment. He said, 'Okay then, say what you need to say.'

Dibbler's quiet extended for a while.

'I'm not perfect,' Brian said.

'Don't say that,' Dibbler said.

'I mean it. I'm not.'

'To me you are.'

'How?'

Dibbler studied Brian.

'I'm not this perfect image partner person.'

'I think you are,' Dibbler said.

'But I'm not. That's why I'm telling you, if you think I'm perfect, you expect me to be perfect, and then I do something that's not perfect and you get all, you know, so that's why I'm saying to you that I'm not perfect. You understand I'm not, right? Like here in the real world where people have to clean and pay bills and work, like, here in the grungy and painful and sharp world—you understand that I'm not perfect. Right? Like. I'm an imperfect person who can't meet perfection. You understand that. Right?'

Dibbler, in the quiet that followed, tried to piece together what he wanted to express, but it was too much and too many.

In the end, he said, 'Did you remember, though, to take off work? For the twentieth?'

❖

Dibbler helped his mother move some things around in her garage the following afternoon; she was making room, she said. She didn't know for what, she just felt she needed the room.

Afterward she took him to lunch.

Dibbler told her the twentieth was coming up.

She shook her head.

Food was delivered, and his mother was still shaking her head.

They ate.

As they ate, she said she thought Dibbler had this image of marriage in his head, that two people come together and that's it, they're a pair, and they take on the hardships of this Earth, and that they're always on the same page, and that a marriage survives whatever you throw at it, she said. I think you have this easy image, and I think you're chasing it and I think, she said, when you finally have it, it's not going to be like you think. Some days, it might, she said, some days might feel good, and some might feel great, she said, but that doesn't spare each other from the real stuff. It's all about the real stuff, she said. Moving the relationship into marriage doesn't leave that stuff behind.

She played with her salad and drank from her coffee.

Dibbler said nothing. His face was red fire. Then he said, 'Brian will be a great husband.'

'That may be, sweetie, but the people we love will always hurt us. A ring doesn't stop that; a big romantic gesture won't stop that. Openly committing, in front of friends and family and God Himself won't stop that. That's just what they do. People being people means someone, someday will hurt.'

Dibbler wasn't touching his food. He was listening. He attempted to eat and found he could not. He couldn't sit still; he couldn't sit with what his mother had just said.

He stood to leave.

He said, 'There's a person for everyone. When you're together with this person, nothing is hard anymore, there's no insecurity anymore, no worries anymore. When you're together with the person that's *just* for you, your minds can be at peace and trust can be at peace, and you can believe every word they tell you. You can trust every time they say they love you that they *actually* love you. You can just believe them. You don't have to sit there, when they say I love you, and convince yourself they love you. You don't have to second guess. Brian is my person.'

His mother said, 'I'm so sorry to say, sweetie, I'm really so so sorry to tell you, every person that you will ever love, whether you're aware of it or not, they will lie to you and hide something from you, and if they don't step out of the relationship in the physical, they will do it in the mental. They will have fantasies of others, and they will have fantasies of you, but in the fantasies, you're different, you're a little more the way they want, not how you actually are, and they'll try to micro-adjust you, to make you how they want you, and I know it so profoundly to be true that you will always encounter it in your lovers, because we do it too, don't we, hon, lying, hiding things, picturing our lovers in a way they aren't, micro-adjusting them. We do it, too, and are we going to stop lying and hiding things? Are we going to stop imagining our lovers as people they're not?'

The waitress brought the check.

Dibbler's mother said, 'Well, are we?'

❖

The following week, Dibbler was opening registers by himself and worked through the morning. It was slow, then Ruthie clocked in, and the door in the wall opened, and Dibbler was asked to come inside, please.

The supervisor had Dibbler sit and said, 'So, I'm just going to get into it right from the start, if that's okay? This stuff is always, yeah, that's okay? If we just get into it?'

The supervisor pulled several forms from a printer and placed them before Dibbler; each paper held walls of legal jargon.

'So, unfortunately, Andy, I am notifying you that your wages are being garnished by the company named here, looks like Recovery Debt Collections, at this amount here, which says if you read there, it says thirty percent plus an additional five, so here's the total of that, which is thirty-five, so thirty-five percent of your pay is being garnished, Andy, this is me giving you notification. That's what this serves as.'

'But then, no. They were waiting for a check.'

'Yeah, it doesn't tell me any of that, unfortunately, it just, this is really just a notice. I wouldn't know.'

'I was actually just going to send them a new check this afternoon. The mail probably lost it, that's what I'm thinking,' Dibbler said. 'And that can't really be my fault. So.'

The supervisor turned the notice over for Dibbler to see.

'None of that's in here; it just says what I said.'

'Well then, can we pause that, because I definitely sent the check, that absolutely happened. I put it in the mail, absolutely, and then I'm thinking it got lost, and what am I supposed to do, follow the mail until it gets where it's going? Am I going to follow the check while it's on conveyor belts and getting scanned and then ride in the truck with it from center to center until it's delivered? Is that my responsibility? So, I don't–this can pause until I can, well, this afternoon actually I was going to send a new one. So.'

The supervisor was unsure how to proceed.

The supervisor said, after an awkward moment, 'So. Starting this week's paycheck, you'll see the deduction in the payment details.'

'It's already going, then?'

'Processed this morning, yep.'

'Well, you think something like that, they'd give you better notice, you know, a call that this was going to happen would, you know. I don't think I ever was told this was going to happen on this date at such and such a time. They never gave me direct notice, and if I wasn't given direct notice, it would be on this date at such and such a time, then can something like this even go on? You know? Legally?'

The supervisor apologized and said he didn't know about any of that and sent Dibbler on his way.

'Oh,' he said before Dibbler was out the door. 'Thought it worth saying, this doesn't affect the offer for management training. That's still on the table. If there was interest? We're sympathetic that sometimes we fall behind, for one reason or another.'

Dibbler stood with the thought.

'But we're going to need an answer on that soon, well, any day before the twentieth, even the morning of the twentieth, we can still book you in and get you out there on your way to success. Just. So you know that none of this money stuff, we're still interested in you, Andy.'

Dibbler walked out of the office.

We're still interested in you, Andy ...

Dibbler was home before Brian that evening.

He turned the TV on for company and started dinner for him and Brian, and the time Brian usually came home from work came and then it was gone, and there was no Brian.

Dibbler waited until dinner was cold; then he ate and waited in the living room with the TV. He flipped channels to busy himself and saw *Forever in Love* was on. It was on the proposal scene, and Dibbler stopped flipping and let it play.

On the TV, the lead guy was walking the lead girl along rock and sand and up the side of a calm pond at sunset. The horizon was throwing warmth and color across their faces, and it was only them, and the rest of the world was empty; the rest didn't matter to the lead guy and the lead girl, and they stopped in the sand and the rock, along the water, and the lead guy lowered to one knee and the lead girl crumbled and wept openly and freely and the lead guy opened for her a ring box, and in the ring box was a beautiful and simple and timeless ring, identical to the one hidden away in Dibbler's closet.

The lead guy gave the lead girl a proposal speech, identical to the one Dibbler had prepared at Marty's apartment.

The movie shone in Dibbler's arrested eyes; there were goosebumps across his arms.

He left the movie on and watched and waited for Brian, then he showered and put away dinner in the fridge and then he stood in the kitchen.

In the quiet.

He looked out the window onto the street, looking out, waiting. Now and then, people walked down the sidewalk and cars passed, but none were Brian. Then an hour had passed, and Dibbler wasn't sure how that happened, and he shut off lights and got in bed and waited in the dark and in the quiet, and now and again he rose and slid apart the hanging blinds and looked out onto the street for Brian's car. More time passed; the amount made Dibbler uncomfortable.

He crawled back in bed.

He'd only just fallen asleep when Brian came in with door and shoe noises and undressed and brushed his teeth real quick, then slid into bed.

All the chaos of his entry lingered then fell to quiet.

Dibbler said into the quiet, 'Everything okay?'

'Just client stuff at work. Ran long. Go back to sleep.'

Brian adjusted and searched for comfort in the sheets and found it, then there was peace in the bedroom.

Dibbler said, 'You don't do the client stuff, I thought.'

A moment.

'What?'

'I didn't think you still did that,' Dibbler said. 'You said you didn't.'

'I was helping out. Everything's fine. Back to bed, babe.'

Brian kissed Dibbler and said love you and rolled away and returned to comfort.

Quiet moved in.

'The twentieth is Friday,' Dibbler whispered.

Brian said mm-hmm. He was already half into sleep.

Dibbler rolled and found comfort on his own, on his side of the bed, apart from Brian, away from Brian.

We're still interested in you, Andy ...

❖

On Thursday, Dibbler was coming into the apartment from work as Brian was coming out of the apartment for some destination unknown to Dibbler.

Brian said he was off to have some *me* time.

'It's not Wednesday,' Dibbler said.

'Well, I just hadn't seen you, so I was going to tell you, I was thinking maybe *me* time can be Thursdays too.'

'More *you* time? Not less, more?'

'It's been helping. I really feel it in my day.'

'Well, I don't know that it's helping *me* any,' Dibbler said.

Brian shuffled past. He stopped to say, 'Oh. Was something funny with your paycheck?'

'No.'

'I saw it go in the account. I swore you worked the same hours. It wasn't very much.'

Dibbler thought about the garnishment. 'It's a payroll mistake; it's being fixed.'

'Yeah, because this is the one rent comes out of, so, keep on them on that. Okay? So, I'll see you tonight then,' Brian said.

Off he went down the hall.

'You have tomorrow off, right? Tomorrow is Friday, the twentieth.''

'What? Oh, yeah, sure.'

'Well, is that yes?'

As Brian exited the building, he shouted back, 'I'll see you tonight.'

Dibbler stood in the empty hall outside the apartment and listened to Brian's car start and drive, then he hurried inside, settled his bags, hurried back out, and locked the door. Out of the building he ran, straight to his car, and began tailing Brian from a good distance, so as not to be seen. It took a moment for Dibbler to catch up, but when he did, and when he was a few cars behind, he didn't let Brian's car escape his sight.

Dibbler followed Brian onto the highway, a few exits down, then off again through the quiet side of town, where he stopped at a 7-Eleven. Dibbler saw whatever Brian bought, he had to point at it behind the counter to purchase it, and it went into a bag, then Brian pulled out and turned into neighborhoods, down curvy and cozy roads to an apartment building next to a ball diamond.

Marty's apartment building.

Dibbler parked back a ways.

Marty was waiting outside for Brian and smoking a cigarette.

Brian parked, and Dibbler watched the two men hug and go inside laughing, carrying the 7-Eleven purchase, just so happy to see each other and laughing the whole way into the building.

Dibbler waited in the car with the radio off, waiting and watching the building, watching the lights in Marty's windows on, then off for an hour, another hour, then on they came again, and he watched the two men smoke cigarettes out of Marty's bedroom window, joking in the window and smoking and affectionate with one another.

Dibbler watched all of it, unmoving, perhaps catatonic; perhaps in Dibbler's mind there occurred a collision, perhaps it was still occurring, or perhaps there were multiple collisions.

Many.

All at once.

Dibbler, very gently and very quietly, shifted into drive and took the car home and went into the bedroom without turning on any lights.

He drifted, he sank into bed.

He was a corpse until he heard Brian's car pull up, heard the door open and close, heard him come in the building, up the stairs, down the hall, heard the apartment door unlock, heard Brian go in the kitchen and mess around in the fridge, heard a cabinet open, a plate, heard Brian make food, eat, heard Brian come in the room and undress and bang his knee, heard him say sorry, then go and brush his teeth and felt him and heard him settle in bed and whisper good night.

Dibbler did not whisper it back.

He let Brian find a comfortable spot, then said, 'The other night you never said what makes *you* happy.'

'Oh, I didn't?'

There seemed no intention from Brian to share. He was lying with his eyes shut and his breathing was slowing for sleep.

We're still interested in you, Andy ...

'Can you say?' Dibbler said.

'What?'

'Can you say what makes you happy?'

Brian said, you make me happy.

You will always encounter it in your lovers because we do it too, don't we, hon, don't we, sweetie, lying, hiding things, we do it, too, don't we?

'You're happy?' Dibbler said.

'I'm so happy,' Brian said. 'Love you, babe.'

Dibbler looked at Brian for a long time, lying there with his eyes shut.

Are we going to stop lying and hiding things?

Brian said, 'Okay, I'm going to roll over now. I have to wake up early. Night.'

'You didn't take tomorrow off?'

Brian said, 'What's tomorrow?'

Are we going to stop imagining our lovers as people they're not?

Dibbler said nothing.

Well, are we?

What's in Your Head, Chris Cooper?

The documentary in question concluded filming on June 19, 2011, some twelve years after the disappearance of forty-one-year-old Christopher Cooper from his residence in rural Larton, Illinois, near the heart of the state. The film, upon its release, reminded the nation of the case which, like so many others, had garnered sympathy and prayer and headlines, then faded entirely from public mind. Silver Peak Productions held the film's copyright until the company's liquidation in March 2020, when its catalog of films and trademarks and assets were sold to **Warner Brothers Entertainment, Inc.** in a deal that served only to satisfy debt. The film's only physical copy, which rested in Warner's shelved archive, was reported lost during a reorganization in late 2022, and its whereabouts remain unknown despite the letters and emails and efforts of Christopher Cooper's family and close friends hoping to locate and initiate the release of the film to the public for awareness and, more importantly, closure. For the purposes of this publication, numerous solicitations for comment were sent to

Warner Brothers and the original Silver Peak production team, including director David Jay Torres and writer Carol Long. **All solicitations have thus far gone unanswered.** Out of respect for the missing, the following transcript of footage and audio are given to the reader wholly unedited and precisely as the film is believed to unfold. As far as this interested party is aware, **this transcript is all that remains of this relatively undiscovered film** ...

PUBLICATION OF THIS TRANSCRIPT PAID FOR BY THE CHRIS COOPER FUND

Transcript Rec No. #AOD1122901

© April 14, 2011 [Silver Peak Films INC] All Rights Reserved

TITLE: *What's In Your Head, Chris Cooper?*

{Begin Transcript 00:00:09}

The film's first images, arriving from opening titles and from black, are given of Christopher Cooper's bedroom in warm morning sun with no soundtrack. Captured only are the outside noises of passing cars and morning birds and the quiet inherent to an empty room and, beyond, an empty apartment.

A line of text overlays the emptiness. It reads:

On March 4, 1999, Christopher Cooper vanished. He has not been seen since.

An older couple comfortably sit in their living room, they are identified as MARY ANNE COOPER [MOTHER] and RICHARD COOPER [FATHER]. Gray has taken their hair, and age has taken

their mobility. They live confined, it seems, to the armchairs in which they are seated, staring at the camera.

Mary Anne Cooper Voice Over: Sometimes you just wanted to shake him. Like you wanted to get your hands around him and shake loose what he was thinking, shake those thoughts right out of his mouth, my gosh, haha!

Richard Cooper: You could go weeks without a word from him. Then he'd call, always out of the blue, and he'd ask about ya, ask about his brother and sister, you know, he'd always check in on ya and them, see how you and them are doing. He was good about that, and then you'd try to ask about him and he'd say, well, you know, and tell you he was fine and everything was fine and that's about all you'd get outta Chris. You could poke for more, yeah, we'd poke, wouldn't we? We'd poke with questions. But that's all he'd give ya. That he was fine. *Everything was fine.*

A woman late in her midlife is then on camera; her hair is large and brown and thinning.

She is on a couch and labeled as NANCY COOPER [YOUNGER SISTER].

Nancy Cooper: Chris lived inward. His world, where I think he lived, where he spent all his time, was in his head, and you know how some people say, you know, they're trapped in their head, or they'll say they can't get out of their head, how some people will tell you that? Chris, I think, I don't think he was trapped in his head. I think that's where he preferred to be.

An older gentleman in wrinkled clothing sits at a desk in a small office and smiles for the camera while it records him. He is identified as DUTTON BLOOM [JOURNALIST, LOCAL PAPER]. The office lacks organization and tidiness and appears to have no filing system other than stacks of papers and newspapers and folders here and there and about. The walls hold plaques and framed stories. The older man's skin is dried and starved, and his teeth keep much buildup and coffee stains. The camera records the older man holding up a copy of the original, aged newspaper reporting Chris Cooper as missing.

The headline reads LOCAL MAN, 41, VANISHES. An unclear black-and-white photo of Chris rests beneath the headline.

Dutton Bloom: I was right here when the story fell on my lap. They don't usually come that way. Usually I'm seeking out a story, but that one didn't come the usual way. That one sought *me* out, I like to say. Well, so, that day a buddy of mine called and asked had I heard a guy out Larton way had gone missing. I said no. No one was talking about it yet. It hadn't been picked up; it was still early. That was the first time I heard the name, Christopher Cooper.

DUTTON escorts and points out plaques and awards throughout the office for the camera.

Dutton Bloom: I got a job after college working for *Daily News*, up in Chicago. I thought, wow, mid-sized paper, it was a good-sized paper at the time. I thought that was where I'd be until it was time to retire. It was a good group of us, the staff. I did a few years of that, maybe five or six years, and—what I could never—what I couldn't—some writers can keep themselves outside a story. They can look at something upsetting and look at it for months, years, decades. Some stories go that long. Sometimes longer. Some writers look at bodies and victims and horrible things that happen to children and families and otherwise good people, sometimes for no reason at all, and they can keep that from affecting them at best, or at minimum can stomach seeing it over and over and over. Tolerate it maybe? I could never. I couldn't tolerate it, what people can do to one another. So, I came down Larton way. Ten years I'm reporting on county fairs and farmland and rural county life before that phone rang and I was given Chris Cooper's name. Then it was like there I was, back to tolerating the bad stuff. But this wasn't gore or bloody photos keeping you awake at night. This was the fact this person, this son and brother and lover and friend, disappeared. Like God Himself plucked Chris Cooper off this earth, and it could be that we never know what happened, or it could be we'll never know what he was thinking, or it could be there are parts of his life we'll never have access to. And. How do you tolerate a thing like that?

The camera finds a small home in a small neighborhood of a small town. The day is bright and sunny. The home is the shade of lemonade, of piss. Then we're inside the kitchen, at the kitchen table, with JEANIE DANVERS [VOLUNTEER INVESTIGATOR], who's in a turtleneck and looking right into the camera with thick glasses and frizzy mom hair. In her hands is a warm mug of tea.

Jeanie Danvers: They showed a picture of Chris on the evening news, and they were saying what happened, and there were police on and my mom, I was a teenager at home still, my mom says to us girls, me and my sisters, we were all in the living room watching this on TV, she tells us she's giving us a curfew now. She wants us home before dark every day. I think it really unnerved her. And I remember my older sister throwing a stink and going well how long do we have the curfew for, and my mom says in that sort of final way that moms say, until they find him. Sometimes I'll be here looking at a report or I'll be between records or following up or, and, I'll think, gosh, I would still have a curfew today, haha, you know, if I wasn't an adult with a family of my own, haha. No, I know that's not funny, I know. It's just a thought I have. Now and again.

JEANNIE shows the camera to her home office down a skinny hallway. Inside she flips on the light for the camera to see years of research and documents. She wanders through it, poking and peeking through it.

Jeanie Danvers: This here, these folders, I made friends with the deputy and, well now I'm close with the sheriff too, Daryl Beuford, he wasn't sheriff back then, but these here the deputy, I'm blanking on his name, gosh, was a short fella, but back then he made copies for me. I made him cookies. Well, I make cookies for all the guys at the station now but, so. This is the missing person's report Chris's sister, Nancy Cooper, made back in 1999, you can see the date there. Gosh, I cannot remember that gentleman deputy's name, he passed, oh, five years ago maybe? Had to be five or so. But. I make cookies for all those guys now, when I need something on the case, haha!

JEANIE is back at the kitchen table, shaking her head into the camera.

Jeanie Danvers: It was after my son was born, my first one, that's when I really got interested in the case, maybe it was a shift in my seeing, because I was seeing everything as a mom all of a sudden. And, too, it was, well, it was that there was nothing, I mean a complete lack of anything. There was no evidence pointing any which way, and that really just–it unsettled me, you know, maybe I–maybe I couldn't accept that? It's like. Everything we do leaves a trace. Everything. A gas receipt, a footprint in the mud. Everything we do is recorded, if it's by a register, by the environment, by people, our loved ones and the like. But. Chris left nothing. And, well, so the case had already gone cold when I started looking at it, so I was starting when everyone else had sorta thrown up their hands about it and moved on to other things, other cases. He left a puzzle, absolutely, and we're left looking for pieces that fit that puzzle. I'm certain the pieces are out there. We just have to find them. So. No. I don't accept that there are parts of him that we won't ever know, no, I don't accept that. Whatever inward life he had, he left a trace of it. I don't accept otherwise. I won't.

MARY ANNE and RICHARD sit with photo albums and turn pages for the camera to see Chris as a newborn, as a toddler, as a kindergartner and on through elementary school ages, photos both in school and out of school, at home, at birthdays with birthday cakes and candles and family gathered, photos playing in the yard, Christmas morning photos, photos reading books under blankets, photos of Chris sleeping in funny positions and in funny places.

Mary Anne Cooper: Christopher was–he was an easy baby. Yeah. Just–he never cried, wasn't much of a fusser. At least for me. He was for you.

Richard Cooper: He was for me, yeah. Always fussing when he was with me. Yep. Yeah.

Mary Anne Cooper: When he was old enough and walking around, he was in whatever room we were in. It didn't matter. The kitchen, the bathroom, wherever you were, he was too. He did not like being alone one bit.

Richard Cooper: He loved to sit and watch me in the garage, or he'd be doing something else in the garage while I was working on this or that. If I went in the fridge, he was right behind me, or he'd trade me for her, if she was doing something. But. He was always following around one of us. Oh yeah. Mostly it was her, though. Mostly it wasn't me. He was a mom's boy, absolutely.

Mary Anne Cooper: Richard would be at work, and I would be doing something in the kitchen or doing laundry or house stuff, you'd kinda forget Christopher was there. You'd be cooking or doing dishes, something loud, something with some noise, and it would cover him up. A moment or two of that and you'd, I swear, you'd forget he was there. And. I did. One time. Sorry, I– um, one moment.

Richard Cooper: Yeah, just give her one moment.

Mary Anne Cooper: Sorry about that. Um. I just. I think about this a lot. So. I went for groceries and left him home all by hisself, just a four-year-old all alone at home, he was so quiet all the time and he never needed anything from you, never asked for anything from you, so it was, I mean I feel awful about it, but I just forgot he was there. When I got home, it was maybe forty minutes, an hour I was gone, he was in the living room, and I could see he'd been crying and stopped already, his little cheeks, they were bright pink, and the tears had already gone and dried. That I'd forgotten him, or that I'd left him, just this tiny little person all alone, I think that really affected him, maybe damaged him, even? Gosh. I think about that, Richard says I shouldn't but I think about that, because after that, all he wanted was to be alone.

Richard Cooper: We hoped when he started school that he'd open up more.

Mary Anne Cooper: We did. But when he didn't, we both sorta accepted he just would never be that way. When I had my second boy and then my daughter and time went on, and they were just the neediest and loudest and they loved talking you up, just loved it and, so the house filled with kid noise, but Christopher was, like, just this, I hate to say it as a parent but as soon as he was in school, it felt like he was just this other person in the family at the breakfast and dinner table. How was your day? Good. What'd you learn today? Stuff.

Richard Cooper: But we never had to get on him about homework or too much TV or games. He studied and read, and he was responsible, even young, such a good kid, never had a bad grade to scold him over. The other two we scolded plenty for grades and roughhousing and behavior, haha. The other two made you wanna pull hair out, haha. But Chris. Nope. From a parent's perspective, he was just a kid on autopilot. We tried getting involved in his life. But. He just. I don't know. For whatever reason, he wouldn't let us in. So. We both let the space between us be there; we didn't mess with it. We allowed it, maybe it was bad of us, I don't know. But. We allowed that space.

Mary Anne Cooper: In high school it only got worse, the distance.

A middle-aged man is seated in a comfortable armchair in an apartment. He's not in shape, but neither is he out of shape, he's somewhere in the middle. The title below him reads ANTHONY COOPER [YOUNGER BROTHER].

Anthony Cooper: Chris was five years older than me, so, we never shared much time at home together, because he was in school, and then when I was in school. When I was going into a grade, he was already on his way out, grade school, junior high, high school. When I was a freshman, he was just graduating. I was always just missing him by a year. He got a job too, pretty young, I think he was bagging groceries at fifteen, so he was doing that at nights, and I remember Mom saying did I hear that Chris got himself a car, and I remember it in the driveway, it was green. This old green car. He would wash that old beater like it was a Cadillac every Saturday, haha. But. So, no. I don't–I don't remember him home all that much as soon as he could drive. So. No, we weren't all that close. As kids. Like ships passing for years.

A man locked in a terrible slouch and in a ball cap and street clothes is seated in a living room; he's not given sound and appears to be asking the camera a question, if how he is sitting, is it okay.

Then he's seated nice and framed for the camera. Life has added weight to his cheeks and his belly. For the camera he gives a bright smile and broad shoulders. The title below him says his name is RONNIE HARRIS [BEST FRIEND].

Ronnie Harris: I got that question so many times, when all that happened, in interviews with the papers and everything, it was everyone's first question, it was yours, too, and I honestly don't know the answer. I cannot for the life of me remember, like, a-a-a first day, a first meeting, like an actual first meeting with Chris. I know it was kindergarten, we both had the same teacher, but I can't remember what or how or, I just look back and all I see is us, just, always being friends. Like when you go back in your head as far back as you can, before it gets–before you hit a wall, when your memories kinda really start, he was always just a part of mine.

Images of RONNIE and Chris are given; one has the pair in a fourth-grade shoebox diorama presentation on dinosaurs, another has the two with Nerf guns in someone's back yard, another has the boys, now entering high school, with their homecoming dates, smiling and awkward.

Ronnie Harris: Chris was always up for anything and he mostly, kinda, followed my lead. Like, when I super got into hockey, I wasn't on a team or anything, it was really just me rolling around the driveway in roller blades with a puck and a stick, haha, but sure enough, Chris got roller blades and a stick, and then he was out skating around with me, and, but that stuff, sports stuff, it came pretty easy to me. Chris would be so excited but he, just, didn't naturally have that–that ability. So. He had to try harder. I know it made him feel like he was always behind or always catching up. And we all loved him anyway. My family did too. He was polite to the point where he'd kinda hover out of everyone's way, if that makes sense? Being so close in age, we grew up together through those milestones young guys go through, and it was great having that, um– Sorry, he was just my best friend in every way you can mean that, and I'm just so glad I got that with Chris, but I think he made it a point to keep himself out of people's way, hovering through life out there, out away from everyone. After a while, I would say this was sophomore year, I would call and tell him come over, and it was one Friday, he says I can't, I'm busy. And then it was more Fridays, and then it was Fridays and Saturdays. So, people ask me that too, if I knew, and no, no, I had no idea about any of that before. But then eventually I stopped asking him to hang out, and in school he was, I would say distant, and all I knew then was he was keeping me out of something, so to me it really felt like junior year, Chris was living two lives.

The camera is close on NANCY.

Up close, NANCY's skin and body look tired.

Nancy Cooper: We always just thought if Chris wasn't home or at Ronnie's, then he was at work. You never had to worry if Chris was going to do the right thing, far as anyone knew he always seemed to do the right thing, didn't party, didn't drink and drive, wasn't out late, no one worried about Chris. I think, maybe, deep down he wanted people to worry about him? Like, not for his safety you know, nothing like that, but maybe just the attention of when you worry about someone? I don't know if I'm saying that right. But. He was missing that, I think.

The camera has released NANCY of her close shot and now includes full view of the couch.

Nancy Cooper: So it was, yeah, it was a shock when I came home from softball one day and Mom's in the laundry room crying, I was eleven maybe, so Chris would have been seventeen or almost eighteen, and Mom's on the step by the dryer with tissue and sobbing and she says your brother just told me he's gay, and I don't think Mom knew a gay person in her whole life. So, she's just sitting there shaking her head and crying, and I asked so why's she crying about that. She says I don't know, hon, I really don't know.

ANTHONY COOPER is leaned forward on his knees, shaking his head at the camera from where he sits in his armchair. The rest of the room around him and the camera is out of focus, but it is small, this room, and it is bare of life, it's sterile and near empty.

Anthony Cooper: None of us thought it, not one time, but when you look back and now you know, it explains some things, not all of it, but, it kinda became this thing in the house that everyone danced around, trying to avoid it best you could and, so, poor Chris now had just another thing about him that people were ignoring, and I think he finally realized that, hey, he really didn't have reins on him, you know, this seventeen-eighteen year old. Mom and Dad were basically letting him do whatever, whenever, because they honestly trusted him but, I think, too, they also, I mean Chris coming out handed Mom and Dad something they didn't understand and, so, I think they shut down to it.

The camera records a small restaurant on a busy city street. A good amount of foot traffic is coming and going, and horns and cars are loud and full.

Inside the restaurant, in a booth, the camera pleasantly frames a man who has entered his later years gracefully and with great care. Age has crept into his face but in a way that endears, in a manner it makes the gentleman appear honest-natured and warm.

We are told this is NICHOLAS WEBBER [PARTNER], and for the camera he is at ease and neither far nor near.

Nicholas Webber: It was at the grocery store actually, there in town. He started working there, he was the bag boy, haha, that's where I first met Chris. I was on registers, they called me a checker. I was a year older, Chris was a junior, I think when he started, I was a senior. Yeah. I would be ringing customers out and he'd be right there bagging, and this place walked your groceries out to your car, so he'd do that, too. In any one shift we would see each other a lot. Of course, we talked, but it didn't start that way, no, he was the shyest. Was so, like, sheepish, haha, I'm not kidding, he was sheepish. I was out of the closet, I was out at fifteen actually, so the whole town knew I was gay. I was used to people being, just, like, like they'd catch it from me or something, they'd avoid you. Chris knew I was gay, and once we finally started talking, like as coworkers who were also friends, he had so many questions about it. And friends are always having a question about it every now and then, too, just a question that pops up here and there, your straight friends, but Chris, I remember, he had question after question, and I kinda *knew*, kinda didn't, before Chris came to his own realization. I had a vibe here and there. I wasn't certain but I suspected. But I was going to let him find his own way to it. We did get close pretty fast and, honestly, I was kinda hoping he was gay, haha! But. I think I was the first person he told. Yeah. We were dating, like boyfriends, maybe three or four months before he came out to his mom.

MARY ANNE COOPER and RICHARD COOPER are shown in wide frame in their living room. Daylight has changed, and lights have been brought in.

Mary Anne Cooper: Well, we knew Nicholas, "Nick," Richard did–didn't you do Little League with Kenny Webber? Kenny was Nick's dad. I thought you did Little League with Kenny.

Richard Cooper: For many years, yeah, Kenny and me, we did Little League coaching from, oh gosh, had to of been eighty-two to eighty-eight, so six years, and we knew his wife Donna, I mean, they lived right up the street from us, basically.

Mary Anne Cooper: So, when Chris brought him to the house once or twice, we knew Nick already. Just. Not like that.

The camera returns to NICHOLAS, at a close angle.

Nicholas Webber: He wasn't my first kiss, but I know I was his, and we did all those romantic-sappy dates, haha! Chris would surprise me with flowers or take me up to Chicago to see the buildings. He knew all my favorite foods, books, movies, I was always telling him. But. I didn't know any of his. He never shared. It was always a guess. Birthday cake flavors, his favorite dinner, he always just seemed fine with whatever I would get or make. You could ask and he would even just say get whatever. So mostly I got whatever. So. Everything with Chris was easy, that's why I fell for him so hard in the beginning.

The camera finds Chris's elderly parents now with remorseful expressions.

Mary Anne Cooper: We did not know what to do, all of that was so new to us and, I think, Richard struggled with it a little more than I did.

Richard Cooper: Well, no. I wasn't–it wasn't struggling so much, it was just, as a parent you were just so afraid to do the wrong thing that you ended up doing nothing, and we didn't know about gay anything. It's, like, do we worry, do we, because you see how they're treated, and, but we didn't think like that right then. And the last thing you want to do is ask him about it so, yeah, you end up cornered, and so when we made him start following the same rules as his brother and sister, no girlfriends or boyfriends over after dark, he was so, I mean, I'd never seen him so mad.

NICHOLAS is halfway through a cigarette in the restaurant booth; he ashes the tip.

Nicholas Webber: It was that whole summer before Chris went to college, he was in a fight with his parents every week, sometimes all week. They were giving him rules he hadn't had before, like a curfew and that. It's not like they were making it hard for us to see each other, but Chris took it as, like, for years and years and years they'd given him too much space but, so, not only were they all of a sudden paying him attention, but it was in the form of rules, so he had a hard time with that. But then he was at college, so that all stopped when he went downstate. I stayed here for community college, but he was usually back for holidays, and I went and visited a few times, so the distance wasn't too hard for us.

NICHOLAS now shows the camera uncertainty as he recalls further.

Nicholas Webber: I didn't notice anything wrong. Except whenever he wasn't home, when he was at school, I had a, there was a feeling in the back of my head that something was, maybe, a little funny. And I honestly thought I was just too much in my head about it, but, I look back and I think my gut knew something I didn't yet and it was giving me signals that, I don't know, I didn't understand. It was clear that he was going through something down there at school. I would ask about his classes, and he would say it's good, classes are good. He wouldn't talk about what he was studying or what classes he liked or didn't like, even if you directly asked him, no, but in the moment, it never felt like he was giving you non-answers. It's only when, later, you're replaying conversations in your head, you'd go, oh, he didn't really answer my question.

MARY ANNE readjusts how she's sitting; it could be she's been sitting for hours, or maybe years, sitting in that chair. RICHARD is nodding along with what she's telling the camera.

Mary Anne Cooper: We only found out because the school sent a letter at the end of his first semester that said, basically, Chris was being expelled from the university. He was failing all his classes, and it sounded like he just wasn't even going to classes.

Richard Cooper: And the whole time we're going, well, that's the whole point of going to school, the classes, and he wasn't working, and we know that because he was always calling us for money, so we were so confused, if he wasn't going to classes, what was he doing all day? Because we were paying for his school, we were paying for him to eat, we were both so, just, dumbfounded.

Mary Anne Cooper: Honestly, I think if we hadn't gotten that letter, would he of told us? I don't know. But. No. He never told us what he was doing with all his time. To this day, we don't know.

NANCY has her arms out, where she's sitting on the couch, and she's wagging her finger at the camera.

Nancy Cooper: When Chris was kicked out of school and came back home, I don't think my parents offered any kind of support. All they could see was how careless he'd been with such a big opportunity, throwing away college. So. They gave him the silent treatment, and when they weren't giving the silent treatment, they were giving anger. I would be in my room doing homework and I would hear them fighting, screaming things and things slamming, and it wasn't all my parents, Chris gave his fair share back to them. But. It made you feel so small, hearing them saying the most awful things to one another.

The camera searches the family living room walls and hovers over captured moments of a family growing older together. From photo to photo, the smiles dim and their posture shrinks, and the distance between them, between the family in the photos, between each and every member, grows more and more.

Nicholas Webber: Chris was probably back from school a few months when, finally, he said he couldn't take it and we got a small apartment in Clinton City, thirty minutes up the highway. It was this tiny, tiny one-bedroom with hideous green carpet, and we had a TV and a radio and nothing in the fridge, haha! But we didn't need much else. It was close to my work and the community college, and Chris had gotten a job in retail, and that wasn't far from us. We were both, just, entering our twenties and finding routines and still making time for fun. Chris and I were getting an idea of what our lives would be, and we were really excited about that.

NICHOLAS nods his head to a question the camera did not record, he answers the question.

Nicholas Webber: It was, yeah, right around then was when he got into painting. He'd talked about it before, I would say a few times, but us being out on our own, I think, gave him the room to finally try and, instead of talking about it, actually do it. Away from family. He thought they would be judgey, I think he didn't like the vulnerability. Them seeing his work. So. He would do opening or closing shifts at the store, and when he was home, he was working on some painting. I'd bought him an easel and paints for his twenty-third birthday, and you'd never seen someone more happy with a gift, I swear it. And then, when he was fired from his job, that was all he was doing, was being at that easel and painting on canvas. Sometimes. Um. Sometimes I'll think, I hate to say, but I would sometimes wish I had never bought those for him, if I'd known painting would be such a curse for him in his life. I think that. But you can't know a thing like that on the front end. Can you?

ANTHONY is sitting on the edge of his chair, practically off the cushion, practically in the camera's lens.

Anthony Cooper: I mean, I'm not a art person, it's a bit of a shame that Chris was born into a family of mostly art illiterates. I saw maybe one painting of his when he was just starting out, and, of course, I wouldn't know a good painting from a bad painting, but his was okay, I thought, just okay, but, if I was a art guy I don't know I'd gravitate toward the sort of images he painted, dark paintings, but, really, we were all hoping painting would be a way for him to empty out all that stuff he was carrying around, sort of release it onto canvas. I think, too, maybe that's why he took to it so, I don't want to say obsessively, but he was kind of obsessive, so, I think maybe with painting he was chasing that, too. An end to the–whatever was living in his head and heart, but I don't know there was ever an end to it, I don't know the stuff he carried around was infinite or not, but he definitely chased it.

RONNIE accepts coffee from a film crew member and thanks them. No audio is provided of this exchange. RONNIE settles.

Ronnie Harris: Chris and I reconnected, was two or three, maybe four years after he'd been back from college and he was living with Nick a while, this was when he wasn't working. There wasn't a falling out, I think life took us different directions, so, no, it wasn't–there wasn't anything we needed to reconcile, it was just, hey, how you been, and we were back as friends. Just like that.

RONNIE seems to correct a statement made off camera, he is assertive with his correction.

Ronnie Harris: Well, Nick was supporting the both of them on one income, and I know Chris was looking for work, maybe not the most proactively, but it was job applications here and there and interviews, and second interviews, and third interviews. Without a degree, though, he kept hitting wall after wall, so, enough times of that and how proactive about getting a job are you really going to be, though, right? So. He let painting consume his time, all of it.

NICHOLAS holds a wounded look for the camera

Nicholas Webber: It was hard. Yeah. Because. I was burning out keeping us afloat, and I know he was trying for jobs, for a while, I know he was trying so hard, but then, it was like, he gave up trying and then it wasn't fun anymore, then everything felt like work, and that's when the arguments really started. We would be arguing one month and good another month and then arguing, and then good, and it was a roller coaster, honestly, and we were mid-twenties, late twenties, and we were like this old couple already, haha. Sorry, I don't mean to laugh, but it was, it was funny, these two twenty-six, twenty-seven-year-old gay guys acting like a fifty-year-old married couple, arguing and way too sedentary. The relationship felt, yeah, it felt sedentary, it wasn't moving forward. And. Chris had never been with anyone but me. Maybe that kept us together longer than we would have been? And one day, I got a little brave and I said, look, I love you, I love you so much, but I think you should go talk to someone, I think you have things that need sharing that, for one reason or another, you can't share with me or friends or family, but these things **need** sharing. I'm meaning a therapist when I say that to him. If he was depressed or if there was something else going on, I didn't know but I suspected. Like. Really suspected. And that–that really set him off but, when he came down and was settled, he said he would try and get it together.

NICHOLAS is given a wide shot; he is surrounded by emptiness. His wounded look has advanced to sorrow.

Nicholas Webber: When it was clear to me that he was just saying he'll get himself together, that he wasn't actually doing anything to get himself together, to get a job, to, sort of, take ownership over his own life and his choices, or talk to anyone, when I could tell none of that was going to change, that's when I decided, yeah. We loved each other, that wasn't why I left, it wasn't a love thing, no one was cheating, no one was–I wanted stability, and peace, and I wanted that for him too, and that apartment had none of those. So. Yes. I did. I left.

RONNIE offers the camera relived pity, pity for Chris.

Ronnie Harris: He was devastated. For a long time. And I would try and get Chris out and get his mind off it, but it was almost like he'd lost interest in, I don't want to say life, because it didn't feel that doom and gloom, but he, there was some wind out his sails, for sure. I mean. Nick was a safe space for him, probably the only one he'd ever had, and now he didn't have that.

First MARY ANNE is given her own close shot, then RICHARD, both seem to have gained comfort in front of the lens.

Mary Anne Cooper: After Nick was out of his life, it seemed like Chris was just trying to find his way. I pushed him to talk to someone too, the way Nick had. All those thoughts and things rotting in his head.

Richard Cooper: He didn't need to talk to anyone; if he'd just hunkered down and got himself together, he'd been fine. He coulda been tougher and not so sensitive to things, he'd been fine.

MARY ANNE smiles at the camera, smiles through her husband's opinion, which differs from hers.

Mary Anne Cooper: He found work, but it wasn't anything he was interested in, it didn't get him excited, not like when he was making his paintings. There were a few jobs he went through in those years; he was only half-invested in any of them. That's how he came to work for his brother.

Richard Cooper: Anthony started his business right after he was married and, right away, offered Chris to come work for him. He was so excited and so happy to be in a place where he could offer that to his brother, and Chris did, he took that offer.

Photos are shown to the camera. They capture moments of ANTHONY and Chris opening a small restaurant, working side by side, cooking, office work, waiting on customers. Together.

Anthony Cooper: It was bumpy at first, but once we ironed things out, Chris was a good employee when things took off. The dynamic wasn't boss-employee, it was a good dynamic, it was brothers with tasks to get done. And we were busy, my gosh. I really wasn't ready for how quickly the restaurant grew, and my wife and I were newly parents too, so it was hectic, oh yeah, and I know on the side and in his free time, Chris was wanting to get his paintings in galleries and, so he was working all day with me and then all night on trying to get his work seen, and all the time was getting rejections. No one wanted his stuff. He had a pile of all these rejections in his closet, all his rejection letters. Over the years, there must have been hundreds. I want to say he kept every one. I think police have all them now.

ANTHONY begins with a smile for the camera but, as he recalls for the camera his experience working with Chris, the smile fades.

Anthony Cooper: He had the balance in a good place, I would say. His work with me wasn't distracted and, I know it wasn't his passion, but I didn't notice a lack in the quality of his work, even as hard as he was working on his art stuff, I never noticed a dip, until I did. He was four or five years in with me at that point, and the business was steady and doing real well, and he was slipping. It was gradual, and it was worsening.

Leaning forward slightly, Nancy clasps her hands together, a gesture of anticipation.

Nancy Cooper: Chris really just needed a win, with his painting, but he wasn't getting one. Not one. So, here's Tony with this booming business, making good money, taking care of his wife and his young kids, and here's Chris, alone, pursuing something for years and getting nowhere. It tormented him, he told me once. It really tormented him that you can work so hard on something and be so passionate about it, and you can allow it to consume your life, and still, after all that, get nothing for it. You know, we equate hard work with success, that if you just do the hard work, you will have your success, and he was watching our brother's hard work pay off as success, and, so what happens when a person puts all of themself into something and they get nothing but rejection? Every time. Always. I mean, really? He never had one, not one win. Not one. So. You gotta think that broke him. Just broke him. And it's like, do you quit? Do you keep going and, maybe, hope for success? Chris wrestled with that, all the time. Painting had arrested his life, and it wasn't moving forward. It was this endless, exhaustive routine of work, paint, work, paint. Where was the joy for him?

Ronnie tilts his head to the side, listening intently to the interviewer's question.

Ronnie Harris: I would see Chris, maybe, once a month? If that. He wasn't allowing himself much free time. When you did finally get him into a social setting, and sometimes it would be work to get him out of the house, he would be, kinda present, kinda not? You could see he was with you when you were talking, but sometimes you could tell he was in his head, distracted. He'd talk about work, with his brother, and that all seemed it was fine, but I did notice Chris was thinning out. I wasn't concerned, exactly, I did ask him about it, but not, like, in a worried way, just in a way that–just making sure he knew. Because he didn't seem to be aware of it. When I really got concerned was when it would go longer than a month and I wouldn't see him. I think the longest stretch was four months, I didn't see him. And I saw him out in town, at a gas station, I think it was, and he looked, I don't know, tired? Not sleep tired, but life tired? If that makes sense? When Nick came back into his life, it really saved him, I think. Honestly.

NICHOLAS weighs his words before he gives them to the camera.

Nicholas Webber: It was nine years I didn't see him, but it felt like no time at all. But. In some ways it felt like a hundred years between us.

A nod of agreement takes NICHOLAS, then he recounts the following with conviction.

Nicholas Webber: He called me actually, out of the blue and so unexpectedly. Before I knew, it was a two-hour phone call, just us laughing and catching each other up. I think it was a week later, we had dinner at his place, and we thought, should we give this another go? And the feelings were all still there, for both of us; that didn't change one bit. We talked through, you know, learned mistakes from our first relationship. I thought Chris had really grown, even if his friends and family didn't think so, and he was working for Tony and, yes, he did talk about his painting a little, kind of how he was ready to give that up. He'd put so much time and so much effort and was no further than when he started fifteen, twenty years before. And I told him there was no shame in that, but it needed to be his decision. I wasn't going to have Chris quit just to have me back in his life, but I also said I don't want to have things the way they were before, where I was supporting us, again. So, all I said was there was no shame in giving his all and deciding he'd rather do something else. That's when he decided the easel and paints were going up in the closet, and that's where they stayed, as far as I knew. He said he was ready to focus on work with Tony and see where there was room for upward movement there. So. We did, we decided to give it another shot. It was a few months later, we bought our home together.

MARY ANNE and RICHARD deliver their answers with light tones and with smiles.

Mary Anne Cooper: We really hoped this time it would click for them, and we really came to love Nick as another son. Nick got Chris coming around the family more, so that was, we really enjoyed that.

Richard Cooper: Having everyone together, having Chris there and involved, it felt like a fresh start for everyone, really. You could feel good about where things were headed; you didn't have to worry.

NICHOLAS prepares to speak, then stops, then, finally starts with a fragile smile and a slouch in his posture.

Nicholas Webber: We finally had the stability and the peace we didn't have before. That was enough for me, and for a while, it was enough for Chris. Everything, then, was pretty much normal. We became that old couple we acted like in our twenties, haha! It was quiet moments at home, it was mornings together, it was. Just. It was really good. Some of my favorite times with Chris were from that second time together. And I remember thinking, worrying actually, well, I felt guilty about him giving up painting. I would look at him and feel guilt, but it —I thought he was doing well, he looked like it, like really looked like he was happier, without painting I'm saying, but, that's why I was so shocked when Chris came in the house one day; he had a letter and was saying his work was going on exhibit.

ANTHONY's speech is rushed, he's trying to get everything out at once, very quickly.

Anthony Cooper: Chris was in one morning saying he needed to talk to me in the office, so we went in and sat, and he said he was sorry, that he'd, well that was when someone'd agreed to show his work. What was it called? Well, it was his only collection that was ever exhibited, it was, oh, it was, uh, *Echoes in Empty Rooms*, that's what it was called, his collection. He said it was being exhibited and, pretty bluntly, that he was quitting to focus one hundred percent on painting, and the first thing I said, I'm not kidding, was, is Nick okay with that? Not even worried about him quitting, just, was Nick going to be okay with that!

With a solemn look, NICHOLAS is shaking his head in disappointment.

Nicholas Webber: Of course, I was happy for him, of course I was, but in the back of my mind, I was, like, wait, didn't you stop all that? Didn't you–had he been painting and pursuing galleries and not telling me?

NANCY's gestures for the camera are sharp and alive with frustration.

Nancy Cooper: We were all saying it, *do not go all in on this thing*. Don't quit your job, don't–but I don't think Chris was ever going to listen to us. I don't know, if it was me, I would either. I can't imagine how he felt, finally having something to show, something to tell him that, all those years, which amounted to most of his life, all those rejections, he now had something he could show that said all that, all of it, wasn't a waste.

There's a heaviness in NICHOLAS's voice as he speaks, his gaze is fixed past the camera, beyond it.

Nicholas Webber: *Echoes in Empty Rooms*? Did I see his exhibit, before it came out? I did. Yes. He never called it a collection, or ever called it paintings. He always called it his work, or his art, or his pieces. So, I did, I saw his "work." It, um ... it took me by surprise. There was so much pain in it. Um. I couldn't look at all of the collection. Some was–Chris didn't know that ... I told him I did see all of it, but. Some unsettled me, and the rest I just couldn't. I think about that a lot too. That's something to really feel guilty about, huh?

NICHOLAS leans forward and speaks in a soothing tone, trying to ease the interviewer into an answer that holds pity.

Nicholas Webber: That year was when things really changed for the worse. The exhibit didn't do well, and, still, he was spending all this money on those sorta events, conventions where you get a booth and people come and look at booths, and that broke my heart too. He would stand there over his work, looking and smiling at everyone passing, and no one would stop, or maybe one person would stop? He didn't have crowds like the others, and he would bad-mouth the other artists at home and get so angry. He would try to hide the anger, but he was not good at that.

NANCY attempts to hide the concern in her answer but fails.

Nancy Cooper: Nick would come over sometimes without Chris and, I loved Nick, I still love Nick, we chat every now and then, still, and back then he would come to the house and he would talk about my brother, and one time he did share that Chris had developed anger issues, never anything physical, never ever, but Nick would share things that Chris had said, and I didn't think they were okay. He was my brother, and I loved him, but I was– I kept telling Nick, sit Chris down and tell him he cannot say things like that to you, but I don't know there was much communication going between them by that point.

NICHOLAS holds a tissue in his lap; he's looking at it as he speaks for the camera.

Nicholas Webber: We did a year of that before I realized it, that we were right back where we were before, like, full circle or cycle, role for role, me supporting us.

Moments pass before NICHOLAS begins again.

Nicholas Webber: He couldn't believe I was leaving again; he begged me to stay. But. I couldn't. I did it once and, I mean, if there was any sign that Chris would change, I would've stayed in a heartbeat, but I said he could have the house. He didn't want it, he couldn't afford it, so we sold it and he moved into an apartment. Not far from our first apartment together, it was the same area.

The atmosphere in the Cooper family room is changed; it is now somber and cold as MARY ANNE and RICHARD are filmed.

Mary Anne Cooper: We didn't hear much from Chris after he moved from the house. Everything felt like it did when he was a kid. If you got him on the phone once a month, you were lucky.

Richard Cooper: He didn't start coming around the house again until, well it was because I fell off the roof and hurt myself pretty bad.

Mary Anne Cooper: Richard came in the house hunched over saying he fell and groaning and I said what the goddamn hell were you doing on the roof, and he says replacing shingles, and I start yelling at him, he was almost sixty, going on that roof, and you know what he says? You want to tell them what you says? He says get me to a goddamn hospital. So I did.

Photos of MARY ANNE COOPER, NANCY COOPER, ANTHONY COOPER, and Chris show the family at their father's hospital bedside.

The camera's wide shot catches, now, in frame, a wheelchair beside RICHARD COOPER.

Richard Cooper: Well, they checked me in, and I remember thinking I'll be out in the morning, but I ended up staying three months, right? That was three? Yeah. It started with walking. They would get me out of bed and my legs wouldn't quite do what I wanted, and it escalated pretty quick after that, where I couldn't get on my legs at all. Doctor told me one morning, I won't forget it, he held up a scan of my spine and said the fall had caused a series of traumas that, he was sorry to say, were not correctable, but he said, there were some exciting studies coming soon. Well, I'm still waiting. So.

NANCY has just tended fresh tears with a tissue and is smiling through hard memories for the camera.

Nancy Cooper: The family definitely came together when Dad had his accident to support him and Mom and help around the house. Chris came one morning and said how can he help, and he helped out, and I thought that would be it, we wouldn't see him for another few months, but he was at the door again the next morning, and then the next, then it was every day he was coming. It was all of us together.

NANCY has collected herself, is now composed, free of sorrow. There is an optimism as she begins.

Nancy Cooper: Chris would sit with Dad, and they would talk for hours, and they became, I think, closer than they'd ever been. They talked about a lot of things, but I know they spent most their time talking about Dad's injury. Chris would ask a lot of questions, like, what does it feel like, not feeling your legs, or was Dad angry in any way about not having control of his legs? I would tell him, I wish you wouldn't ask him about that kind of talk. He still did, and Dad is not a talker either. Growing up, Dad was the quiet authority, but for Chris, for him coming around and spending time with him, he opened up about all of it. I think it led to big emotions and all that. But Chris, yes, about the injuries, he was so curious, and I thought he was trying to help Dad process, to talk about it and not keep it inside. But. When I heard what he was planning, it kind of all made sense, why he was around so much, why he was, basically, interviewing Dad about his injuries, asking the man to sit and think and answer questions about this thing that had changed his life indefinitely. When I heard about the painting he was doing of Dad, correct.

ANTHONY is wide-eyed, glaring into the lens, arms folded tight across him. Halfway through, as he speaks, they unfold, and he displays significant frustration.

Anthony Cooper: He didn't ask Dad, he didn't! Chris painted him and used all the stuff Dad had expressed to him, and I saw the fucking thing, Chris showed me and he–he– Look. If you looked outside and saw a beautiful day, beautiful sun in the sky, beautiful blue above you, Chris told me once he didn't see those things. He asked me why couldn't he see it, automatically, beauty, the way I did, the way most people do, he said he needed to talk himself into seeing it, and sometimes, then, he still worried he wasn't seeing beauty the way we do, most people. That's how that painting of my father read, and I told you before, I'm not an art guy, but that's exactly how that goddamn painting read; it had no beauty in it. I was so mad. I was. So. Mad. It was such a fuck you. To all of us. I just. Because. Sorry. One second. Because. Sorry. Because it broke my dad's heart, being painted that way. Like. Here's the tragedy of his lifetime forever in a fucking depressing painting, and here Dad was just thinking he was getting closer to his son, when he was really just a subject to Chris. And all we've ever done is help Chris and been there for him, and he does that? I will tell you, no one else will, but I will, Chris was the most selfish fucking person. Everyone says how tortured and wounded he was, and maybe he was those things, but he was a black hole, sucking everyone in and never letting anyone escape. I still feel that way, like there's this constant black hole keeping us from escaping the sum of him ... So he did that painting, I could of–I was fucking furious.

NICHOLAS appears spent from the interview, his face is blank.

Nicholas Webber: Chris called and said he had another painting going on exhibit. He was very excited about it on the phone. He wouldn't tell me what the painting was, I guess, well, he said his brother was upset about the subject of the painting, and he didn't want that to affect what I thought, so he said I would just have to see it. He said judge it for the paint and nothing else ... and I told him congratulations, I said I was very happy for him, but I wouldn't be seeing it. I was still hurt, and I said I didn't want to see any more of his pain on display. That made him very quiet.

NICHOLAS has shrunk inward, shrunk from the camera, shrunk so very far away into himself, but still he looks in the lens and speaks.

Nicholas Webber: He said okay. Then he hung up. That was the last thing he said to me. Imagine? Those being someone's last words to you? "*Okay.*"

NANCY speaks slowly and deliberately, carefully considering each word.

Nancy Cooper: There was an exhibit date and a whole press thing from the gallery, I want to say it was in the paper. Not a big national release, as I understood it, more of a local release was how it was advertised. So. On the day, I drove up the hour to Chicago, to the gallery. I didn't want to pass any sort of judgment on the painting on what Anthony was saying, I wanted to see for myself, but I went in, and I didn't find it on a wall. I asked the gallery guy, and he said he didn't have any paintings from that artist, and I said excuse me? He went in the back and made some calls and come back out, maybe, ten minutes later shaking his head. Well, we found out later the exhibition of Chris's painting was canceled, and, but not only that, no one could get a hold of Chris. We collectively allowed him a few days where he wasn't answering any one's calls without, you know, being too nagging; we didn't know if maybe the painting was pulled or scheduled wrong or what could have happened, so we let a few days go by, if maybe he was upset and didn't want to talk. We didn't know. Then, when it was a week and still no answer ... that's when I went over and found his apartment unlocked and, all his stuff was there, dishes in the sink. I remember seeing a bowl of cereal that had probably been sitting days, a week maybe, like Chris had taken a few bites, however long ago, and got up and left, but his car was there.

The camera sees NANCY has gone cold where she sits, her eyes big and empty.

Nancy Cooper: I called police that same day.

The camera follows a husky gentleman in a windbreaker coat and jeans two sizes too big; they're choked tight by a belt with a gold buckle. A hat atop his head hides most of his salt-and-pepper hair, but not all. The gentleman leads the camera into a diner.

Then we're seated at a booth with the gentleman while he enjoys his coffee; he's identified as CHESTER MCFLUTEY [RETIRED STATE POLICE INVESTIGATOR]

Chester McFlutey: I remember I was at my desk and my lieutenant was on the phone and he comes out his office, real big guy, with this look and he says that was Wayne Casey who phoned, who was Larton County sheriff then, and he was asking for some help, he says. Those guys had come headlong into something like this before, when all those church folk went missing years and years ago, and we'd helped then, we'd supported those cases. So. The call came again, they needed our help down Larton way again; someone went missing we was told. So. We were pulled in almost right away.

Photos of Chris's apartment as a crime scene are given in sequence. The photos carry age in their quality, and each was taken with immense flash. We are shown Chris's kitchen, which is neither disheveled nor clean, but somewhere between, and his bathroom and bedroom and living room, which are sparse and without personal touch.

Chester McFlutey: In the apartment, we found his wallet, which still had money and Chris's IDs, in his bathroom was all his medications and things you'd generally need if you were leaving, they were all left behind. We found food left out, unchecked messages on the answering machine, of course we found all his paintings. Nothing indicated to me or the other investigators that Chris was planning on leaving for an extended period of time.

MARY ANNE wipes at her eyes with a tissue, RICHARD reaches and takes her hand in his.

Mary Anne Cooper: We were just home, Anthony was over and I was fixing supper, and the phone rang and it was Nancy and she says, "Mom, Chris is missing." The worst words I've ever heard.

Richard Cooper: I thought, well, they'll prolly find him broke down on one of those back roads outta Larton, or maybe a car accident where he can't get to a phone. It felt, that first day or two, any minute someone was going to call and say, ope, we found him, you can stop worrying. That they would *not* find him–that never occurred to me

CHESTER now appears to be in a home office, seated comfortably. On the desk before him is an open file. He does not reference it as he speaks; he recounts everything, it seems, from memory.

Chester McFlutey: We were able to determine, pretty early on, the last anyone had seen Chris was nine days before the sister phoned police and reported him missing. An eyewitness confirmed Chris had purchased a half-gallon of skim milk and a box of cereal from a Wal-Mart near his residence at approximately ten after nine on the night of February twenty-third. We believe that is the last anyone saw Chris Cooper.

A pair of glasses now rest on CHESTER's nose to examine photos in his hand; he removes his glasses to show the photos to the camera.

The photos display a younger Chester on scene with investigators.

Chester McFlutey: From our interviews, we understood Chris to be relatively independent, that for friends or family to go stretches of time without hearing from him was not unusual, but from an investigation standpoint, we were nine days behind, and that's not a place you want to start from.

News footage plays of police outside Chris's apartment, then trades for footage of community searches venturing into grassy thickets and rolling fields and tree lines.

Nancy Cooper: Behind Chris's apartment and some streets back was cornfield, and that opened up into countryside, so police started searching there and in the general vicinity, and we expanded from there. I think, at one point, we had two hundred folks from Larton walking with us. Some were driving outside of town, looking, some were combing fields, so we had full support of the community. Everyone wanted a job to do, everyone wanted a way to help.

Aerial archive footage shows searches of rural roads, bodies of water, and vast empty country outside of town. Police and volunteers trudge through all manner of environment.

Nancy Cooper: I don't think I went home once those first few days; we were out searching with everyone all day, and when the sun would set, we'd get out the flashlights and keep going and, sorry, I don't like remembering all that, because, you were looking and the whole time you're thinking, please don't let it be me who finds something I don't want to find, you know, don't let me find him like that, sorry ...

CHESTER is sprawled back in his chair, hands over his large belly; the fatigue of the time appears to have returned upon the case's recollection.

Chester McFlutey: Three full weeks of searches, everyone was wiped, some guys were going home to grab a few hours' sleep and then coming back out, but all that and we found nothing. No trace of him.

A news segment shows an anchor reporting on police and volunteer search efforts. Though the anchor, a lovely female, is not provided audio, the scrawl beneath her reads: SEARCH EXHAUSTED, NO LEADS.

Mary Anne Cooper: Well, police packed up, and then it was Nancy organizing searches, without their help. She would get folks together every day, and when they couldn't do every day, they did weekend searches, but police, when they weren't finding anything, they left us high and dry.

Richard Cooper: I woulda given anything to be out there searching with them. I really woulda. It's like two tragedies, I can't walk and I can't help, and not helping, I don't care about walking but not being able to help my own missing son, stuck in this chair? That's the worse of the two. That's the true tragedy of my life. Make a painting of that.

Bright redness has collected in ANTHONY's cheeks and ears and neck; his body is having a physical reaction to his retelling.

Anthony Cooper: The absence of Chris, him not being around, we'd been used to that, but when that first month went without him, it was like all of a sudden, we weren't used to it, if that makes sense?

NICHOLAS appears to have already cried and stopped. There is a tissue balled in his hand, which he squeezes over and over.

Nicholas Webber: You replay interactions, you sit and you ask yourself what could you do different, you know, all sorts of rationalizing and, really, just, generally not accepting what's in front of you. But the thing is, the situation doesn't care if you accept it or not because there it is right in front of you, even if you're choosing not to look at it. And, really, you just want him back.

CHESTER gathers photos and reports into the open file on his desk.

Chester McFlutey: We just weren't sure what kind of case we had; we knew Chris was missing, and that's about all we knew.

The camera follows CHESTER along the sidewalk outside of Chris's old apartment building. The color has changed with time and repainting. Chester takes big long steps, wide, looking over the property, re-scanning the grass and the building's siding, the windows.

Chester McFlutey: Investigators were able to determine, in the year leading up to his disappearance, Chris was having significant financial issues. These weren't small amounts we're talking, and Chris had made no efforts to mitigate or reconcile his financial strains and, in fact, they were worsening. Chris was receiving food stamps; this was a surprise to his family and friends. This was something he didn't talk about with them. So, when we told them he was receiving aid from the state, this was news. We also understood Chris to be somewhat of a depressed individual. Let me be clear, no one explicitly said he was depressed. But. What was described to investigators of Chris's, sort of, character, his behavior, that read to investigators as depressed. You know, did he, maybe do something to himself? We explored that possibility. Another theory we had at the start involved, maybe, Chris leaving everything behind for a new start, maybe he was embarrassed about aid from the state, or failed relationship, but, without his vehicle or wallet or IDs, and really no other evidence supporting that theory, we put our efforts into other leads.

RONNIE is standing in his kitchen, leaned up against the counter. He's smoking out an open window over the sink and ashing into the drain.

Ronnie Harris: It was the year after Chris went missing that a journalist, that was Dutton Bloom, from the *Clinton City Gazette* called me up and asked me some questions, asked me personal questions about Chris, and asked if I'd heard about the gentleman who'd been murdered up in Minooka, which is upstate, hundred, hundred fifty miles or so, and I'd seen on the news but didn't know too much. There was another gentleman too, they'd just found, up in Wisconsin, just past the state line. Found him in a ditch. Both guys very similar looking to Chris, both loners, both gay. Mr. Bloom says to me if you lined up those murders with Chris's disappearance, the locations of them, you see they all sorta follow the highway, something a serial murderer might follow. Both men were abducted from their homes in the middle of the night. So, I went straight to police. That seemed, to me, okay, here we might finally be on to something?

The camera is now in CHESTER's vehicle with him at the wheel, it records him driving up the highway with thick sunglasses.

Chester McFlutey: We were aware when the story ran about the possible link with a suspected serial killer, and we did look into a potential connection between Chris's disappearance and the murders of Dale Gradwahl and Stephen Amalfatino. Chris's description shared many similarities with the victims of those murders. Absolutely. We never said they didn't. We were open to the possibility, heck, we talked about it ourselves before. So. If the family tells you we were closed off to the idea, that's just downright not true. But after the story went, myself and my investigating partner made a trip up to Whannell County and spoke with lead investigators of those homicides, compared cases, everything we had, for *two* full days, and, ultimately, after thorough review we determined, outside of speculation, there were no other pieces of evidence linking these cases together. We determined our energy was better put elsewhere. The family did not like our decision. But I told them, in my job I have to go on facts, that voice in my head and the voice in my heart, they can be wrong as much as right. So. We deal with facts. The facts didn't point us that way. The facts, as we've always said, pointed at the brother.

The camera follows CHESTER into the Sheriff's Department building. He waves at familiar faces as he weaves through desks and comings and goings, until he reaches a back room.

CHESTER shows the room to the camera.

Chester McFlutey: This room was our home, yeah, for that whole time.

The interview continues in this back room of the Sheriff's Department, CHESTER is seated along the edge in a folding chair, looking at the room's entirety.

Chester McFlutey: During our investigation, we discovered there had been a number of disagreements between Anthony and Chris, surrounding a painting that Chris was planning to exhibit. We learned from several sources Anthony had gone to Chris's apartment to confront Chris over the matter. Eyewitnesses placed Anthony's truck on the road to Chris's apartment complex on the night of the fourth, further corroborating the timeline we put together. However, Anthony

Cooper stated, and to this day maintains, that Chris was not there. He stated he knocked and waited thirty minutes, then found the door unlocked and Chris nowhere to be seen. If Chris had, in fact, been there, if there actually had been a confrontation, that it could have become physical, we don't know. The evidence is inconclusive. There were, photographed at the scene, several, we called them collisions, on the west living room wall of Chris's apartment, which indicate impact of a body or large object. In a corner, also, was a very small pile of debris, about a quarter inch wide, that appeared to have been swept into said corner, collected there, like someone cleaned up a mess or swept it in that corner, and, we believe, forgotten. Investigators identified, from this debris, pieces of broken ceramic, matching a broken lamp found in the garbage bin outside the apartment complex. But. Not the bin immediately outside Chris's building; this lamp was found in the next bin over. So, whomever tossed this lamp took extra steps to toss it in the next one. If this lamp was broken during an argument between Chris and Anthony, and maybe the fight escalated and a crime was committed by Anthony and he cleaned up and missed his sweep pile and claimed Chris was already missing by then, whether these events are in fact what happened is inconclusive.

MARY ANNE is already shaking her head at the camera, in full denial, when the camera is on her next. RICHARD is nodding, fully in agreement with his wife.

Mary Anne Cooper: We never thought, when police started asking us about Anthony, not for one second did we think he was involved. No. Anthony loved his brother, we know him, he wouldn't do something like that.

Richard Cooper: We thought, wow, what a waste of time when they could be, all those resources, putting them into other leads, more viable leads? Everyone thought that, because it was, it was a waste of time.

NANCY is in her back yard, looking into the tree line at the edge of her land. Between the trees there is emptiness and nothing else.

Nancy Cooper: Do I think Anthony had anything to do with Chris's disappearance? Absolutely not. When people ask me that, I always tell them family can know each other, in and out, and, honestly, Anthony is the exact opposite of Chris. Anthony shares everything, there's no interior life that Anthony is hiding, he's a book that's all the way open. No. Anthony didn't have any involvement. If he did? Well. I won't entertain that question until there's proof of that, otherwise, like everyone says, what a waste of time, right?

NICHOLAS thumbs through photos of him and Chris from where he sits. When he's finished, he answers the camera's question.

Nicholas Webber: I don't know what happened to Chris, and I don't see much point in speculating. He's not here. That's, what else is there than that?

CHESTER is followed out of the Sheriff's Department building, to his vehicle, and then home.

He stands in the doorway of his home office for a moment. Then he shuts the door.

The camera records him smoking on his front porch, where he sits on a bench swing.

Chester McFlutey: Unfortunately, years and years have come and gone, and theories have come and gone, and Chris is still not here, and we still don't know. You, kinda, need to manufacture your own closure, because, on something like this, you don't know if any will be given to you. You hope it will. You can't lose hope for closure, that it's coming. You can't lose hope for that, but it might not come. Until there's new evidence or until someone comes forward with information, the case has gone as far as it can. When I retired, I had to make a lot of my own closure, for this case, for a dozen others, too, and only now and again do I have trouble sleeping. Only now and again.

MARY ANNE clings to her husband's hand, nodding and serious in expression. RICHARD is trying to find comfort again, adjusting how he's sitting.

Mary Anne Cooper: I believe that we'll find out what happened to Chris. I really do. I have to.

Richard Cooper: Whatever it is better hurry up and show itself, is all I'm saying.

Mary Anne Cooper: Richard has a heart thing now, and I've replaced both my knees.

Richard Cooper: I'm saying the both of us, well I don't know how much time we got left but there's more behind us than there is in front of us, haha, I can say that for sure. So. It better hurry.

Mary Anne Cooper: It's like, you feel like life kinda owes you that, at least, it owes you the truth or an explanation for taking Chris from us and all the years without him. Feels like you're owed that before you make your final departure.

ANTHONY acknowledges a question from the camera.

Anthony Cooper: I would tell him, if he came back, you know, I love you, you're my brother. Whatever you need, you know, if he'd left for some reason, I would tell him that reason doesn't matter, you're family.

Dusk burns through the trees in NANCY's backyard. She goes inside and speaks to the camera in her kitchen, now staring at the back yard out her kitchen window.

Nancy Cooper: I think whatever monster Chris carried around inside, I think it, maybe, convinced him of things that weren't true, the voice he carried around inside him, the one that tells you you're not good enough or it tells you you'll always be alone, maybe one day it was louder and–I don't know. If he were here, I would just hold him. Until he knew it was okay.

Fresh tears have found NICHOLAS, but he does not let it affect his answer; he gives it despite the tears rolling down his cheeks, and he keeps his focus despite them.

Nicholas Webber: It's like waking up every day with a void in your heart that will never be filled, not knowing what happened to someone you love so deeply, and also, there's this lingering guilt, you think should I have stayed with him, at the expense of my happiness? Just to keep him? I would, I would go back and stay with him, and I would live in misery for him, if it meant he would be here. And it affects every aspect of your life; your relationships, your work, your sense of self. You have to learn how to navigate life a new way, a harder way maybe? A way where, now, you're aware how easily bad things can happen? How, now, you're aware life doesn't owe you a thing, an explanation, an insight, so you can't expect what you're owed, what you believe you're owed? Maybe that's how Chris saw things?

The film's final shot is of NICHOLAS forcing a smile through his sadness.

The film ends with images of Chris throughout his life, and a message asking any individuals with information pertaining to the disappearance of Chris Cooper to please come forward.

A phone number is provided.

{End Transcript 01:56:24}

ABOUT THE AUTHOR

Aj Saxsma, born in Illinois in 1987, is a queer writer. He lives in Los Angeles with his husky. His literary work has earned awards from Almond Press UK and has been published in several genre magazines. As a screenwriter, his work has been an official selection for the Independent Horror Film Awards, Hollywood Screen Film Festival, Los Angeles Cinefest, and Los Angeles Horror Competition. He's also written the narrative scripts for four video game projects produced by Oculus for the Oculus VR system.

Printed in Great Britain
by Amazon